"A novel that is rich and elaborately woven like the most exquisite mantel lambrequin you can set your eyes upon, albeit the story flows so naturally like the river into the sea of fantasy and reality. Each character brought into life by the author, carefully and intricately. It is not an ordinary read; it is extraordinary. My own experience in reading this masterpiece is like staring intently into Van Gogh's *Starry Night*. The whirlpool of colours, the words of the book, and its characters bring me into a dimension of time and place I have not seen but I feel I know well. You find something about yourself in every character. You move from the past to the here and now just as much as each character is faced with the same challenges. The city shapes of Van Gogh below the night stars are like the books' chronicles when it jumps to certainties of the present times.

"The narrative put together as a whole picture melds fantasy into substance so perfectly and snugly. The fact that it is set in a medical frame of reference is so unique and gives this novel its distinctive edge. I did not foresee how this could be done but this book has done the mix of fiction and the medical sciences superbly.

"If you are looking for a novel that will allow you to experience the wonders of times past and largely how characters from the 'then and now' can hold much similarities despite the difference of periods in the millennia, then let this meticulously written novel take you to a journey of friendships, men and women of passion, loyalty, ethics, the medical practice and profession, its dignity, career dedication, human relationships, love, life, and death."

—Petite Paradero
Psychologist
The Philippines

"The Book of Drachma will keep you glued to the pages as you follow the gripping tale of a modern day cardiologist, along with the shattering revelations of a fifteenth-century healer, and behind both lies the hand of the mysterious Drachma.

"Written with an easy flow, this novel will stir your emotions as well as capture your imagination and keep you treading a thin line between reality and fantasy till the line itself is blurred. Intensely potent and written with a combination of wit, humour, and with a philosophic touch, *The Book of Drachma* is immensely enjoyable and a compelling must-read."

—Subha Majumder
IT Recruiter
Mumbai, India

COAPTATION

The Book of Drachma

COAPTATION

Second Edition

Timothy H. Cook

Published by Drachma Publishing

Published in the United States of America

ISBN: 978-0-9991403-2-1
1. Fiction / Fantasy / General
2. Fiction / Medical
15.05.12

Dedication

This book is dedicated to the memory of Margit Mårtensson Cook.

Acknowledgments

I would like to thank a number of persons, without whose help this book would not have become a reality. First and foremost, I want to thank my wife, Sara Cook, for putting up with me during these sometimes trying times.

Then I would like to acknowledge again the work that Michelle Ogle put into this opus. Special thanks need to go out to Diego Green and Michael Thayer for their efforts. And then there are my faithful blog readers, who did, in fact inspire me along the way, including Just Me 99, Cayman, Legacy, Angie, Stories, Alex, Volataire, Tawna, Diane and Psycho. You know who you really are.

Chapter One

As she drove the unfamiliar streets of suburban Chandleridge, Judy tried to remember why she had decided to go. Something in those dreams that night seemed to compel her, but just what it was she couldn't say. The dreams seemed to have nothing whatever to do with Josh and nothing at all to do with death and funerals. Somehow, underneath it all, there was a connection, one she could sense as easily as she could her own pulse. The harder she tried to pin it down, though, the more elusive it became.

It had warmed a little in the past two days, and some of the snow and ice had begun to melt, leaving the streets safe but messy. Shiloh Chapel was not hard to find. It stood out from the modest houses in the neighborhood like a rich uncle at Thanksgiving. Judy turned into the curved driveway of the funeral parlor, then into the parking lot at the side of the building. She was surprised to find only a handful of other cars in the parking lot.

There should be more people here, she thought as she got out of her car and walked toward the main entrance.

She hesitated before entering. A sensation tugged at her consciousness, one of fear, embarrassment, and some loathing. Having come this far, though, she realized it would be silly to

turn back now. Overriding her apprehension, Judy stepped into the funeral home.

Inside was cool and dim with a strange mixture of smells, some floral, some medicinal. Judy felt tense, ill at ease, and a little confused. A tall, balding, elderly man directed her in hushed tones to the visitation room down the hall. She nodded then followed his direction, entering a large, carefully lit room.

Within the room were ten or twelve adults and two children, most seated in chairs facing the front of the room where the half open casket was laid, surrounded by a large array of flowers. Beside the casket stood Earl and Janie, with two older women Judy did not recognize. Janie noticed Judy the moment she stepped inside the room, smiled, and beckoned Judy to come over, which she did awkwardly.

"Oh, Judy, thank you so much for coming." Janie's voice was gratitude and sorrow incarnate. "You'll never know how much this means to us. All of you at the hospital have been real family to Josh and Earl and me. I'm just so…so…"

Janie swallowed, fighting back the emotions, unable to get the words out.

"It's okay, Janie. I really felt I needed to come. Josh was always much more than just a patient to me." Judy was surprised by her own use of the past tense. The reality of loss had not fully registered in her mind yet. "Josh was family to me too."

The two women embraced like grieving sisters, each giving and receiving raw comfort. Tears flowed freely from Judy's eyes.

The organ began playing quietly, interrupting the intensity of human contact. Judy gently stepped back then directed her attention to the casket, stepping over to look down at Josh's still features.

That's not you, Josh, she thought. *You're somewhere, but not here. You and Bob, you're somewhere…* She felt a cold chill sweep through her as she sat down near the center of the room.

The service went on with Judy paying little attention. She focused her gaze on the little bit she could see of Josh's face. Over and over in her mind, like a chant, ran the thought that Josh was somewhere, not here—somewhere, just not here. Her eyes remained focused, but her thoughts became less coherent, less verbal. Odd sensations flowed through her, feelings of distance, of coldness, of danger, of need. There was something else, too, something subliminal but powerful, compelling.

"Above all," the minister continued in his eulogy, "Joshua believed and trusted. Those that gave him care were his family. Through the pains of his illness, through the misery, he was never bitter, for he always felt secure in the simple knowledge that those looking after him did care, as they would care for their own…"

Judy's thoughts drifted back to the dreams, the dreams that shouldn't matter but did somehow. The forest, the dappled path, the warmth, the smell of newly turned earth. She had walked down that path (wasn't that just the way Bob had described it?), following a compulsion too powerful to resist. The path had led into an ancient wood, deep with mystery and promise, alive and breathing. She had walked toward the sound of running water. By the stream the stillness of the deep woods was even more profound. The only sounds were the running water and Judy's own breathing.

Standing still and taking in the heavy silence, Judy had waited. For what she did not know, but the importance of the moment was unmistakable. Nothing in day-to-day living carried this much weight or power. Only in the twisted logic of dreams did the arrival of the old man make any sense. He stood there by the stream, appearing as old as the trees but with a sparkle of youth in his eyes. He smiled at Judy, his smile both warm and dangerous. Judy opened her mouth to speak, but no words would come.

"Good morrow, lady healer," the old man said, his voice resonant with age and passion. "I bring you greeting from another age. Be assured, lady, Master Gilsen is yet alive and safe.

His purpose, which you share, shall become clear in the fullness of time."

She noticed that the old man looked much like the one who died so dramatically in the ER. But the voice—it seemed the voice of the ancient forest speaking.

"You shall receive a sign when your time does come, and you will know by my presence what it is to be."

She tried again to speak but could not.

The old man smiled at her, turned, then walked into the depths of the forest, the stillness returning.

The eulogy caught Judy's attention again as the minister read from the book of Ecclesiastes:

"A good name is better than precious ointment; and the day of death than the day of one's birth. It is better to go to the house of mourning, than to the house of feasting: for that is the end of all men; and the living will lay it to his heart. Sorrow is better than laughter: for by the sadness of the countenance the heart is made better. The heart of the wise is in the house of mourning; but the heart of fools is in the house of mirth. It is better to hear the rebuke of the wise, than for a man to hear the song of fools. For as the crackling of thorns under a pot, so is the laughter of the fool: this also is vanity."

Judy found herself reacting to the words with grief and rage. *No, Josh*, she thought, *No! This is not the end, not your end. There's more. Somehow I know there's more, and it's got something to do with Bob and that old man. I just know it!*

Tears started streaming down her cheeks. She reached into her purse to pull out a handkerchief, and as she pulled it out, a small coin clinked down on the floor. As she stooped to pick it up, she saw that Janie had noticed and smiled at her through her own veil of tears.

The preacher continued, but this time the words rang like chords of truth through Judy's consciousness.

"To everything there is a season, and a time to every purpose under the heaven: a time to be born, and a time to die; a time to plant, and a time to pluck up that which is planted; a time to kill, and a time to heal; a time to break down, and a time to build up; a time to weep, and a time to laugh; a time to mourn, and a time to dance; a time to cast away stones, and a time to gather stones together; a time to embrace, and a time to lose; a time to keep, and a time to cast away; a time to rend, and a time to sew; a time to keep silence and a time to speak; a time to love, and a time to hate; a time of war and a time of peace."

Something stirred deep within Judy's consciousness, an awareness of the same compelling sensation she had felt earlier. As the minister read the words from Ecclesiastes, the feeling rose almost to the point of recognition then retreated to its emotional depths as she regained her sense of place and time. A sense of continuity and purpose remained, though, like an aftertaste.

She thought about Bob's inexplicable absence. There seemed to be no trace, no reason, no sign, and yet she knew with absolute certainty that the answer lay somewhere in the convoluted sequence of events and circumstances that tied together Josh and Bob, the coin, the note, the old man in the ER, and her dreams the other night.

Oh, Janie, she thought, *how unbearable this must be for you! Not just to lose your son, but to lose with no explanation his trusted physician and friend.*

She looked in Janie's direction then realized why she really had decided to come to Josh's funeral. She had to give Janie an answer, however vague and sketchy, to her dismay. Bob was the one physician Janie had truly come to trust with Josh's care, and for him to disappear without a trace or word the same time her son was dying would be cause for more grief than anyone could bear alone. The problem, Judy realized, was how to put what she felt into words that would make sense, because really it did not make sense except in dreams.

The brief service ended with a gentle but moving rendition of the "Pie Jesu" from Faure's Requiem, sung by a young woman Judy did not know but whose face and voice seemed familiar.

As she filed out with the others, Judy was able to catch Janie's attention.

"Janie," she said, "I need to talk to you, soon, in private."

Janie nodded.

"After the graveside," she said, "follow us home. We can talk."

During the drive to the cemetery and throughout the short, cold service, Judy found herself trying to compose her thoughts, trying to think about what she would say to her new friend in need.

The trouble, she thought, *is I can't make the logical part of me understand and believe what the irrational part of me knows to be true. So, how am I supposed to make someone else understand any of it? It's about like trying to explain your religious beliefs to a stranger.* No matter how she tried, she could not find words to adequately explain her convictions about things that made no sense, even to herself. Even as the service was ending and as she followed the family members away from the gravesite, her mind remained unsettled, wrestling with elements of logic, conviction, and emotion.

Lagging behind the others on the path, Judy became aware of another presence beside her. Startled, she turned to see a very old man in a long, flowing, grey overcoat striding silently along with her. She stopped, and as she did so, the man turned and faced her. In the midst of the white mane of beard and hair, Judy saw the now familiar smile.

She opened her mouth to speak, but before she could do so, the old man held up a slender, long finger in an obvious gesture of caution.

"Nay, m' lady," he said, "do not speak now. I have come to advise you and you alone. Be assured, your time shall be soon, but for the present, go about your way as you had intended,

keeping your appointed tasks. You shall find the words you need, and further, you will discover, beneath my likeness, a message of import for you alone. Heed well that message! It will provide both the key to understanding and the means to accomplish that for which you are needed. Fare thee well for now, m' lady. We shall meet again."

Before Judy could think to respond, the man turned and walked away back across the slush-covered cemetery into the grey of winter.

Judy stood and stared, uncomprehending and trembling slightly. After half a minute of standing still amid the gravestones, she rejoined the others getting into their cars and noticed Janie and Earl in their maroon sedan and followed as they drove out of the cemetery into the wide avenues and narrow side streets of the suburbs. Judy followed the Crabtrees to a neat, modern house at the end of a short lane. Janie eagerly invited Judy into their home and led her into the living room.

"Here, Judy, let me take your coat. Just take a seat anywhere. I'm so glad you've come."

Judy sat down somewhat awkwardly in the closest chair and looked about the tidy living room. On the piano was a picture of Josh, which caught her eye. It appeared to have been when he was about sixteen—a formal picture, with Josh dressed in a dark suit and tie, smiling stiffly. Judy found herself reacting to the picture much the same way as she had to seeing Josh's body in the casket—it just wasn't Josh. As she stared at the picture, Judy again tried to compose in her mind what she wanted to tell Janie, but all she could think of was that this just wasn't real, that there was more, much more to the story, and that all those weird coincidences had meaning. And now, that man in the cemetery! She was sure that there was more. How else would he even know her business? She had told no one.

"That was taken when he graduated from school. He was eighteen at the time." Janie had returned and noticed Judy staring

at Josh's picture. "He never did like the picture, but we have so few of him. He was always so shy around cameras."

"Oh, Janie. I'm sorry. I don't mean to stare. I was just kind of caught up in my thoughts."

"I can believe that. We've all had a lot to think about lately, haven't we?"

"Yeah, that's for sure. I don't really know what to think about a lot of what's happened, but I did feel we needed to talk. You know we kind of got a start back then in the hospital, when we were trying to page Dr. Gilsen, and we were discussing all the strange things that had been happening."

Janie nodded. "You're right, Judy. It seems we got started on something important, something unfinished."

Earl stepped into the room at that moment.

"It's been a cold, miserable day out there," he said. "Would either of you like something hot to drink? Some coffee, tea, or cocoa?"

"Why, thank you, Earl." Judy smiled. "A cup of coffee would be great."

"Coming right up. How do you take it, Judy?"

"A little cream, thanks."

"Janie, you want a cup too?"

"Yeah, Earl, that would be wonderful."

Earl turned and went back toward the kitchen, leaving the two women to their concerns. He would have felt uncomfortable discussing much of anything at the moment. He too remembered the last time they started talking about the strange series of coincidences that surrounded Josh's final illness and how the discussion had made him so acutely upset and more than a little confused. He never had told Janie about the dream he had had that night either. Altogether, it seemed better that he stay out of this discussion. Emotionally, he was just a little on edge, and he didn't want to risk losing it. Making coffee just seemed safe.

Janie, for her part, smiled as Earl went back toward the kitchen, knowing full well what he was trying to avoid. As he turned to walk back, Janie said over her shoulder, "Dear, maybe you could bring some of that fresh bread in with the coffee. You know, the stuff Aunt Grace made."

"Yeah, okay, I'll cut some up and bring it in."

As Earl walked into the kitchen, he found himself fighting to hold back a flood of memory and emotion. Ever since Josh's death, he had been stoic, in control, had not shed any tears, and mostly listened as Janie had talked and wept, comforting her and making all the phone calls and arrangements for visitation, the funeral, and taking care of notifying all the relatives and friends. Overall, he was "holding up real well," as Janie's Aunt Grace had said.

Something happened when he walked into the kitchen, something subtle and powerful. As he tried to perform the simple task of making coffee, he found himself unable to carry through with the most mundane action, could not even think how to proceed. All alone, and face-to-face with the pent-up emotions of the past week, Earl began to weep. His hands shook too badly to hold anything, so he sat down at the kitchen table and put his head down. His whole body shook as he sat and silently cried— pure emotion, with nothing verbal to dilute it.

It was in the midst of his pure, wordless sorrow that the dream came back to him, just as it had the night before Josh had died. The setting was the same, the feeling identical, and just as real. He was there again, the same dimly lit room with the musty smell, the tall window framed by rich burgundy velvet curtains, the faint sound of a harp from a distance. The man was there, too, the old man with the long grey cloak and the wild mane of white hair and beard. When he spoke, it was with the resonance of the ages, his words filling Earl's whole awareness.

"Master Earl," he said, "I have come to you through the ages. Your son shall not have died without purpose. However, the

import of his death shall not be known to you until the hour of your own. You do have a task, though, in this time of great turmoil. Heed well what I shall tell you, for you must give a message of promise and power to the lady healer. Her task shall be the more immediate, and through your words she will understand the truth of what she does already believe only in part."

Again, as with his first encounter, Earl tried to speak but could not.

"Nay, Master Earl, do not try to speak, only listen. Your message to the lady healer shall be simple and direct. You will tell her that you have seen my face, and I have said that her path will be made clear and is to be shared with Master Gilsen, the healer. You shall further know that the time to speak shall be when you both together recognize my face."

The old man then turned his clear eyes directly on Earl and spoke in a voice as ancient as thunder. "I am Drachma, the Elder of the Forest, and I have spoken!"

As he had the first time, Earl recovered his wits, shaken but convinced that what he had seen and heard was no ordinary dream. Unlike the first time, though, he could not attribute what he had seen to long hours of staying awake under stress. He had naturally assumed that the dream had been a kind of rehashing of the experiences that had gone on during their long vigil with Josh and his surgery, that all this talk of Drachma and ancient coins and the impressive performance by Dr. Greshin, the "lady healer," had been the fertile ground from which sprang his bizarre and disturbing dream.

Why now? he wondered. *Why this replay?* It made no sense whatever.

Slowly Earl got up from the table, collected his thoughts, and started to make himself busy cutting up the homemade bread and making coffee. He still trembled inside, but at least externally he had recovered a measure of composure. He glanced at the

clock and noticed that he had been out in the kitchen at least a half hour.

Judy and Janie, deep in thoughtful conversation, had not really noticed Earl's absence until he returned with the coffee and bread on a tray. Janie took notice of the still scared look on Earl's face but chose to say nothing, hoping Judy would not realize something was wrong.

"Thanks so much," Judy said, as Earl set his tray down. "This is so thoughtful of you."

"Oh, it's nothing really," Earl said, rather candidly. "I'm just not too good at conversation these days. I just prefer to busy myself with doing things."

"Ah, yes, that's understandable, but thanks anyway. Won't you at least sit down and join us for coffee?"

"Oh, sure, I'll do that. Here, yours is the one with cream. And please, have a piece of the bread. Aunt Grace makes some of the best bread in the world. Here…"

Judy took a piece of the buttered bread, feeling somehow, strangely, that this simple act carried some weight, a message perhaps that she did not comprehend but recognized nonetheless. Earl was right, though, the bread was delicious. It had a warm, sweet taste that reminded her of something from years ago. She couldn't help but smile just a little as she ate her piece.

As the three of them sat and shared their coffee and bread, the conversation gradually drifted back to the hospital and things they had already said, but eventually, without any conscious attempt on anyone's part, the talk turned to Josh's final struggle with life, and to the mysterious loss of Dr. Gilsen.

"I just don't understand it, Judy. I just can't figure where he might have gone, and without saying anything to us. It's not like he didn't realize we were there. I mean, he had been faithfully keeping us up to date on everything that was going on with Josh. I don't know, I just don't know…"

"Now, Janie, don't take this wrong." Judy hesitated. "I know somehow, don't ask me how, but I know, sure as I know my own name, that Dr. Bob isn't gone in any usual sense, and his disappearance has something directly to do with Josh. You see, I had these dreams—"

"Dreams?" Earl interrupted. His look betrayed a sensation of panic that was triggered by the mention of dreams.

"Yeah," Judy continued, "but not like any ordinary dreams I've ever had. It was like they carried messages for me that were supposed to make some sense of all the weird happenings of the past week, but I couldn't make myself believe any of the stuff. It was just too crazy."

Earl could barely get the words out, fearful for what she might say. "Ah...these dreams...what were they like? What... what were these messages?"

"Well, each time there was this path, a path into the woods, and it was springtime, warm, and I could smell it in the air. There was something compelling about the woods and the path, something I couldn't resist. I followed the path deep into the woods, deep where it was dark and silent except for a flowing stream. Each time I would walk to the edge of the stream and wait, wait for something I was sure would be there. Then he would be there, across the stream, the old man—"

"The old man?" Earl couldn't help asking, the edge of fear still in his voice. "What was he like?"

"Well, you remember me telling you about the old man who died in the ER? This man in the dreams looked a lot like him— old, with long, white, straggly hair and a white beard. And his voice, it was weird. His voice was exactly the same voice that we heard come from Josh just before he had his seizure. It was the kind of voice that captures your attention and carries so much authority that you couldn't argue if you wanted to."

"And...and what did he tell you, this old man?"

"Well, it was strange. He seemed to know who I was, and he told me that Dr. Bob, or Master Gilsen as he called him, was safe, and that I would be sharing some kind of great purpose with him, though the man never said what it was, only that I would find out in time. It was weird, too, because each time he addressed me as 'lady healer.'"

Earl's jaw dropped open as a flash of insight and recognition caught him unexpectedly.

"Also, this old man told me that he was Drachma. Drachma, the Elder of the forest, he called himself. No matter how I tried, I couldn't shake the notion that this was not just my fevered imagination, not just a result of stress and long hours."

So it's Judy who's the lady healer, Earl thought. *In some crazy, unbelievable way, it all may start to make a little sense.* Thoughts raced through Earl's mind as he tried to sort out what his own dreams told him in light of Judy's revelation.

Janie noticed the familiar look on Earl's face, the one she had seen so often when he was puzzled and trying to figure things out in his mind before saying anything.

Janie reached out for her husband's hand. "Look, Earl, I can tell by your expression that Judy has said something that's touched an area too sensitive and awkward for you to want to think about. Why don't you just tell her? It might make more sense than you think."

Earl paused, head lowered, before speaking. "Well, I guess you're right, but this is not easy for me. As you know, I'm not one to believe in crazy, off-the-wall kinds of stuff."

"I do know that. And that, I'm sure, is what's making all this painful for you. I can see it."

"Okay, I'll tell you, but try not to be too upset that I didn't tell you sooner."

Janie nodded and squeezed his hand.

"Anyway, Judy, you're not the only one who's been having strange and powerful dreams. The night before Josh died, the

night after we had been talking at the hospital, about all those weird coincidences and strange Greek coins and all, I had trouble falling asleep. I just kept tossing and turning, felt like my brain was running ninety miles and hour, and I couldn't shut it down. Finally, not wanting to wake Janie, I crawled on down to the rec room downstairs, turned on the TV, and lay back in the recliner. There wasn't anything good on TV, of course, but the noise was kind of soothing, and I eventually drifted off. Then it got really weird, 'cause normally I don't have any smells in my dreams, but it was a smell, a real strange, musty, old kind of smell, and a sound, the sound of a harp playing down the hall, that woke me, if that's the right word.

"Anyway, I found myself in this dream, in some old, cool room with stone walls and a real high ceiling. There were tapestries on the walls and a big, tall window with lots of frames, bordered by long drapes of maroon velvet. Strangely enough, I wasn't scared. Rather I was kind of calm and relaxed. That was, until the man walked in…"

"The man?" Judy could not help but interrupt.

Earl nodded. "Yeah, and it sounds like the same one—tall, lean, very old but bright, with long, white hair and a beard like a mane, and with a voice no one could ignore."

Judy drew in a breath but said nothing.

"The man walked up to me and spoke, and when he did, my sense of calm vanished, replaced by a feeling that's hard to describe, not fear, not awe in any typical sense—more like the feeling you might get if your favorite movie star or the president suddenly and unexpectedly sat down in your living room and started to talk to you like an old friend."

"Yeah," Judy said, "I recognize that feeling. I felt the same. I can't explain it. Anyway, go on, tell us what he said."

The conversation was interrupted by the sound of someone on the front porch. Earl looked at his watch.

"The mail's kind of late—has been since before Christmas."

"You stay, Earl," Janie said. "I'll go get it. It's bound to be mostly cards, anyway."

Earl took a sip of his coffee as Janie went out to the front porch to get the mail. Judy sat, silently, feeling suddenly very awkward, but also a little vexed at the disruption of what seemed a very important narrative. Earl seemed relieved, if anything, drinking his coffee and taking another bite of his bread.

Janie returned quickly, the door slamming shut behind her, a gust of cold wind blowing into the house.

"Whew, it's gotten a lot colder and windier out there just in the past hour," Janie said, returning to the living room. "Look, Earl, here's a really strange envelope for you."

Janie handed Earl a fairly large, cream-colored envelope then put down the other mail on a side table.

"Well, if this isn't the most peculiar thing," he said. "Janie, take a look at this."

Both women stared at the object in his hand. The envelope was about five by seven inches and made of a most distinctively textured paper that felt old and stiff. Judy immediately recognized the paper but said nothing. On the front there was no address, simply a name, in large, ornate script:

Master Earl, esq.

On the back, the envelope was held closed with a singe large, wax seal, equally ornate but unreadable.

"I'm not even going to ask how the mailman delivered this with no address or stamp," Earl said. "I guess I'd better open it, though. You never know these days what might be inside."

Earl's hands shook slightly as he tore open the envelope, preserving the wax seal. Inside was a single sheet of similar paper, folded in half. As Janie and Judy looked on, Earl unfolded the paper. Inside, on the upper half of the page was an engraving in exquisite detail of a man holding a staff, the wind blowing

his hair and beard, his deep-set eyes looking intensely toward the distance.

Judy and Earl's recognition of the figure was simultaneous. They looked at each other.

"It's him, isn't it?" Judy asked.

Earl nodded, unable at first to speak.

After a few moments, Earl was able to regain his voice and composure. "What he said, Judy, was that when you and I both recognize his face, I was to give you a message. I was to tell the 'lady healer' that her path would be made clear and that it will be shared with 'Master Gilsen,' and that this message was of power and promise."

"And what he told me," Judy continued, "was that under his picture would be words that would make me understand what I was supposed to do, and give me the means to do it."

They all looked. Under the picture, written in a hand Judy now recognized, were the words:

> A wise old man shall he be,
> Riding as if a Knight alone.
> Join him on his steed,
> Showing to him my seal,
> Affixed hereon in crimson,
> The path shall be
> Into the trees,
> Then following yonder stream,
> Hence, to shelter,
> Now, go, m' lady,
> We await!

For the better part of a minute, no one could speak. Finally, Judy said, "I guess this means I'd better be going. It's all a bit scary, and I don't know if or when I'll see you again, but when I do, I know we'll have a lot to talk about."

"You bet we will," Janie replied, "and listen, Judy, you be careful. We're counting on you. Keep in touch somehow."

"I sure will, Janie, one way or another."

Jane went to retrieve Judy's coat. As she did, Earl turned to Judy and handed her the letter.

"Here, Judy, from what it said, I think you better hang on to this."

"I think you're right, Earl." She took the paper, and as she did so, she gave him a quick embrace. "Thanks, Earl," she said, "for everything."

Janie helped Judy on with her coat then saw her to the door. Before stepping out, Judy placed the paper carefully in her purse, and then gave Janie a heartfelt hug.

"Remember," she told Janie, "I'll always be thinking about you."

Janie said nothing, her eyes overflowing.

The weather had changed dramatically. As Judy stepped out onto the porch, the icy wind cut through her inadequate coat, blowing new snow into her face. She stepped quickly out to her car in the driveway then slipped into the driver's seat, slamming the door briskly. The snow had not yet accumulated enough to require scraping, so she was able to start the car and back out into the street without having to get out again.

As Judy headed back the way she had come into the lane, the full fury of the snowstorm lit upon her. She really began to fear for her safety, though, when she made a right turn onto the main road and realized that, not only was her visibility rapidly declining, but she really didn't know where she was or how she got here. She continued on, however, fearing more to stop, and made what she felt were probably the correct turns to take her back toward the city.

The storm did not abate. Rather, traveling became ever more treacherous as the streets became slick and invisible in the whiteness. After another ten or fifteen minutes, Judy realized

that she was completely lost. There were no landmarks of any kind she could see, and the road ahead gave only a vague notion of guidance. She began to panic. Up ahead, slightly off to the right, there appeared to be some buildings, perhaps a farm, that she could half make out between wipes of the blades on her windshield. Judy decided to try to get at least that far then concede her need for help. As she gently stepped on the brake, though, the car completely lost all traction and began to drift sideways. Judy furiously tried to correct her direction of travel, making the car skid even more wildly. Completely lost and out of control, she could feel the car start to fall down the embankment. As it rolled, she could see nothing but whiteness, whiteness with a few drops of red.

Chapter Two

Bob woke from his long, intense, and dreamless slumber to the muffled sounds of horses' hooves and excited voices. As he opened his eyes, he saw light streaming in through the window high overhead. The noises seemed to be coming from just outside the wall. He could not make out any words, but could tell that there were at least several people outside and probably several horses.

I can't believe this, he thought. *I'm still here, wherever here is, in this cold, smelly room with these ancient soldier types running around and acting scared out of their wits.*

Quite without warning, the realization dawned on Bob that he appeared to have lost everyone and everything he had, including his place in time and space, that this was no dream, and he was not likely to find his way back anytime soon. The recognition came with searing grief as intense as anything in his recent experience, along with a sense of total helpless abandonment. He sat on the bed, head in his hands, trying to collect his thoughts. All he could think about, though, was how totally alone he was. He had never really been this alone before, never in a situation where even rudimentary communication was a major struggle. He thought about Josh, and what might be happening with him, and he thought about home and realized that all during

Josh's ordeal, he had not called his wife to tell her anything of his circumstances. Deep within himself, he felt well up an almost uncontrollable urge to cry out in anguish and outrage. There was something else, though, a nameless, ancient something that he felt almost like some primordial heartbeat, something that had to do with that path in the woods and springtime, something that kept him from crying out and seemed to provide him a gentle hint of reassurance.

Bob's brief reverie ended as the door was flung open, and what entered was the oddest assortment of persons Bob had ever seen. Along with Sean and Michel, his two guards, were four others. The tallest was a man of at least sixty years of age, sallow and balding, thin as a rail, and carrying a bow very much like those held by the hunters Bob had encountered earlier. Beside him was a brown, wiry man, no more than four feet in height, walking with a slight limp, and with a large, bulbous head, curly black hair, and dark, deep-set eyes. Behind these two walked a younger man with red hair and a powerful face and physique. The one that caught Bob's eye, though, was the youth. Slight of build, looking no more than eleven or twelve years old, he had the eyes and composure of one much older, but more than anything, here was the very image in perfect physical health of Josh Crabtree!

Bob shook his head then stared again. The image had not changed. He was still there—Josh as he might have been— staring back at him. Actually, all the new arrivals were staring at Bob. He certainly did not look the part of a purveyor of great power worthy of the respect and protection of Drachma and the earl. If anything, he looked lost, confused, and frightened.

For a while, no one spoke, each one lost in his own thoughts. Eventually, Sean took it upon himself to make introductions.

"This, my fellow guardsmen, is Robert of Ewe Ass. As you have been told, his safekeeping has been our bounden duty, and too, as you have said to us, your duty shall be the same." He turned toward Bob. "Robert, by order of our earl and his agents,

you are to be turned over to the safekeeping of these men, who shall provide you passage across the island.

"This," he said, indicating the tall older man, "is Master Woodsman Martin. None know the forest as he does—its land, its rivers, or its dangers. This swarthy little fellow is called Stoneheft. Do not be fooled by his size, for he is quite stout and can take many men of greater stature. Of that I am a witness."

Sean paused then indicated the young, red-haired man. "This handsome lad is called Kevin, and, I am told, has the eyes of an eagle and the ears of a fox. The youth I know not, but he is named Tom and comes directly from the earl with his blessing and brings you his greetings."

Bob nodded politely then asked, "Do you mean to tell me that you folks, who don't know me or anything about me, have been expecting me? That just doesn't make sense. I think you've been expecting the wrong person—some kind of magician or wizard or something. I'm just a doctor, a physician."

"So you have said," answered Sean. "But in truth, it is not we who have been expecting your arrival."

"Who, then?" Bob sensed that this might be a sensitive issue.

Sean visibly tightened. "The earl himself, I believe, but more than that I cannot say. I am certain, though, that you shall learn all in good time."

Bob looked again at his strange welcoming committee then shook his head in disbelief.

"All right," he said, "you guys seem to be making the rules in a game none of us seems to understand, and I'll try to cooperate. But tell me this. Am I a prisoner, or what? It would be kind of nice if I at least knew what my status was in all of this."

The men looked at each other, comprehending nothing but the question, "Am I a prisoner?" the other words rolling past them like so many meaningless syllables.

"No, Robert of Ewe Ass," Sean finally answered, "you are not a prisoner, for we are not at war, and you have committed no crime.

Nevertheless, we have been entrusted with your safekeeping by our liege and know only that there are powers that would seek to destroy his efforts."

Oh, great, thought Bob. *That's what I really wanted to hear. As if I weren't confused and nervous enough already.*

After a moment, Stoneheft stepped forward.

"If I may be so bold, my good men, as to suggest that the way may be arduous and that we should avail ourselves of the shelter we now enjoy. We have simple provisions for our journey, but we should eat and drink now while we may and while greater supplies are at hand."

"Aye, Stoneheft," Michel replied, "you should prepare well now, as we have stores here that should more than suffice and from which you may take what you might need. I am certain that our good stranger could use both victuals and a warmer garment than he now possesses for your travels to come. Wait here. I shall return from the larder anon."

Michel turned and walked out through a narrow doorway on the far side of the large room then returned moments later carrying two canvas sacks. He laid the contents of the two bags on a low table, beckoning the others to join him. On the table he spread out the food, which included some dried meats, fruit, and hard loaves, as well as a flask of wine.

"Come eat and drink, Robert. I know you have had nothing since your arrival."

Bob followed the others toward the table. He did not feel hungry but thought that eating even a little might settle his continuing nausea. What Michel spread on the table did not look appealing, but he picked out several pieces of dried fruit and broke off half a loaf then, after eyeing the others, began chewing on the fruit. The taste was vague but not unpleasant, a little like apple but different, slightly spicy. As Bob ate, Michel poured flagons of wine for all the men and a smaller cup for Tom. Bob tentatively tasted the wine. The flavor was intensely sweet and heavy but also

rather pleasant. As he ate and drank more enthusiastically, he found his nausea and apprehension easing.

As the company ate, Martin and Stoneheft spoke quietly. With the few words he was able to discern, Bob could tell they were discussing possible routes of travel. The others remained quiet and self-absorbed.

Michel finished eating, took a final gulp of wine, and then went back to the provisions room, returning after a minute with a garment made of animal skins.

"Here, Robert," he said. "This cloak is not comely but will shield you well from the cold. Your journey shall be safe, I know, among these guardsmen and less cruel with protection from the winter."

Bob took the cloak with mumbled thanks and after a moment's inspection was able to figure out how to wear it.

Nothing seemed strange anymore. There was no longer anything normal for Bob to compare to his present circumstances. The fact that he was on horseback, trudging through the snow in the middle of winter on some remote island in the company of primitive warriors who had treated him alternately as a captured prisoner then as some sort of expected hero hardly seemed any more absurd than ancient Greek coins and mysterious messages from dying patients. Bob ceased trying to figure his situation out. It seemed better for now to let things happen and adjust as well as he could.

It was nearly midday as the small band left the village, heading out over the surrounding, snow-covered fields, the wind swirling about the riders, stinging their faces with cold moisture and bringing the faint smell of the sea across the hills. The clouds were low and blew swiftly from southwest to northeast. Martin and Kevin rode ahead of Bob, and Stoneheft rode with Tom in the rear. Bob's mount was a sturdy gelding, dark red-brown in color

and chosen for its even temperament and easy ride. The company moved along the low stone fences that edged the covered fields for the better part of two hours, no one saying a word until the woods appeared ahead and to the right. On Martin's signal they halted briefly as he and Kevin conferred. Then with a gesture he led them toward the forest.

As the company entered the great wood, what caught Bob's attention was the silence. The sound of the wind and even the muffled sounds of the horses seemed engulfed by the powerful quietude of the forest. It was as if the silence itself represented a presence worthy of respect, and in whose domain they had just boldly trespassed.

The party moved ahead along the path under Martin's direction into the ever deepening stillness. Bob felt physically warmer out of the wind and drifting snow but within himself felt trepidation, like a coldness that had nothing to do with the temperature or the wind. Glancing back, he noticed on the faces of the riders behind him a look of similar apprehension. He wondered now about those powers Sean had mentioned before they set off. Somehow, though, despite his apprehension, he could not believe that the presence he perceived here in the forest was an evil one.

The riders followed what appeared to be a well-worn path when first coming into the forest, but, as they rode further in, the path became less clearly identifiable, and the more it seemed as if they were entering a more remote realm, cut off from the civilizing influence of roads and maps into a region in which they were treading uninvited. Martin, though, at the head of the little band, proceeded with cool assurance. Kevin, just behind him, seemed more wary, glancing quickly from side to side, his attention drawn to sights and sounds the others did not perceive. Bob and the other two riders, more tentative than those in front, remained several lengths behind but continued on without speaking. The sense of intrusion intensified as the group began a slow, steady ascent into the mist-enshrouded slopes of the upper forest.

After one full hour of climbing, Martin turned the group into a small clearing, then halted and dismounted. He signaled the others to do the same. The mists at this altitude were thick and cool, limiting visibility, but there was no wind. As Bob dismounted, his body instantly reminded him of his unaccustomed arduous hours in the saddle. His legs cramped and buckled beneath him as he tried to stand. Stoneheft was immediately at his side, helping Bob to his feet.

"Aye, Master Robert, 'tis plain that a horseman you are not, as is true of all healers I have had chance to meet. Allow me to aid you upright."

With Stoneheft's aid, Bob slowly stood erect, sensation returning gradually to his limbs. He dusted the snow off his clothes as he regained balance. The others in the company, also grateful to be standing back on the ground, stamped their feet and rubbed their hands. Silently, Kevin returned to his mount and took down a saddlebag filled with provisions. He passed out dried meat and fruit to the tired, hungry travelers, each one taking his rations then returning to stand by his mount and chew the tough meal.

After quickly downing his portion, Martin addressed the others.

"We are yet hours from any true shelter and safety. I do not fear any ill weather, but this is not a part of the forest in which my men can offer full protection or guidance. I am in hopes that we can yet gain another three or four hours' travel before nightfall."

"Where, then, are we, Martin?" asked Stoneheft. "I know by our climb that we are high in these hills, but I do not know the feel of these parts as you do."

"As well you might not," he replied, "for we are nigh the crest of Firebarrow Ridge."

Tom inhaled involuntarily, choking on his mouthful of meat. All eyes turned in his direction then, after he had recovered his breath, back to Martin.

Without fully understanding why, Bob's uneasiness abruptly increased. The look on Tom's face was one of alarm, much like the old man's face in the village when Bob had mentioned the name Drachma.

"Aye, well, Martin," Stoneheft continued, "you told me this course might be the truest one. We trust you to know the best. You have been appointed as the earl's envoy."

Stoneheft tipped his hat in a sort of clumsy salute to their leader. The others in the band caught the apparent gentle jest and smiled. Even Tom could not quite suppress a shy grin at Stoneheft's expense. The effect must have been what was intended, for all could sense an abrupt easing of tensions.

"Come, then, my good fellows," Martin announced. "We are off again. We must avail ourselves of what daylight we still have to get to proper shelter."

With Stoneheft's help, Bob saddled up again, as did the others. The riders were sore, but eager to get on their way. Martin remained in the lead, with Kevin again keeping watch behind him. The other three rode in a clump two lengths back. Despite the release of tension their break had provided, the riders still sensed that this was not a light venture they were on and kept conversation to a minimum.

The path continued upward for several miles before leveling off. The woods had thinned some at this altitude, and Bob noticed that, in places where the mist had lifted, he could see beyond the ridge that they were on several high, shrouded peaks, with occasional glimpses of a lofty, ominous presence, at least as high above them as they had already climbed since leaving the village.

Stoneheft noticed Bob's attention caught by the mountain.

"That'd be Croftus Knob, Master Robert, greatest peak on our fair isle, truly a sight be it winter or summer. We would then be riding along Firebarrow Ridge, as Martin has said."

"I see," Bob said, nodding. He thought about asking how high the peak might be but instead kept quiet.

An icy wind began to blow again as they rode the ridge, chilling their hands and faces. Bob was able to tuck his hands inside his cloak while still holding the reins but wished he had something to protect his face from the blast. The path that Martin chose took a slight turn downward to the left, rounding a large outcropping of bare rock. The path itself became more irregular and slippery, but in the lee that the rock provided, the wind was less severe.

It was in that period of slight respite that Bob first sensed another presence. It was nothing he could quite hear or see, but it was definitely there close by. He turned and looked behind, but there was nothing he could see, and it appeared that Tom and Stoneheft did not see or hear anything of concern. Bob thought again that the best thing to do was just to go along and let things happen and say nothing.

For a while the sensation abated, and the journey went on uneventfully. Then, as the path once more turned into a sheltered woodland, Bob felt it again—peculiar, subtle but undeniable. As the wind abated, he could perceive something at once familiar and unclear. He again looked around but saw nothing new. He shook his head as if trying to clear his senses, but it was still there.

Tom and Stoneheft looked at the stranger. There was obviously something he was seeing or hearing that they did not.

"What is it, Master Robert?" Stoneheft asked. "Do you hear something?"

Bob shook his head. "No, nothing, nothing at all."

But there it still was, like the presence of someone nearby that he should know yet could not see. As he closed his eyes he heard, faintly, but clearly...

"Bob, where are you? Bob..."

Yes, he knew that voice!

Chapter Three

The doorbell rang, and Marilyn Gilsen's heart skipped a beat, knowing it would be that detective she talked to on the phone that morning. She shook her head to clear her mind, got up and straightened her outfit, and then went to the door.

At the front door were two people.

"Good afternoon, Mrs. Gilsen?"

"Yes that's me, you must be Detective Bryant. Do come in."

"Yes, I'm Edgar Bryant," he said. "And this is Detective Lewinsky." He indicated the slight but attentive woman at his side, and displayed his badge.

"Nice to meet you both. Do come in. Can I get either of you a cup of coffee?" She shook both their hands and led them into her kitchen.

"Thank you, that would be nice. Just black for me, and for you, Chris?"

"Oh, I'm fine for now," the woman spoke, looking around at the cluttered home of the Gilsens. It had the look of people who were self-absorbed and intelligent but who did not entertain. The kitchen was busy but functional; the living room was one that was used for just that—living, with books and periodicals scattered about randomly.

Marilyn went to the coffee pot, got down a pair of mugs, and poured some coffee for herself and Detective Bryant. As she turned toward them, she said, "Why don't we just sit here in the kitchen? You know, I'm not used to talking to cops, and this whole business has got me upset."

"Why thanks, ma'am. Here, I'll take that. Sure let's just sit down here." His manner was polished and polite, if a bit condescending. "Now, you indicated to me this morning that your husband has disappeared, isn't that right?"

"Uh huh, that's right…or that seems to be right, or at least that's what the hospital indicated."

"The hospital? Why don't we just start back at the last time you saw him. I assume your husband is a doctor…"

Marilyn noticed Detective Lewinsky had taken out a small notebook and was beginning to write stuff down.

"Yes, his name is Robert Gilsen. He's a cardiologist and works mostly down at Memorial." At this point, Marilyn had to stop. She took a sip of her coffee then fought back a flood of tears. "I'm so sorry. It's just that this is so unlike him…it's just not… just not…" Marilyn just excused herself, got up and found the Kleenex dispenser, grabbed several out of the box, blew her nose, and then sat back down, trying to collect herself.

"That's all right, just take your time. We're not in any hurry."

When she was able to speak again, she recalled, "It was the night of the third, he came home late, as usual, and seemed somewhat preoccupied—"

"Preoccupied, with what?" It was said innocently enough but got the attention of Chris Lewinsky with her pad at the ready.

"Well, he seemed more than usually tired, and dwelt on his life, our life, and what seemed to be missing. It was as if he sensed there was more to be had."

"Oh, and what do you suppose he meant?"

"Oh, I don't really know. It's not as if we lack for anything, but…he did make a point of saying we never seem to sit down

anymore to a meal, without interruptions, or expectations, unless we're out of town somewhere, like at a conference or something. And you know, that much is probably true. Our interactions always seem to be interrupted by his work. But don't get me wrong, Bob loves his work."

"I see. Did you discuss anything? Did he mention anything going on at work?"

"No, not that I recall. He just kind of wistfully talked about something missing from our lives. Then he got ready for bed. Well, he drifted off to sleep. I think it was more like his head hit the pillow and he was comatose, but that's not unusual. Then I eventually fell asleep too, but not before noticing how peacefully he was sleeping, like he was actually enjoying it. Then there was that phone call in the middle of the night, also not unusual, but I could tell this particular phone call got him upset."

"Upset? How?"

"Well, it's hard to say, since I was still not quite awake, but it was typical hospital business, something about someone having trouble in the ER. Anyway, he then got up and left for the hospital, and that's the last I saw of him."

Detective Bryant sipped his cup of coffee thoughtfully then asked, "And the following day, or days, did he call or in anyway try to get in touch with you?"

"Uh, no, not once, which is also unusual. He normally calls me at some point, you know, just to talk, see how my day is going, and let me know when to expect him home." Marilyn fought a lump in her throat and took another sip of her coffee.

Chris Lewinsky was madly scribbling away on her notepad.

"I take it then, Mrs. Gilsen, that he left no note or anything to indicate that there was anything unusual going on in his life."

"No, nothing at all, other than his preoccupation, which I just wrote off to his being tired and working too many hours. No, other than that he seemed quite normal."

"Then you said the hospital called you to let you know he... what?"

"I got a call from the director of hospital security—I'm sorry, I don't remember his name—asking if he was here. I thought that was kind of strange. I'd never gotten a call from hospital security. It made me wonder if there was some kind of trouble. But he said no, just that 'they'—meaning the nurses and all—were trying to get hold of him, for the last several hours, and no one knew where he was. Why security got involved, I don't know."

More scribbling in her notepad.

"Then what happened, Mrs. Gilsen?"

"Well, later on that same day, this was the fifth, and I hadn't heard from Bob, I got a call from the administrator asking me if I could come down to the hospital. I thought, *This is really odd, especially when the administrator*—I think his name was Ken Purcell, or something like that—*called personally.* All this time, I'm getting a bit frantic, wondering what's going on, what's happened to Bob."

More frantic scribbling.

"Anyway, I went down to the hospital and met with Mr. Purcell. He told me that Bob had apparently just disappeared. He was making rounds at the hospital and then was nowhere to be found. He asked me if I had any idea where he might have gone. Then he asked if Bob and I had any trouble (as if that were any of his business). Then he suggested I call the police and make a missing persons report. So that's what I did, and that's why you're here."

"Ah, yes, that's right. In any event, what I have to do is ask you some of the same things that Mr. Purcell did, but if any of this is 'none of my business,' we can just leave it at that for now."

"Okay."

"First of all, I need to find out if your husband had gotten any threats, you know, from upset patients, former partners, anyone…"

"No, not that he told me about, and I do believe he would have said something. Actually, Bob's patients loved him, to a fault, and as for former partners, he didn't have any. He's always been

solo. For a while he tried to recruit a partner, but no one wanted to work that hard, and eventually, he just gave up."

"How about financial difficulties? Any creditors, any bad debts?"

"No, he paid off his student loans, the only thing we owe on is this house."

"Any gambling, any women, any—"

Marilyn just chuckled. "You don't know Bob, do you? I really don't think he had any time for any of that. Only mistress he ever had was medicine."

"Well, you've certainly painted the picture of a solid citizen and husband. Unfortunately, that doesn't give us much to go on. No bad habits, no bad finances, nor girlfriends. Just a model husband who up and disappeared from work.

"One more thing, Mrs. Gilsen, do you two have any children, any family we should know about? Are there any family members anywhere else we should contact?"

"No, not really. Bob and I have been unable to have kids. His family members aren't too close and live up in Canada, and I'm the only one left in my family."

"Any close friends who live either here or elsewhere?"

"Oh, he keeps fairly close track of one of his friends from residency and fellowship, a Dr. Andrew Richter. He lives now down in southern Ohio, down by Cincinnati. But he's probably as busy as Bob. Anyway, I don't recall Bob mentioning Andy recently."

"Well, I think that we'll just leave you alone now, and thanks for the coffee. If you can think of anything, no matter how insignificant you think it might be, please don't hesitate to call. Here's my card with my phone numbers. I'm sure something will turn up sooner or later. Also, if I think of anything else to ask, would it be okay if I called?"

Just then the phone rang. Marilyn got up to answer it.

"Hello…Yes, this is she."

Something inside him told Detective Bryant not to leave just yet.

"Yes, I am." Her tone of voice said this was no ordinary phone call. Marilyn Gilsen suddenly looked pale and unsteady. Edgar Bryant helped her sit down in a nearby chair.

"I see, and when was that?" She hesitated. "And you'd like to meet me to talk about it? When and where?" Again she paused. "Okay, noon tomorrow at the hospital cafeteria...and I'll ask for...how will I know you? ...All right then, good-bye."

She was visibly shaken when she hung up the phone.

After a brief pause, Detective Bryant asked, "Now, if I may be so bold, who was that on the phone? It didn't appear to be anyone you knew. Yet it was someone who had your home number."

"Yes, you're right about that. It was someone from the hospital, actually someone visiting a patient in the hospital. He said his name was Carlo something, and he had a strange accent. He said he had information for me about my husband, said he'd meet me at the hospital cafeteria—tomorrow at noon."

Chris Lewinsky had gotten out her notebook again and was busy writing.

"I must say, Mrs. Gilsen, it looks as if you are going to need some company when you go to meet this Carlo person. I think Chris and I better accompany you tomorrow. How about if we pick you up at eleven thirty?"

"Yes, you're right. It would be better if I weren't alone. You know, this has got me kind of scared. I mean, if this person has my number, do you think he also knows where I live?"

"That would be a distinct possibility. I think we can have extra patrol cars cruise this neighborhood, or we could have you stay somewhere else tonight."

"I appreciate the offer, but I think I'd better stay here, just in case Bob should come home, you know."

"Yes, that sounds reasonable," Edgar said without conviction, "but we'll definitely have extra patrols in the neighborhood tonight. You've got my card. Please call if anything disturbs you."

"Thanks, I guess I'll see you tomorrow, here?"

"Yeah, we'll pick you up at eleven thirty."

After the detectives had left, Marilyn found herself exhausted, shaky, and more afraid than she had ever been in her life. She couldn't sit down, so she paced about her house. She heard creaks and groans from every corner. She tried reading and watching TV to no avail. Her mind kept going over the possibilities and improbabilities.

Oh, Bob, she thought, *Where are you? What have they done to you?*

Chapter Four

Craycroft's head throbbed with pain. The light was already trickling in through the windows overhead.

Cursed drink! I've slept far into the morn, he thought, sitting up and tossing the covers aside. His head hurt even worse when he sat upright. It was hard to concentrate, much less plan what he was going to do with his day. Nevertheless, beneath his pounding misery was an insistent and irritating voice that seemed to be reminding him of something important, something he needed to do.

Ah, bother! he thought. *I must clear my head before this day's trials begin.*

With resigned effort, he heaved his bulk erect then found his cloak and put in on. He frowned at his fireplace, noting that it was cold, grey, and lifeless. He stooped forward, reaching into the tinderbox. His temples screamed in pain as he bent over, but he was eventually able to get a small blaze going. He coughed, sending more shooting pains through his head. Moaning miserably, he sat down on the floor, pressing his temples hard with the heels of his hands, easing the agony only slightly.

After several minutes, his headache subsided enough for Craycroft to get back up, throw two larger logs into the fireplace,

and then prepare himself a light meal of bread and cheese. The nausea did not allow him to eat much, so mostly he sat and again tried to collect his thoughts. There was something he needed to do…

Then he remembered.

The book! he thought. *I never did find the book.*

In fact, he did not remember coming back to his quarters after his evening revels with the apprentices and musician, but what he did remember of the evening did comfort him ever so slightly. He closed his eyes, and the almost painful beauty of the harpist's music came back to him. For a moment, he was back in the thrall of the melodious magic of the evening. Then his pounding headache brought him back to the reality of the present cold morning.

Ah, yes, I must again seek out the book, then perhaps find audience later with the earl. There are too many unsettled questions, too many difficult choices for me alone. And what of Drachma's most dangerous summoning of powers? I am surely unfit for all of this!

A loud knocking at his door interrupted Craycroft's thoughts.

Ah, who now? he wondered as he reluctantly got up to answer the summons. *There have been more than enough crises here of late.*

At the door was a young messenger Craycroft did not know.

"Well, lad, what brings you?" he said, not too amicably.

"Ah, Master Craycroft, you are needed," the youth sputtered. "Councilor Rust says it is a matter of some importance, and we should not delay."

Oh, God, not him again! Craycroft thought but outwardly held his composure.

"Very well, lad, we shall go. First let me get my satchel, for who knows what his summons may bring?"

As he prepared himself to go out, Craycroft felt a familiar sensation of dread come over him, overpowering even the pain in his head.

"Well, Councilor, I am here. I must tell you that I do not feel very well this morning. It is my hope that your summons will warrant my coming out on this miserable day."

Craycroft's words were tempered with a slight smile, and Rust was able to detect the subtle chiding as he let the master in.

"Good morrow, Master. Surely you know me well enough by now to believe I would not trouble you without reason. Please, come in from the cold. I have made a comfortable fire in the parlor."

The parlor was in fact pleasantly warm. Without asking, Craycroft sat heavily in a chair near the fireplace.

"Now tell me, Councilor, what is the issue of such urgency that you sent a messenger in haste for me?"

"Ah, my good friend, it is truly a matter of which I have little knowledge, but I hope that you are able to enlighten me enough that I shall be able to carry out my tasks as the earl has directed."

Craycroft felt a tightening in his stomach. Whatever Rust's news was, he knew it would be, at the very least, unpleasant.

"You see," Rust continued, "I received this message from the earl last night." He reached behind him and took a small paper from the table. "I did attempt to summon you then, but you were not in quarters."

"True, I was out."

Craycroft took the paper then frowned as he read the terse message to Rust from his liege.

> Councilor:
> Convene the council on the morrow
> Upon my order.
> Inform the members of the following:
> I am ill, and presently unable to govern.
> Master Craycroft has full knowledge
> of present matters, and shall

Govern in my stead.
Heed him.
Drachma the Elder has summoned
Powers for our aid, and such
Have arrived upon the Isle.
Master Falma and guardsman Kerlin
Are upon a further quest for our aid,
But are by report lost in a winter storm,
Whereabouts not know
Anything further you must know, ask it of Craycroft.
Shepperton,
The Earl

Craycroft felt a mixture of embarrassment, frustration, and anger as he read the letter. "I knew that the earl appeared tired, but he did not tell me he was ill. I must go attend to him. You say you received this letter last night?" Craycroft realized, with no little remorse, that even if Rust had found him last night, he would not have been fit to care for the earl's needs at the time. He wondered to himself why the earl had not summoned him directly if he were ill enough to relinquish rule of the island.

"True," Rust answered his question. "It came at the end of the third watch, quite late." Discreetly, the councilor avoided asking Craycroft's whereabouts the previous night. "It is well you should see to the earl's needs, but pray, tell me some of what I must know before you go. If I am to convene the council as directed, I must ask for your help. I know little of what the earl mentions in his letter. What has Drachma done? What aid has he summoned? And what of Master Falma…an old man, on a perilous mission… lost in a winter storm? What do I tell the council of all this?"

"Let me tell you this, Councilor—I do not envy your position. But let me also say that I am aware only of some of what has transpired and do not feel worthy of the trust the earl has placed in me at this time. What I am able to tell you is that the earl and Drachma have perceived a peril to our people of a

magnitude greater than others discerned, and that this threat is intimately connected with the deaths of our painters and potters, and further possibly relating to the death of Lord Vincente, and even our beloved lady Felicia."

Rust stared at the master, regretfully realizing that the earl was right to choose Craycroft. There was no one else in any way as capable to govern without risking dissention in the council.

"What, then shall I say to the council?" he asked.

Craycroft though for a moment, then answered, "Tell them, word for word, what the earl directed you to say; and further, that you have conferred with me, and that matters are now such that no action will be required of the council, only that these things are told them for their edification. This is in hopes that wild rumors can be contained before action would be required of the governing body."

Inwardly, Craycroft groaned under the weight of this unexpected new burden. He was meant to teach, tell stories, and to heal, not govern. His head throbbed anew with pain.

"Then Master, may I request your presence at the council meeting? I am quite certain that there will be questions I am ill-prepared to answer."

"Ah, good Councilor, today I think not, for as you must realize, my duty takes me anon to the side of our liege. I know not what ails him, nor what it may take to return him to good health. I fear I may be wasting precious time here now. I must be off. Rest assured, though, your summons was not in vain." A feeble smile appeared briefly on the master's face.

As he got up to leave, he handed the paper back to Rust. "Here, you may wish to keep this safely in your possession. The earl's seal is there for verification before the council if it be needed. And, good friend, one more request—will you have Father Henri offer a special prayer for the earl today? I must now do what I am able."

Stepping back outside, Craycroft felt somewhat ill himself, but at least he knew the nature of his own malaise.

The atmosphere at the earl's chambers was thick with strain and worry. Craycroft's arrival was obviously anticipated, and he was shown quickly to the earl's side. He was not prepared for what he saw, felt, and smelled.

"My liege! You did not tell me you were ill. I would have stayed to help you."

Before Craycroft, in the bed, lay the earl. But this was not the same man he had seen just two days earlier. Here was a desperately ill man who no longer looked the part of ruler. His grey hair fell in strands of perspiration about his drawn face. He breathed through pursed, dry lips, darkly purple in color. Every breath seemed an effort and was punctuated by paroxysms of coughing which sapped his failing strength. An audible rattling sound was present with each inspiration, and there in his presence was that unmistakable, sickly sweet odor.

"Ah, my dear friend, Craycroft," he said between gasps, "that is precisely...why I did not tell you I was ill. You...had more important things...to do...than to attend...to this dying man."

"Oh, my liege, nothing would be more important than your care. I feel so ashamed I did not come sooner."

"Nonsense. What could you have done...in truth...for me?"

Craycroft only shook his head.

"Listen, my friend, I am glad that you have come. Now... come closer, so I may tell you...what you will need to know."

"My liege," he answered as he approached the bed, "pray let me do what I may to ease your discomfort, then we may talk of what I need to know."

"Very well...if you must...but there may not be much... time."

A spasm of painful coughing seized the earl, bringing up from his burdened lungs a large issue of bloody pus. He lay back, exhausted.

Craycroft quickly examined his patient, finding the circumstances all too similar to Felicia's recent illness. Talking to the servants, he found that the earl had, indeed, been ill on and off for the past week or more but had kept his illness concealed from all but his closest attendants.

As he had done with Felicia, he sent a servant off to fetch some warm water and salt. From his satchel he brought out what was left of the aromatic oil, then put together the apparatus for inhalation that he had used with Felicia.

The earl was able, between racking spasms, to obtain some measure of comfort, and was breathing more easily when Craycroft pulled up a chair close to the earl's bed.

"Now, my liege," he said, quietly, "you may tell me what I must know of our present circumstances, though I must tell you I do not truly feel worthy nor capable of the tasks you would have me carry out."

"Ah, then you have seen Rust?"

Craycroft nodded.

"Well, that is good. What I must tell you…is…to use whatever means you may need…to seek Drachma's knowledge and counsel. He has told me that he will keep you informed… about what he is doing. He does know that I am ill…and that I… have appointed you to govern…in my stead."

"Very well," Craycroft replied. "I shall do what I am able. But tell me, what of Falma and the guardsman? What do you know of them?"

"Little, I am afraid. What I was told was…that young Tom is safely in the care of Drachma and his woodsmen, but Master… Falma and…Kerlin went elsewhere, and into…a winter storm." The earl lay back, exhausted, and without saying another word drifted off into uneasy sleep.

Craycroft did not pursue the matter further. Sleep, such as it was, would be the best thing for the earl at this moment. But the thought of old Master Falma, frail as he seemed, out on horseback

caught in one of the island's infamous winter storms was more than he could bear. He had to find out more. Whether he wished it or not, he was now responsible.

As the earl slept, Craycroft made use of the time to make the rounds among the earl's servants, in order to find out as quickly as possible whom he needed to contact for information, and to get things accomplished. He was somewhat surprised to find the servants very willing to help. Evidently, the earl had prepared his staff for this time of illness, and now, as his illness had become graver, they seemed glad that someone was in a position of authority prearranged by the earl himself.

Within the space of two hours, Craycroft had learned enough of the servants' names and positions to feel sure that he would be able to obtain what information he might need to begin to carry forth what he knew of the earl's wishes.

As he reflected on the current state of affairs, though, what Craycroft discovered was just how lonely he felt. He had just lost one dear friend, and it appeared as though his liege would also die soon. Good Master Falma was lost in a storm, and now, young Tom, who had shown such promise, was also away on some mission he was only just beginning to understand. He could not count Rust or any of the other councilors among his friends and feared that the earl's choice of leadership might not sit well at all with the council.

And now, above all else, he was thrown into an alliance with the powerful and unpredictable Drachma himself. This at a time when Drachma appeared to have played his most dangerous gambit, calling upon powers none had ever before invoked.

As he pondered what to do next, Craycroft realized the headache which had plagued him before had eased and become just a gnawing in his stomach, somewhat like hunger, enough so that he sent one of the younger servant boys after some food and drink. He dispatched another youth toward the council chambers to await word of the council's actions or requests.

He returned his attention then to the earl, finding that his liege had awakened. The earl appeared not well, but more comfortable than before. He sat down again in the chair by the earl's side.

"My liege, how do you feel?" he asked.

"Weary, but better...I thank you. Now tell me...is there anything you need to know? I know you well enough...to believe...I have chosen well."

"Ah, my liege, I do not feel worthy of your trust. Neither do I feel capable of my new duties."

"My friend...let me tell you a secret. If you felt yourself... capable, I would not...trust you to...govern."

The earl sank into his pillow then abruptly sat back up in the throes of another racking spasm of coughing, violent and draining. He finally lay back once more, drenched with perspiration and horribly dusky in color.

Craycroft took a clean rag and dried the earl's face and chest, then prepared another breathing treatment. His own hands shook as he held the steaming flask close to the face of his liege. Beads of sweat ran down his forehead into his eyes, clouding the scene before him. Feelings of grief, rage, and impotence welled up inside.

No, this cannot be! he thought. *I am no ruler. I am not even a healer in the presence of my lord's greatest need.*

"Master Craycroft..."

He turned toward the doorway to see who spoke, but his vision was still blurred. He set the misting flask down, rubbed his eyes, then turned again to see that it was young Simon, the servant he had sent for food.

"Master, I have the food you requested."

"Ah, yes, thank you, lad. Set the tray there on the table, if you will."

The boy nodded. "Very well, sir." He set the tray down. "Also, Master, I was given this message to give you."

"Message?"

"Aye, Master, from the bird keeper. I was told to give it to you or the earl."

"Very well, bring it here to me."

The boy came hesitantly toward the sickbed, handed Craycroft a small cylinder, and then immediately stepped back two paces.

"Will there be anything else, sir?" he asked.

"No, that will be all for now, thank you, lad."

Simon bowed quickly, then turned and left the room.

Craycroft looked down at his hand, then unsealed one end of the cylinder as he had seen the earl do before him. A small piece of paper was curled up within the cylinder, which he was able to remove with a needle that he kept in his satchel. There again, on the paper, was the familiar script, and a short message:

Our Summons has been answered.
A healer, possessing great magic,
Has arrived on the Isle.
Safe conduct to the Castle shall be
Provided.
There may be more to tell.
Drachma

Craycroft read the note again, shaking his head. He looked at the earl, asleep once more. He clenched his fists, crumpling the note.

No! he thought. *That is too much to hope for.*

Chapter Five

The snowstorm began to let up enough to see a few lengths ahead. There were no details visible, but Falma could just make out some shapes to suggest the edge of the mountainside to the right. He had not seen nor heard from Kerlin for some time now but could think of nothing to do but keep going slowly along the same direction in the faint hope that Kerlin might find him. He felt certain that if he stayed still, he would die of the cold. He knew just as certainly that he was lost with no sense of place or direction. There was no sound but the breathing and padded steps of his horse, and no landmarks to be sent.

Falma kept going steadily along what seemed to be a path for the better part of an hour, even as the snow gradually receded. The mountains now lay behind him, and ahead were low, rough hills. He could see up ahead what appeared to be some farm buildings and a small wisp of smoke rising from close by.

At long last, he thought, *some shelter for my weary bones, with perhaps a fire to warm me.*

Strangely, as he trudged directly toward the buildings, he seemed to be getting no closer. They remained in the distance and only indistinctly visible. He stopped his horse and rubbed his eyes clear then looked again. Now he could no longer be sure.

What looked earlier like buildings might just be rocks and woods. He sat still, with frustration and despair nearly closing in. He considered turning around and going back the way he had come.

No, he thought, *just a little farther, just to be certain.*

Reluctantly, he urged his horse forward again.

Then there appeared something definite ahead, a small, dark shape that was moving. Falma blinked and rubbed his eyes again. Yes, there it was, something moving toward him, a person, perhaps! His heart pounded in anticipation as he urged his mount forward.

Now he could definitely see—it was a person, walking slowly in his direction. As he came closer, he could tell that it was a woman, but dressed in very peculiar clothing, and with her hair cut short, like a soldier or page. Then he could see that she had been injured, was bleeding from a cut over her right eye, and that she had been weeping. He stopped his horse and dismounted stiffly.

He had truly never seen anyone like this before in all his life. She was garbed in clothing of a most unusual sort, but of a quality beyond the means of any but a highborn lady.

"My good lady," he said, "what ails you? You are hurt..."

Judy stared at this feeble old man who had just gotten off his horse. She rubbed away the blood and tears from her eyes. Her hands and feet were numb, and her forehead throbbed miserably, but here in front of her was certainly the man described in her letter, though frailer appearing than she would have expected.

As the man came toward her, she opened her mouth to speak, but what came out was a racking spasm of coughing.

Falma backed off a space to let this strange young woman catch her breath. After a moment, Judy's breathing eased, and she was able to speak.

"I'm sorry. It's just that I've been in a car wreck, back there by those farm houses." She pointed in the direction Falma had seen what he thought were buildings. "I'm not really too badly hurt, just shaken up a bit. I don't really know why I started walking in

this direction, but there was no one home at the farm, I didn't want to just stand around. I guess it's a good thing I did, huh?"

Falma stared at her, dumbfounded. He could understand only a few of the torrent of words that came from her mouth and almost nothing of her meaning.

Judy noticed his look of incomprehension.

"I'm sorry," she said, opening up her small purse, fumbling with numb fingers for the paper she knew was inside. "Let me explain. You see, I got this paper in here that said you would find me. I'm sure that sounds pretty weird…ah, here it is. Here, read this. Maybe you'll understand it better."

She handed Falma the paper from her purse, which he took cautiously. He rubbed his eyes, then focused on the writing, the familiarity of which hit him like a blow. He blinked then looked again at the script.

> A wise old man shall he be,
> Riding as if a Knight alone.
> Join him on his steed,
> Showing to him my seal,
> Affixed hereon in crimson,
> The path shall be
> Into the trees,
> Then following yonder stream,
> Hence, to shelter,
> Now, go, m'lady,
> We await!

Falma's hand shook as he gave the paper back to Judy. "My good lady, there is no need to show me the seal, for I recognize the hand that wrote this. It is Drachma's work. That I know, and know too that he has reached beyond all reason. Alas, I am no knight, just a weak old man, whose name is Falma, but my horse can easily carry us both, though I have no saddle fit for a lady such as yourself, and I know the way shall be arduous. If you should prefer then, you may ride, and I shall walk alongside."

"That's nonsense, Mr. Falma. You're in far worse shape to walk than I am, and as you say, that horse can carry us both quite easily. We'll both ride, just like the note here says. By the way, my name is Judy, Judy Morrison."

She held out her hand, which Falma gently held, as he bowed and kissed her gloved fingers.

"I am honored, m' lady. Let me welcome you to Shepperton Isle, though I am hardly fit to do so, and the weather has become most inhospitable."

"Oh, you'll do just fine, Mr. Falma, but you'll have to pardon me. I have no idea where Shepperton Isle is or how I got here, though I must admit, a lot of very strange things have been going on lately, and somehow this fits right in."

"Ah, lady Judy, you are likely very far from home, as your speech suggests, but as to how you came to be here, that Drachma himself must try to answer, for it certainly appears to be his efforts that have brought you to this time and place."

"Yes, this Drachma person seems to have been sending a lot of strange messages, and in the most unusual ways."

"Aye, of that I have no doubt."

After consulting the note again, Falma decided that the nearest outcropping of the forest, back slightly and toward the far side of the mountains, must be the trees mentioned in the letter. With some effort, they were both able to get on Falma's mount, with Judy sitting behind and with her arms around the old man's waist for support. Bringing his horse about, Falma headed off toward the forest again. For the better part of the next half hour, neither rider spoke, each thinking his own thoughts, trying to come to terms with the bizarre nature of their journey. Without realizing it, they began following a path that ran by the edge of a forest stream, partly frozen over. The path led gently upwards, along the side of the mountains. Without the storm to hinder them, the way was not particularly arduous, though the strain on Falma's old body became more obvious as they went along,

for it had been a longer, more strenuous day than any he could remember in years.

"I hope you will pardon me, my good lady," he said at last, "but I am weary beyond measure, and if we do not find shelter soon, I fear we must stop for a spell, or I should drop."

"Oh, of course, sir, that would be fine with me. You stop whenever you need to. I think we're both kind of lost and tired, though we do seem to be following the stream that the note talks about. Maybe the shelter will be coming up soon."

"Aye, perhaps just around yonder curve of the path."

"Sure, let's go for that and see."

As she spoke the total absurdity of her present circumstances struck Judy. Just this morning (or was it really this morning?) she had awakened in her own bed in the city, later had driven out to attend Josh's funeral, and things just got weirder and weirder since then. Now here she was on horseback in the middle of winter, on some unknown island with an old, frail man who spoke like some character out of a movie, smelled funny, and called her m' lady, and all because of some peculiar note written by an even more mysterious ancient forest person who called himself Drachma. On top of that, she left her wrecked car in a snowdrift, who knows how many miles back, with little hope of being able to locate it again anytime soon.

It did turn out that Judy was right about the shelter. As they came around a slight rise and curve in the path, there was ahead of them to the right a low, simple building, little more than a hut, but sturdy, and with a thin trickle of smoke rising from its chimney. Nothing could have been more inviting to the two travelers than that sight.

Judy dismounted easily then helped Falma to the ground. They tethered the horse to a post then walked into the hut without knocking. What appeared before them brought tears of startled gratitude to Falma's eyes. There in the middle of the deserted hut was a table with two chairs. On the table was a wineskin with two

goblets and a tray laden with bread, cheese, dried meat, nuts, and dried fruit. In the corner, a welcome fire burned in the fireplace.

"Ah, lady, I can see we are expected. I know not the whereabouts of our gracious host, but we will offer him our thanks when we next meet. For now, m'lady, let us rest and enjoy this grand respite from our travel."

Not until she started eating did Judy realize she was hungry. The food was simple and hearty, the wine strong and sweet. Falma ate as one who had not seen food in a week and was grateful that there was ample provided. The wine began to quickly take hold, as he found it increasingly difficult to keep from nodding.

"Look, Mr. Falma, I know you must be just terribly tired. Maybe you could lie down for a while and rest. The fire is warm, and the floor looks a lot more comfortable than your horse."

"Ah, lady Judy, you are kind, but I fear I am a poor host if I should let you watch while I sleep."

"Nonsense, I'll be just fine. You go ahead and rest. I'll just stay and enjoy this wine and warmth."

"Very well, m' lady, but I would ask that you waken me should any come near. It is quite obvious to me that we have been expected."

"Okay, it's a deal. I'll wake you if anyone comes snooping around. Now you just lie here and get some rest. Look, they've even left a few blankets here. Lie down. I'll cover you up."

It was not long before Falma was sleeping the sound sleep of exhaustion, and Judy was left alone again to ponder her circumstances. She thought about how the day had started like any ordinary day, but as the time grew later, it seemed to Judy as if she were falling into a web of weirdness from which she had no way to extricate herself, and no clues with which to orient herself.

Now here she was in a small hut on a snow-covered mountain, apparently on some island, God knows where, with a frail old man who might have walked out of some fairytale and evidently was sent to find her without knowing it.

Though she tried, Judy could not fully believe what she saw, heard, and smelled around her, although there was no mistaking the very real effect of the wine, warming and numbing her inside.

A little too sweet, but not a bad vintage, she thought wryly. *Maybe if I have just a little more, I'll fall asleep, too, and find out that this was all just some really strange dream.*

She sat and sipped some more, letting her mind wander as it would, when she was startled to see there was someone else in the hut, standing by the door.

Chapter Six

The hunting shelter was a welcome site, especially for Bob. The others seemed well accustomed to riding for many hours, but Bob's back and legs were aching to the point of numbness. He had no idea how long they had been riding, except that they had started out in the morning, and now the evening light was fading rapidly. His watch said 12:30, but that meant nothing in his new environment. Once inside, Bob sat in a seat that felt unusually comfortable in contrast to the saddle. Martin was able to quickly get a fire going while the others put together a rough but hearty meal. As they made preparations, Bob quietly observed the others, paying particular attention to young Tom, noting again how incredibly like Josh he looked, but, by contrast, in obvious good health. His features were identical and even his voice strikingly similar.

After eating, they all sat about the fireplace relaxing, Bob staring intently at the fire, the others staring at Bob.

"Tell me, then, Master Robert," Stoneheft interrupted his pensive silence, "what might you be pondering so deeply, if I may be so bold as to ask."

Bob chuckled. "Actually, I was just thinking how much I would dearly love a good cup of coffee."

"Coffee? What is coffee?"

"Oh, no, don't tell me you guys don't know what coffee is. How remote can this place be that you don't even know about coffee?"

Stoneheft turned to the others, who shrugged and stared back blankly.

"I fear, Master Robert, that none here know aught of this thing you call coffee. Pray tell, what is it?"

Bob leaned back. "Well, where I live, a place called the United States of America, or the US for short, coffee is one of those things we just kind of take for granted. Actually, it's a drink made by running very hot water over some ground-up, roasted beans that come from the mountains of certain tropical countries." He noticed their puzzled expressions. "You know, places where it's warm all year round, and they never have snow and ice."

"Aye," Tom spoke, to everyone's surprise, "I have heard of such places, but in truth, I though they were only stories, mere fancy."

"Oh, no, Tom, they're very real and very wonderful. Anyway, in some of these countries they grow these coffee beans on the sides of mountains then sell these beans to the rest of the world to make coffee. I guess in some of these smaller countries, raising and selling coffee is what keeps them going."

"Going?" Martin asked, "What do you mean by that?"

"Well, the money they get from coffee allows for the purchase of things that aren't made in the country, such as cloth and machinery, and helps pay for things such as education and medical care."

A light of understanding shone on Tom's face. "I believe I comprehend. It is much like our painters and potters here on the isle. The sale of their craft allows our liege lord, the earl, to provide for the needs of all here in ways that we would be otherwise unable." The others looked at Tom. It was as if he had said something as awkward as letting out a family secret. Seeing their faces, he blushed slightly but said nothing.

Bob caught none of the unstated message and went on, "that must be quite some business of yours, this pottery. That's the second time I've heard it mentioned since I've been here."

His statement was met with only awkward silence. Each man's eyes avoided Bob's questioning face. The silence persisted until Tom spoke again.

"Tell us, then, Master Robert, if you will, of the place from which you came. Truly it must be a land of great wealth and power."

Bob thought for a moment then said, "Okay, I'll tell you about it, but first, answer one question for me. This may seem like a stupid question, but tell me, what year is this?"

The question caught them all off-balance, as it seemed so impertinent.

"Why, as we all know,' said Stoneheft, "'tis the year of our Lord one thousand four hundred ninety-two."

"1492!" Bob let out a slow whistle. "You've got to be kidding." He could see that they were not. "1492, that's the year Columbus discovered America!"

Again, his words were met with stares of incomprehension.

"All right, then, it looks like I've figured some of this out and probably ought to explain what I can. You see, I'm not just from a long way away in distance but in time as well. Where I came from isn't just a big ocean away, but also five hundred years beyond."

The men gasped, almost in unison.

"How is this possible?" Stoneheft asked. "I have never heard of such a thing."

"I have absolutely no idea, and this certainly was none of my doing. In fact, it would seem that someone on this island has a much better idea than any of us what I'm doing here. After all, weren't you folks sent to get me? That should tell you something. Whoever sent you probably knows something."

"Aye," Martin replied, "you are correct, but, in truth, we did not comprehend more than our task, which was to escort safely back to the earl's castle a man of great powers, held by the village guards. I must tell you, though, that you now have provoked our interest. Pray, tell us more of whence you came."

Bob thought for a moment then said, "Okay, I'll tell you something about the world I came from, but you've got to realize a few things. The first thing is that an awful lot has changed in the last five hundred years, and much of what I tell you, you're going to have a hard time believing or even understanding. The second thing is that you will be hearing things that no one else in the world knows, and maybe you shouldn't be repeating what I tell you to just anybody."

Tom felt the shiver again run down his spine and felt his heart begin to race.

Martin pondered what Bob said then replied, "You are correct, Master Robert, there may be danger in powerful new knowledge. We must all, here in this room, vow to tell none but our liege lord any of what you reveal. Is this agreed by all?"

Martin looked around, and all nodded agreement.

"Do you, Stoneheft, swear this?"

"I do."

"And you, Kevin, do you swear upon your honor?"

"Aye. Upon my honor."

"And you, Tom, do you swear to all here, that you will tell none but our liege?"

Tom swallowed then answered hoarsely, "That I do swear."

"There, Master Robert, you have heard us all swear to this, and we are all men of honor, to that I can vouch."

"Well, I really didn't mean to make such a big deal of all this, but I believe you. Anyway, thanks. Now, let me begin by telling you what is happening this very year, on the other side of that same wide ocean I came across, somehow, to get here. There is a man, named Christopher Columbus, who left the country of Spain with three ships, setting out on a quest to prove two things. He will be successful in one and fail at the other, but his greatest success will be the discovery of something entirely new yet something he will never in his lifetime understand."

Bob now had the rapt attention of all in the room, but nothing compared to the eager gleam in Tom's eyes.

"The first thing Columbus set out to prove was that the earth is not flat but round, like a ball. The other thing he tried—actually I should say will try—to prove is that there is a passageway to India and the Far East by continually traveling west."

"It seems a certain fool's quest to me," said Stoneheft. "Trying to fall off the end of the earth in a ship, indeed!"

"Ah, but as I told you, he will be successful in one of his pursuits, and that would be showing that the world is, in fact, round, like a ball. He never will be able to find that passage to India in his lifetime, but in trying to do so he will discover a new land, which will become known as America."

Tom could not restrain himself, and asked, "but Master Robert, how can it be that the world is round? Would we not all fall off?"

The others murmured their own versions of the same question, chuckling as they did at the impossibility of what Bob was saying.

"Well, let me see if I can explain it to you in a way that might make some sense. First of all, you have to realize just how tiny we are in comparison to the world, smaller than a tiny speck of dust would be in comparison to a huge castle…"

Bob went on to explain in the simplest terms he could the concepts of gravity and world geography to his rapt, half-comprehending audience, but when he attempted to describe the relative size and importance of the sun in the solar system, he could see that he was losing all but young Tom.

"I think I'd better stop here. I can see that this is all a bit too much to grasp all at once. Maybe you have some questions I could try to answer."

"Ah, Master Robert," Stoneheft replied, "what you have said is beyond our ken, though we know you do speak the truth. Would you tell us, though, of this land from which you come? As

young Tom has said, it must truly be a land of great wealth and power, beyond anything we know here on this isle."

Bob thought for a moment, trying to think about what to say, and how to say it. Then an idea came to him. He reached into his pocket and pulled out his penlight.

"You're right when you say I come from a land of great wealth and power, but I should tell you that power is something that exists in everything around us, and it is no exaggeration to say that, contained within a handful of dirt, is more power than you will see in a mighty storm, it's just that the key is in knowing how to find and use that power. Let me give you a small example. In our age we have learned to harness a form of power called electricity. Now this is a kind of power you are already familiar with in the form of lightning. The problem is that lightning is uncontrollable, but we have learned to make use of this same power in smaller, more controllable forms. In my hand here I have what appears to be a simple stick or wand. If you look, though, I can take this stick apart, and inside is something called a battery."

To his astonished audience Bob demonstrated how he could unscrew the top of his penlight and pop out the two small batteries. He then let the others see and feel the objects made of more exquisite handiwork they had could ever have imagined. They were simply awestruck by the materials and craftsmanship contained in objects that to Bob were as mundane as two ordinary AAA alkaline batteries.

"Anyway," Bob went on after Stoneheft reverently returned the little cells, "the most astonishing thing about these objects is that they hold within them what you might consider a tiny bit of lightening, which I can now control. Here, let me show you."

He could see a mixture of fear and excitement in the faces of his companions as they each stepped back a pace.

"Look now, as I press this little button on the top of this wand, it suddenly sends out a light that's brighter than any torch."

They all gasped and involuntarily shaded their eyes as Bob shone the bright beam of light on each of his companions in turn.

"There's no reason to be afraid. It won't hurt you, but when you look at the light directly, you can see that it's almost as bright as a tiny, little sun. Here, I'll let you pass this around and play with it. Really, it won't hurt you."

One by one, beginning with Tom, they each took the penlight and, with Bob's coaching, learned to operate the little on/off button and then shone the light on each other. For the better part of an hour, they carried on like children with an amazing new toy that they just couldn't put down.

At one point in the merriment, Bob did try to resume his little lecture then thought better of it. He found himself thoroughly enjoying the scene before him, in which the simple technology of a penlight provided a joyous and awe-inspiring interface with a future no one could have imagined.

Eventually, they returned the penlight to Bob, who clipped it back in his coat pocket.

"Maybe I'd better keep it safe with me. You never know when it might come in handy, and, unfortunately, the batteries won't last forever, and I'm quite sure we won't find any more of them around here."

They all laughed at that notion, then passed the wine around the room for refills. As Bob sipped his sweet wine, he could feel it begin to numb his senses, and he started to nod.

"Ah, a long enough day for our weary traveler," said Martin. "Listen, I shall take first watch, then you, Kevin, second, with Stoneheft last watch. We must try to make the castle by nightfall tomorrow. Our Master Robert will need good food, clothing, and a comfortable bed as an honored guest of the earl."

"Aye, well said," replied Stoneheft. "An early morrow it shall be."

Bob had no trouble falling asleep on his simple bed of blankets and straw but found himself awake and restless several

hours later. He looked about, and saw that Kevin was up and awake, the rest sleeping soundly. He sat upright then went over to where Kevin sat, tending the fire.

He pulled up a seat by the fire and whispered, "Tell me, Kevin, what is it you're guarding against? Is there trouble on the Island? Are we in any danger?"

"Ah, in these woods, there is always some danger. Thieves and brigands are ever about, with this isle being a favorite place for hiding plunder. But here, upon this mountain, in the middle of a winter's snow, I think those dangers less likely. Yet, somehow, I am not at ease, and I sense that Martin is likewise. There are rumblings of discontent within the council, and we know not if some of the lords might have ambitions of power. If that be, then our work is never safe.

"But rest you well, Master Robert. Your guard is the best on the isle. You are as safe with us as with any. On that I would stake my life. Now you should try to get a little sleep. The morrow comes early, and another long ride awaits us."

"Thanks, Kevin, I'll try."

Bob returned to his bed of blankets, lay tossing for a while, then drifted off again, dreaming of hospital corridors, cardiac monitors, and dying patients. Sick old men, short of breath, with swollen legs…

Chapter Seven

Craycroft could feel trouble ahead. There was something in the tone of voice the page had used that thinly hid fear and anxiety. No doubt, things had not gone entirely smoothly for Rust at the convention of the council. He debated whether he should even answer the council's request to appear, pleading his need to remain in attendance with the earl; but the earl now seemed to be resting comfortably. There was truly little he could do here, and it might seem prudent, at the very least, to address the Council of Lords. After all, their liege lord was still alive, and it was his directive they must accept or risk his wrath. That thought, however, gave Craycroft no comfort. He did not feel ready for political battle.

"Well enough, lad," he said at last, "I shall go with you to the council, but first I must leave word with the earl's servants that, should I be needed, they must summon me at once, for my allegiance is still here with my lord, the earl."

"Very well, sir, of course. I shall await you here."

The master took one more occasion to be certain that the earl remained comfortable, then let his close servants know that they should send at once with word of any change in the earl's condition, or if they should become the least bit concerned about his state.

The day was cloudy, not as cold as it had been, but there was still the cutting wind, carrying moisture toward the mountains from the sea. Craycroft wrapped his shawl about his face and headed out, with the page, toward the council chambers. Along the way, his thoughts were of Falma. He wished he knew more of the old master's fate, and feared the worst. Falma was one ally Craycroft could ill afford to lose now. As he plodded on over the trampled snow, he tried to imagine what he would say to the council if they asked about Falma.

As they reached the council chambers, Craycroft turned to the page. "Hear me, lad. I would ask that you return to the earl's chambers and wait there for any word of his condition. Come at once if the servants give you any tidings, good or ill."

"Aye, Master, I shall go anon. And please, sir, if you are in any need, may I suggest you call upon Sandy. He will serve you right well."

"Right, I shall. I know the lad. Now, be off with you. These are troubled times."

The heavy outer door to the council chambers closed hard behind Craycroft as he entered. There another page showed him into the great hall. He entered deliberately, looking cautiously about the room for signs of friendship, enmity, fear, or disdain. What he saw did not cheer him. Of the six councilors, only Rust seemed at all pleased with the master's arrival.

"Ah, Master Craycroft, it is good that you have come. Pray, tell us, how is our lord, the earl?"

Craycroft looked slowly about the room before answering. "When I left, the earl was resting in fair comfort. He is, of course, gravely ill, but," he added, with careful emphasis, "he is of sound mind and heart. His voice, though weak, still carries the full weight of his authority."

After a moment's silence, Lord Reordan cleared his throat then asked, "Well enough, then, are you able to tell the council what we may expect as to the likelihood that our lord, the earl,

may recover from his illness? As you are aware, Councilor Rust has brought us tidings that concern us all very deeply."

"Aye, my Lord Reordan, I am aware of what Councilor Rust has brought before you. As to the earl's chance of recovery, I can only say that, in persons similarly ill whom I have had the opportunity to attend and one very recently, there would seem to be little hope—"

Craycroft's words were cut off by agitated murmurings among the councilors. This was too much for Craycroft. He raised his arm and spoke in a voice of restrained thunder, "Councilors all! You have summoned me here, away from duties that all reasonable men would deem to be of great importance, and you have not the courtesy to hear me out. I should expect better of you than this."

Sudden silence enveloped the room, but no eyes, save those of Councilor Rust, could meet the healer's glare.

"You asked what I believed in regard to the possibility that our lord, the earl, might recover from his illness. Now hear me out. I have seen persons afflicted with illness of similar nature, and, in truth, none had the good fortune or the touch of providence to recover. However, as you must surely recall from what Councilor Rust told you, our mysterious benefactor, Drachma, the Elder of the Forest, has summoned aid, which has, by his account, arrived upon our isle in the form of a healer possessing great powers. It is my hope, as it surely also is yours, that this healer can be brought to bear his craft in pursuit of a cure for the earl. I can say no more on this particular matter at present, as I have not seen nor have I met this healer. Be assured, though, that the council will be apprised of any further progress in this regard."

The council sat silent for a time, each member pondering the implications of what Craycroft had just told them. Eventually, Councilor Reordan spoke again.

"What you say has certain merit, Master Craycroft, and we do, of course, hope that this healer of whom you speak can restore our liege lord to health, but we of the council would not be true

to our duties if we did not also consider what we should do in the event that, Heaven forbid, our good earl would not recover."

Craycroft could feel a tightening in his throat at Reordan's words, sensing that they were merely a bluff, and that the real point of the councilor's verbal dagger was yet to be thrust in his direction.

"Tell us, then, what you would make of these, our earl's words, brought here by Councilor Rust."

It was a baited question, Craycroft could tell, as he took the paper from the councilor's hand. After scanning the familiar note, he handed it back to the councilor.

"I had opportunity earlier this day to see our earl's letter. Furthermore, I have had opportunity to speak with the earl himself. It would seem to me that the note requires no explanation, that the earl's wishes, whatever we may think of them, are quite clear. What, pray tell, do you find unclear in the letter?"

A brief look of disappointment flashed across Reardon's face as he realized Craycroft would not easily fall for his ploy. He hesitated briefly before answering.

"My good Master Craycroft, we of the council have, as you must know, only the highest regard for your skills as physician and healer, and I do believe we understand why the earl would wish to have you, his trusted advisor, act in his stead while he is ill. What is not clear to us, however, is what our liege lord's wishes would be in the most unfortunate event of his demise. As you well know, the earl is without rightful heir, and you, Master Craycroft, though undisputedly wise in your craft, have neither land nor legacy, and further do not come of highborn parentage."

Craycroft knew the blow was coming, and was prepared, but the sting of the councilor's words still hit home.

"So this, Councilor, is why you have summoned me here, to have me play into your game of choosing the earl's successor? Nay, I shall not give you the satisfaction of venturing my own opinion in this matter. I had no part in the earl's decision to have me act in

his stead, and I shall not make claim to that which is not rightly mine. Rather, you shall have the earl's own decision on this matter. As I have told you, I have had the opportunity to speak with the earl and understand his wishes. However, I submit that you, the Council of Lords, must choose from among your ranks one whom you trust and dispatch him anon to the earl's chambers. There, if the earl be willing to grant audience to one of you, you shall hear from your lord's own lips his wish for his successor."

"Now, then, you may decide what you will, and send whom you will. As for me, I must return at once to the aid of my liege lord. I do not envy your task, nor should you wish mine. I bid you good day."

With that, Craycroft bowed ever so slightly then turned to leave the council chambers.

"Ah, Master Craycroft, one further matter, if you will." It was Councilor Genet who spoke.

Craycroft turned. "Yes, Councilor, what is it?"

"Well, this matter of Master Falma, it is…well, not quite clear to us what the earl's purpose would be to send a man so old and wise yet so frail on a mission out in midwinter. I—that is—we, the council, were perplexed. Would you be able to enlighten us as to the nature of this venture?"

The master hesitated then decided in his own mind that the truth would serve him best.

"My good councilor, you have asked a difficult question, and one that I can answer only in part, for the earl himself has only given me that knowledge that he himself has about the matter, which is also incomplete. What I am able to tell you is that Drachma, in the matter of summoning aid, has great need of Master Falma's wisdom. The whole tale I am unable to tell, but I shall tell you that Master Falma was sent out at Drachma's urging, accompanied by the earl's own forest guard, Kerlin. Be assured that, as I learn more of this matter, the council will be duly informed."

"Now, m' lords, if you will, I must return to the care of our liege lord, the earl."

As the council members muttered among themselves, Craycroft turned and left the hall and council chambers, back out into the chilly wind. Though the encounter was brief, he felt drained. He knew that he had done what the earl would have wanted, but at some cost. He understood that much had changed in the last few days, and changed forever. Some of the simplicity in his life had been permanently replaced by a responsibility he had not sought. His intense hope remained that this new healer would be able to provide a cure for the earl, thereby removing this burden of leadership, for which he felt, as did Councilor Reordan, that he was unfit. Craycroft also knew, but was not willing to admit, even to himself, that the earl believed in his own impending death, and that Craycroft was his own choice as successor.

Halfway back to the earl's chambers, he could see the small figure of the page, hurrying in his direction. His heart pounded as he quickened his own pace to meet the youth.

"Ah, lad, tell me, what is it? How does the earl fare?"

"Our lord, the earl, is resting comfortably, Master Craycroft. That is not the nature of my summons. Rather, it is a messenger who comes, with tidings of some import, as I understand, though I know not the nature of his message. The servants said I must bring you at once."

Craycroft's heart jumped again at the page's words. There was so much at stake, and so much he did not understand. He knew, though, that the messenger must have come from the forest, likely sent by Drachma himself, but bearing what sort of message, he could not begin to imagine.

"Well, then, lad, let us away. Whatever word this messenger bears must surely be noteworthy."

The master and the page then turned and headed back across the great square toward the earl's quarters. On the way, Craycroft

again recalled the events of the previous night, thinking how free he seemed at the time, and now, looking back, how that might have been the last time he would ever be so free.

The messenger was not what Craycroft had expected. Before him stood the tall, powerful, but visibly shaken master guardsman Kerlin.

"Master Craycroft, I fear I have returned from trouble to yet more trouble. I was not aware, when I left, that our lord the earl was this grievously ill. The household servants tell me that you are now the one to whom I should report. I am comforted to see the earl has acted wisely."

Craycroft nodded his acknowledgement. "I am led to understand, then, that you bear important tidings. I would surmise that these tidings have to do with Master Falma and Tom as you were accompanying the good master on your mission."

"Aye, that is correct."

"Well, then, let us sit down here by the fire. There has been much turmoil of late, and I am becoming weary, and I know you must be as well. Ease your burden, then, in this chair and tell me all I need to know."

As they sat down, Craycroft sent one of the servants after some food and drink for Kerlin then listened with concern and not a little trepidation as the guardsman told his tale.

"As well you know, Master Craycroft, I was, in fact, sent by our earl to lead and protect a small company on a mission to the other side of the island, and most particularly to guard Master Falma on this quest. I know not the complete nature of this venture, but I was told that Drachma himself had set its course, and it was the earl's wish that Master Falma go on this journey, as one who could best understand and react to unknown perils in a way that would be in keeping with the earl's own wishes."

Craycroft nodded, indicating his own growing understanding of events that seemed to be spinning ever more out of control.

"First, can you tell me of Tom, as he is not here with you?" said Craycroft.

"Aye, m' lord." Kerlin's use of the term came to him naturally but made Craycroft wince. "Tom was with me early on, then when we were close to Firebarrow Ridge, we were in dense fog when we found Tom's horse was riderless. Then when I went back to investigate, it appeared that Tom had been abducted."

"You say this was close to Firebarrow Ridge?"

"Aye, close to the western side."

Craycroft remembered then how Drachma's home was not far away from that point. "And you say that he was abducted? No sign of any violence or bloodshed?"

"Nay, m' lord, there we only the tracks of several horses converging on the path."

"Ah, well, though it pains me not to know, I would assume that our young friend is probably in Drachma's camp."

"Well, I thought about that, and I think I agree, as that part of the wood is patrolled by none other than Drachma's men, and even though it was not explicitly stated, it makes sense to me now."

"I had been instructed by Drachma himself to take Master Falma on the more northerly route, by Firebarrow Ridge, toward Castle Kearney. Though I was not told the nature of this journey, the instructions I was given did disturb me greatly."

Craycroft, not surprised, grunted his acknowledgment. Drachma's plans always seemed beyond the understanding of anyone else, yet there throbbed a pulse of certainty in all his machinations that went beyond reason toward the realm of faith.

"I was told to take the master along this most dangerous route, and that there was a winter storm expected. Further, I was instructed that, should we become separated, I was to return anon and report to the earl, rather than search for Master Falma. I will

not deny that this upset me greatly, not alone for the fact that I was entrusted with the master's care, but also for the implication that we would, indeed, be separated. Against my wishes, then, did I give my word, as I had sworn to our liege lord that I would take Drachma's instructions as if from the earl himself."

"I can well understand your plight," noted Craycroft, "as I have found myself in similar grievous states of late. Pray, though, continue your tale. I must hear what has happened."

"Very well, I shall. As you must have surmised, from Master Falma's absence, Drachma's words did prove prophetic. We did, upon arriving at Firebarrow Ridge, encounter a most sudden and fierce storm. For a short while I was able to keep close with Master Falma, but then, quite without warning, he vanished, as if swallowed by the snowstorm. I did for a while try to ascertain where the master may have gone, but with no success. Then, as I was in danger of losing the path, agreed in my mind to heed Drachma's order and return here. I have done so, as you see, but not without shame or remorse."

Craycroft pondered in silence what Kerlin had just told him. As both men sat quietly, the servant returned with food and drink.

"I shall say again, in truth, good man, that I do understand your woe. This has become a most difficult time for us all. Believe me when I say you have done no wrong, and that, for certain, we are all playing a part in some plan of Drachma's that defies any explanation. Though I too fear for Master Falma's safety, it is sure that Drachma foresaw this, and shall make use of his wisdom in ways neither you nor I can see if, God willing, the master remains alive."

"Come, now, have some refreshment while I consider what you have told me. Your journey has been arduous, I know, and we shall all need your strength and knowledge."

"My thanks, Master Craycroft. I shall have some, though, in truth, I am not hungry."

As Kerlin ate, and Craycroft sat thinking, another servant came to the door. Craycroft let him in, then asked, "What is it, son? Is it the earl?"

"Nay, Master, it is but one of the lords from the council. He awaits in yonder chamber, says he has a matter for our lord, the earl. I asked him to wait, but what shall I tell him, sir?"

"Tell him nothing, lad. I shall come myself, for I am certain I know his business."

He turned to Kerlin and said, "I am sorry to leave you, but please, stay, eat, drink, and rest here. This is a most vexing matter I have with the council. I am hopeful that it will not take very long to resolve."

"I understand, Master Craycroft. You have my word. I shall await yours, as I am now faithfully in your service."

Craycroft was disappointed, but not surprised, that it was Councilor Reordan who waited in the chamber.

"I see you have come alone, Councilor. If you will, please sit here while I see to the earl's condition, if he is awake and able to take visitors."

"As you will, Master Craycroft. I shall await here."

As he turned to leave, the master thought he detected a slight look of either fear or regret in the councilor's face. Whatever the emotion, it made Craycroft ill at ease. He truly did not want to disturb the earl's rest and decided that if the earl were asleep, he would simply tell the councilor to come again later.

Arriving at the earl's chamber, he asked the servant in hushed tones how their liege had been faring.

"As well as can be expected, m' lord," answered the servant. "His sleep has been fitful, his waking minutes filled with coughing, though the mist does provide for some relief. Of late he has been asleep."

"That is well, thank you, lad."

The master looked into the room, where the earl did seem to be resting, but as Craycroft came in, the earl stirred then opened his eyes. Recognizing his friend the healer, the earl smiled.

"Ah, Craycroft, it is good to see you." He paused for another breath. "How goes the struggle?"

Craycroft approached. "In truth, my liege, I fear not too well. I find myself in the midst of conflict I neither understand nor wish to take part in. Alas, it is just such that brings me to your side now, though I did not wish to disturb your sleep with such matters."

"Ah, truly, you did not expect the council…to accept my choice…without turmoil, did you?" The earl's words were tinged with sorrow. "Alas, I know that brood of ambitious…rogues only too well." The earl paused to catch his breath, "Tell me, who of them…speaks…for the others in this matter?"

"It appears to be Councilor Reordan, m' lord, who seems to resist your wishes most vocally, and it is he who awaits without for an audience with you now."

"What…here, now? Were not my wishes plain enough? What can that…snake…wish with me?"

"I fear, m' lord, that his question is one of the permanence of your choice of leadership, hoping, I am sure, that you appointed me only until the council was able to choose one of their own as a permanent successor. This, despite my informing the council that you are still quite alive, and fully capable of deciding your own orders."

The earl's wrath rose but was interrupted by a spasm of coughing and difficulty catching his breath.

When able to resume talking, both his anger and breathing had eased some. "Ah, friend, you know as well as I that this illness is beyond our ability…to cure. You also know well my wishes…in this matter. Very well, then, send that vulture in here. I shall make things very plain to him."

Craycroft, choosing to stay by the side of the earl, dispatched a servant to bring Councilor Reordan to the chamber. Neither man spoke while waiting for the arrival of the council's representative. As the councilor stepped into the room, Craycroft could not read the look on his face, but his voice carried tones of austerity and importance.

"Ah, m'liege, it saddens me so to see you in this state. Please know that I bring you prayers and wishes from the council for your timely recovery."

The earl, despite his weakened state, glared into Reordan's eyes and held up his hand for silence.

"Councilor, do not shame yourself or the council with your words. The truth shall suffice…"

Reordan opened his mouth to speak, but the earl again raised his hand.

"You and I both know…my time is short, so I will not waste any. Tell me this, and this only…what is it in my sealed order that you and the council find difficult to…understand or obey?"

The councilor cleared his throat, then spoke carefully, "Well, m'liege, it is simply a matter that needs the slightest clarification. We certainly understood your choice of Master Craycroft to govern in your stead while you are…ah…indisposed, but as to a more permanent—"

The earl cut him off. "Enough! Let me make this…plain, both to you…and the council. Hear me, as I shall say it only once. As of the moment you received my message…Master Craycroft, my trusted friend and advisor, is your liege lord. Mark you, this… is for life, and you have…heard it directly from me as my last official…act as earl…of Shepperton. Now, be gone…and take my message…to your council!"

The councilor bowed, and muttered, sotto voce, "As you wish m'lord."

With what appeared to be the earl's most painful effort, he motioned for his servant to show the councilor out. As Reordan left, the earl sank back into his bed covers and lapsed into sleep.

Craycroft silently pulled a chair close to the bed, sat down, and wiped the sweat from his lord's brow. Using the same cloth, then, he dabbed at his own tears.

Chapter Eight

"It is good, lady, that he sleeps, for he is an old man, tired and weak. I am most heartened that you have come. Our need is great. I believe, by this time, you know who I am."

Judy stared at the white-haired man by the doorway. There was no question. This was the same man who had walked along side her in the graveyard. Yet in the meagre light from the fire, seemed younger, and somehow more tangible.

"I guess I do. You're Drachma, aren't you?"

"Aye, that I am. None other."

"That's good. Maybe you can explain to me what's happening, how I got here and all. And, too, what about Dr. Gilsen? Do you know what's happened to him?"

"I can tell you some, but not all, of what you ask, good lady, for my knowledge is also incomplete." He paused to pour himself a small portion of wine. "As I said, I am truly glad to see you, for you have arrived safely, by means heretofore never taken. I do hope that the food and wine, though not befitting your importance, did ease your ache and hunger."

Judy thought for a moment, realizing that she did, in fact, feel warm and relaxed, despite her drastically unfamiliar surroundings.

"Actually, it was really quite good, thank you. I assume, then, that it was you who was expecting us here."

"Aye, that is correct, m'lady, for it was I who sent the note by which you learned the way here."

"I see. Well, then, maybe you could tell me how you knew about me, and about Dr. Gilsen, and how you got me here, wherever here is."

"Ah, you ask much, with few words, lady. My answers, though incomplete as they must be, will require more than a few. Let me begin by telling you that Master Gilsen is yet safe, on another part of this isle, having arrived some three days before you, by similar powers. I am quite certain that he shall be in need of your healing hand. As Master Falma may have told you, you are on Shepperton Isle, in the North Channel, 'tween Scotland and Ireland, ruled by our good earl, in the service of the English king. What you likely do not know is that it is now the month of January, in the year of our Lord one thousand four hundred and ninety-two."

Judy gasped.

"Now wait a minute, that's not possible! How can that be? I was just today…no that just can't be right."

Drachma gazed at Judy steadily, waiting, it seemed, for the reality of her situation to penetrate her understanding. Judy, for her part, could think of nothing to say, and sat, staring open-mouthed at the old man in front of her, waiting for him to continue.

"Ah, my lady, it would seem that, even in your time, an arrival such as yours is difficult to believe and to comprehend." A subtle smile appeared on his face as he continued. "So be it. Well, let me attempt to explain what I am able of your circumstances, though, I must confess, my knowledge of these matters is far less than perfect."

Judy relaxed slightly but held his gaze, waiting.

"As it is upon this isle, I myself bear no title, nor do I have any authority that would be recognized by the crown. Nevertheless,

I have, for many years, acted as agent and advisor to our lord, the earl, and have come to know well the fabric and needs of this, our island. In years past I was a teacher and confidant of nobles, and was, in my capacity, able to travel far and wide, and to learn of many things rare, if unique. Among the things I was able to learn from my travels east was some knowledge of time itself, and how, under special conditions, what is yet to come may be made to touch what is here and now."

Judy understood but couldn't believe what she was hearing, though her circumstances seemed to confirm what Drachma was telling her.

"Are you telling me there are ways to connect the future with the present? That's the stuff of science fiction..."

Drachma studied her, a questioning look on his face, and then he answered.

"Ah, lady, your very presence here must tell you something. It must surely be difficult to comprehend, and perhaps to believe, but for that reason, if no other, did I send you word of things to come."

"You mean, the notes and the coin and that old man in the ER?"

"Old man? Of which old man do you speak, m' lady?"

"The one who died in the ER, some incredibly old man. Now, what was his name? Just a minute...it was...Vincente. That's right, it was Vincente."

"Vincente? Might that have been Carlo Vincente?"

"Why, yes, that was his name. Carlo Vincente."

"Ah..." Drachma pondered a moment. "Then it would appear that there is more to unfold, more doors opened than I had anticipated."

"Look," Judy interrupted his thinking aloud, "you said that Bob, that is, Dr. Gilsen, is alive, in this place and time, and that you've brought us here for some purpose, right? Well, why don't you tell me about that at least? This great need you speak of, what's it all about?"

"In truth, m'lady, it is both great need and singular opportunity that have joined to bring you here. Of the need I may speak freely, but of the opportunity, I am only able to say little at this time. As to our need of your presence here, permit me to explain a little of our history, as it is necessary to understand our present plight.

"Many years ago, a noble explorer named Eustace Fitzgibbon happened upon this island, finding it inhabited by simple shepherds, woodsmen, and farmers, a poor but content lot, who seemed to have no need for dealings or intrusions from without. Eustace, however, saw it as his God-given right to claim the isle for himself and his heirs. With little opposition, then, from the peace-loving inhabitants, he began the construction of the great castle on the other side of the isle, which is our present earl's residence, and from whence he governs.

"Now, as some years went by, Eustace's son, William, inherited his father's domain, and was established as the first earl of Shepperton. As man and earl, William was not loved, but he did possess a great gift of observation and a shrewd mind for commerce. What he saw among the inhabitants of the land was that those who had lived and worked their lives upon the island were stout, of excellent vitality, and lived long lives. This, however, was not true of those who had come with the invaders to rule the land. These persons, which included William's father, Eustace, his lady, Agatha, his brothers and cousins, all, while still youthful, became sallow, weak, and ill, dying at unseemly young ages.

"As a lad, then, William had occasion to sport with some our island's native sons, finding for himself that they were a hale and hearty lot, unlike his own kin, who seemed always to be weak, pale, and complaining. Now when his father died, and he was bestowed the title of earl, William wisely sought counsel on his matter from some of the elders of the many villages. From them he heard always the same story—that the secret of health and strength on this isle was, of all things, the pots. As you might suspect, William was perplexed by their answer but, to his credit,

did not dismiss their replies as fairytales, but rather, asked further. What he discovered was that, as far back as any could remember, each household on the island, and each woodsman and traveler, kept safe with him a special pot, made of certain clay from the lake at the base of our highest mountain. It was said that one drink each day from one of these pots was enough to safeguard the health of man, woman, or child."

Judy nodded, interested in his unfolding tale.

"What William did, then, was to acquire some of these pots for himself and his family, and began the practice of a daily drink from these vessels. It soon became apparent to William, once established in his new habit, that his own health and vitality, as well as that of his family, was much improved. He gained strength and vigor, as well as clarity of mind and purpose, which he had heretofore never known.

"His next venture, though, was truly his greatest deed for this island and its people. What he did was to go, along with an envoy, to the king's court with a gift for the king, consisting of two of these pots and a testimonial extolling their virtues.

"It did not take long for the king, then, to believe the claims William made, and sent an envoy of his own to seek out more of these wondrous vessels. It so became established, then, that this isle should become a protectorate of the crown, to be governed by its earl. In exchange for providing the king and his nobles a supply of these vessels, William, then, was granted great wealth and land holdings, from which he was able to import skilled craftsmen to work in his newly established guilds. These were craftsmen of the highest order, both potters and painters, brought to the isle for the sole purpose of providing large numbers of these pots, not merely wondrous in their healing properties, but now also most handsome in appearance."

"Now, the fame of these marvelous vessels spread to the noble houses of Europe, and those with good relations to the English

king were allowed to establish their own ambassadors on this isle, who, in turn might live in the protection of the earl."

Judy looked at her companion curiously, thinking how odd this story seemed, especially as she had never, in all her years of schooling, heard of Shepperton, its marvelous pots, with their great healing powers, or of their obvious importance to the nobles of the time. Yet, there was no denying the authenticity of what she was hearing.

Drachma seemed to take no notice, and continued. "As you may well imagine, this newfound wealth was to have great influence on all the inhabitants of the isle, for along with the painters and potters and their craft, it became necessary to use the skills of the native islanders for many tasks, to wit: the digging and transporting of the clay, the establishment of paths through the forest, the protection of the earl's men; further it became necessary to ward off and punish poachers and counterfeiters, who have made attempts to sell lesser quality vessels to unwary buyers looking for easier or more expedient supplies.

"So, thus it came to be, over the years, that an island of peaceful farmers, herdsmen, and woodsmen became a society greatly dependent for its wealth and security upon the manufacture and sale of goods, available nowhere else. Thus it was when I first happened upon this island many years ago. It seemed most curious to me how a people could have made its own nobility, if you will, from mere guildsmen, for, in truth, these artisans were revered as lords in their own right, and over generations, given wealth and land holdings, as well as governance through their Council of Lords, whereas the true nobility on the island were the earl, his family, and the foreign ambassadors and their kin. Now, in the eyes of the king, of course, the island was ruled only by the earl. In truth, however, most of the ruling of the island and its inhabitants was through this Council of Lords, as they represented the power to produce and sell the goods that much of the world's nobility had come to esteem.

"So, m' lady, over many years, it became less certain that our marvelous vessels were providing much benefit to the health of humankind. Nevertheless, despite the fact that people, both poor and noble, continued to fall ill and die as their time came, it has remained a fast belief within noble houses that a Shepperton pot will safeguard the health of one fortunate enough to acquire one."

Judy looked back at Drachma, nodded, then said, thoughtfully, "I assume, then, that you're going to tell me how Dr. Gilsen and I fit into this story of yours. It's all rather interesting, I'll admit, but so far has little to do with us in the twentieth century."

"Indeed, aye, m' lady. It is precisely the change in this state of affairs that has led to your summons."

"Do go on. I'm listening."

Instead of continuing immediately, though, he got up, stretched, and went over to the fire. There he put another log on, adjusted the logs with a fire iron then rubbed his hands together. Finally, he looked again at the quiet form of Master Falma, reassuring himself that the old man was still deeply slumbering, then came back to the table and sat down.

"Now, before I continue, my good lady, I must tell you that no one else knows all of what I am about to relate. There are those who by necessity know part, but none know the whole. So, as a word of advice, be most certain of the character of any to whom you might relate any of what I am about to tell you."

Judy's eyes widened, and she nodded. "It seems I haven't really met too many people to tell anything yet, but I'll try to remember."

"That is good, as I do feel that, since I have had much to do with bringing you hence from your time and place, I owe you, at the very least, an explanation of why you may have been summoned."

"Thanks, I guess…please, go on with your story."

"Ah, well, as you now have some understanding of the peculiar circumstances of this island and its people, let me tell you of recent events that have led to our present crisis."

"Our troubles began some months ago, in the spring of last year, when a number of our best young painters and potters became quite unexpectedly ill and soon died. Since then, others in the guild have fallen to a similar fate. As you might by now appreciate, this has been a bitter blow, and one not taken lightly. In the ensuing months, then, our production of pots has fallen to the point where we are in fear that the king's advisors might take it upon themselves to investigate the matter, and I must tell you from experience, that that is not something any with love for this isle would wish to happen. Further, as the malady at first afflicted only those directly making the pots, there has been talk of poisoning, witchcraft, curses, and the like. This has gotten the island's native people stirred to the point of being unwilling to work further toward the making of these vessels for sale to the foreign shores.

"Now this was all tragic enough, but recent events have culminated in worse tidings yet. You see, now others beside the painters and potters have, it would seem, succumbed to a similar fate. The first, of interest to you, was none other than Carlo Vincente of whom you spoke."

Judy gasped involuntarily.

"Now Lord Vincente was a nobleman, not of this isle, but the ambassador from a great Italian house. One who did, in fact, live many of his long years here upon the isle. It was widely known that much of his wealth was made from arranging for the sale of our pots through many of the great houses of Europe, and his family became much loved here in Shepperton. Most especially loved, though, was his gracious daughter, Felicia, a lady of true beauty and virtue.

"As lord Vincente was advanced in age, his recent death was not notably alarming, but striking was the similarity of his last illness to those of the younger painters and potters. But now, a greater grief has befallen us all. You see, his beloved daughter, the lady Felicia, has been similarly ill, and, I am told, very recently has

died herself, a fact that does grieve me more than most anyone here." Here Drachma paused, swallowed another sip of wine. Judy could tell that this particular bit of his story was perhaps a bit too personal. Eventually, Drachma recovered and continued his story.

"Further still, our present and well-loved earl has himself become dangerously ill and has no heir. Word of this has not yet spread throughout the island, but, you may be sure, it will not be long before it does, especially as the Council of Lords has been made aware of our present circumstances."

"So, then," Judy interrupted, "I would assume that you have been led to believe, God knows how, that Dr. Gilsen and I are somehow capable of helping you out with this problem of your people getting ill and dying, and causing financial ruin on your island. Am I correct?"

"You are most perceptive, m'lady. It would appear to be within your powers, not ours, to heal our island."

"Wow, this is just all too weird, too much…look, I'm a nurse. I work in a big city hospital emergency room where I've got lots of help, lots of doctors, other nurses, lab people, and loads of equipment to help the sick and dying. Now here I am, on some remote island I've never heard of, in some other time, with nothing but the clothes I wore to a funeral and this cut on my head. I don't really think I feel or look much like a powerful healer right now."

As Judy's words poured out, Drachma smiled benevolently, and Falma stirred in his slumber. When she paused to gather her thoughts, he responded.

"My dear lady, you do yourself an injustice. While it is most true that your arrival on our isle has not been gracious, and it grieves me that you have suffered injury, it would seem that you do not yet comprehend what powers you do possess. No matter now, for I am certain that you shall find your powers as you need them, both you and Master Gilsen. Of this I feel sure."

His smile was somehow reassuring, even though the words carried implications Judy was not yet ready to deal with. Fatigue began setting in, as Judy stifled a yawn.

"Look, M...Mr. Drachma, this is all too confusing for me now. Maybe after I rest and get cleaned up a little, it'll make more sense, but right now...then again, maybe if I get some sleep, I'll find this was all just another dream."

"Ah, my good lady, if it be a dream, then we are all beholden to the same dreamer, else we could not share as we do. Here, a toast to you, m'lady" he said, raising his flagon. "Then you should rest."

They both took a sip of wine; then Judy shook her head, smiling and saying nothing.

"Now, fear not, lady, I shall have two of my men guard your door, then upon the morrow escort you toward the castle. Peace be with you this night. We shall meet again."

With that, Drachma rose and went to the door, stepping out into the blackness.

Chapter Nine

Now Marilyn Gilsen was really apprehensive. She spent the last night pacing about in her room, thinking about who could have called her, and what he could possibly tell her. What could have happened to Bob, and was he now in mortal danger? And now here was that Detective Bryant again and that infernal note taker, Detective Lewinsky. She took a couple of deep, slow breaths and then went to the door to let them in.

"Good morning, Mrs. Gilsen. We're here to escort you down to Memorial Hospital." The words slipped out of his mouth before he had a chance to retract them. "I'm sorry for the choice of words. Perhaps I should say we're here to accompany you to Memorial Hospital. Doesn't sound so much like official police jargon that way."

"Oh, do come in, Detective Bryant and Detective Lewinsky."

"Please, call me Ed, and thank you, Mrs. Gilsen."

The two detectives stepped back into the Gilsens' home. If anything, it looked even more cluttered than before. Marilyn offered them seats in the living room.

"Well, what do I need to know or do before we go to the hospital?"

"What we'd really like is to be as inconspicuous as possible, but don't worry, we'll be right there, close by. What I thought we could do is to drive you down, then park our car. Then Chris and I will follow you into the hospital, as discretely as possible. We'll let you go to the cafeteria and meet with this Carlo person. What we will do is give you this electronic signaling device, and if you feel at all nervous about what is happening, just press this button here, and it will send a signal, and we will be there right away."

What he showed her looked like a small brooch that she would wear. In the center was a tiny button she could push. The wires from the brooch were connected to a small apparatus, which Detective Lewinsky carefully hid under Marilyn's jacket. Marilyn tried the button, but she heard nothing.

Edgar Bryant, though, pointed to what appeared to be a small hearing aid in his left ear.

"Yep, I read you loud and clear. All right then, we all set to go?"

"Oh, all right, but I don't mind telling you I'm very nervous about all of this. And I don't want anything to happen to Bob as a result."

"Oh, I understand fully. Now did this fellow give you any idea how to find him? What should we be looking for?"

"No, he said that he would find me in the cafeteria."

"Did he say if he would be alone?"

"No, but I got the impression that he was alone, I don't know…somehow, something he said…oh, I don't know."

"That's all right, Mrs. Gilsen. I'm sure we'll have no trouble finding our guy."

"Okay, then I think I'm ready. Let's get this out of the way."

Marilyn got her coat and gloves, and the three of them went out to the waiting police car, a grey, unmarked Taurus. As they pulled out, Marilyn noticed the other car behind them, also a grey sedan.

"Oh, that's detective Warner behind us, he'll stay out of the way, but he'll be there just in case," said Edgar Bryant.

Just in case what? thought Marilyn, but said nothing. She just sat and thought her own thoughts on the way to the hospital, while the two detectives chatted amiably about nothing in particular. She had made up her mind. Though she was nervous, she was determined to go through with this and find out something. At least this fellow, Carlo, knew something about what happened to Bob. That much at least was clear to her, and he didn't sound threatening or crazy on the phone, and he sounded old, like someone's grandfather from another country.

They pulled up to the hospital, and parked in the visitor's lot. It was cold, but the sun was struggling to shine, making the weather a bit more bearable than it had been recently. Marilyn got out as Edgar held her door open. As she stepped out into the weather, he told her, "Now, you just go ahead to the cafeteria. Chris and I'll be staying back a ways, but remember, if you get at all nervous, just push your little button."

What he didn't tell her was that they would be recording everything she said and heard, and that she was wearing a wire.

The main entry into Memorial Hospital was not one Marilyn had ever used, and was quite disorienting, with its large rotunda, and tile floors. It was a throwback to older hospital designs and produced sensations of anxiety and intimidation, which Marilyn was already feeling. She looked around, and could see no signs toward the cafeteria, so she stopped at the information desk and asked the volunteer lady where the cafeteria was located. The volunteer smiled coldly and pointed down the hall and indicated that she would go down then turn left where she would find the elevators, then take them down to the basement.

Marilyn murmured a thank you then headed down the hall. The feeling of intimidation grew as she got on the elevator, and heard the conversation between several young people in scrubs and white coats.

"You know, it's too weird," said one of the group. "Things like this aren't supposed to happen, not here. I mean this isn't New York or LA, where people probably just disappear every week."

"Yeah, it's like some strange kind of story from *The Enquirer*. You know, about some mysterious cardiologist in the Midwest, who's having some affair, and then, well, you know, gets taken out by a paid assassin, and then his body shows up a week later in the river."

"You've got some imagination, Kenny. I just think there's probably some simpler explanation…"

"Like what? You mark my words. We'll be reading about his body in some sordid story while waiting in the check-out line at the grocery store…"

Mercifully, the elevator stopped, and the group got out and left Marilyn behind, shaken by their careless talk. She was disoriented again, looked up and down the hallway, and then saw a sign that she thought indicated the way to the cafeteria. She headed down the way toward the sign.

"Madame Gilsen."

She turned abruptly toward the voice. There was an old man with stringy, white hair, a full white beard, tall, thin with a hawk-like nose, dressed in gray. Despite appearing to be out of place, he seemed to project a certain regal attitude, as if his presence alone were enough. Marilyn stared at the man and said nothing. She began to feel a bit woozy.

"Madame, I am Carlo Vincente," he said with a very small, courteous bow. "Come, let us sit down and we may talk." He led her into the cafeteria, then to a small room, set off from the cafeteria proper. The room was deserted, with cluttered tables, and some stuffed chairs. He then asked her to sit, and he himself then sat down, across from her.

"Now you may be rather alarmed at my presence, as I am sure you were when I spoke to you through your telephone. I am most sorry if I have offended your sensibilities. You see, I am from far away, both in place and in time, and I am uncertain as to your customs."

"Our customs?" Marilyn managed at last to speak.

"Aye, there have been many things to learn in my brief time here, before I am called away, which shall be soon."

"And where is it you're from?"

"From Italy are my origins, but I have spent much time on Shepperton Island. Do you know of Shepperton?"

"No, I can't say that I've ever heard of it."

"Ah, well, no matter. Let us just say it is far away from here, both in distance and time. I would like to thank you for the courtesy you have shown, and of this chance to speak with you. What I have to tell you is a most extraordinary tale."

Despite her initial feelings, Marilyn found herself being drawn in to this stranger's words. He was not some crackpot, and he was not, as far as she could tell, trying to lie to her; nor was he appearing to be any kind of threat. She just nodded and said to him, "Do go on, Mr. Vincente. I'm listening."

"And for that I am grateful."

"Well, as I begin my tale, I would ask that you bear with me, and to hold your disbelief to yourself, as it is truly a tale that I must tell, and it would seem that you are the one I should tell, and then after I have told you all of my tale, you may judge me for what I am, and for what I may have done and also for what I have not."

"Fair enough," said Marilyn, but she thought to herself, *Oh boy, what have I gotten myself into? And what about Bob?*

"Might I begin by telling you that I am a potter by trade but a nobleman and ambassador through assumption—a thing most unusual. I did begin my trade in my youth in a town not far from Genoa in Italy. As it happened, I was well taught by my master, a craftsman unlike any other, if I may be so bold, and one who himself had occasion to study under Yang Xiu, from China; and it was he who told me of the great opportunity in the castle in Genoa, for pots that would be like no others to be had at any price. And we did produce some of Europe's finest pottery, for years. Our fame did spread among the wealthy houses

throughout Italy and Europe, and it became commonplace for visitors from far off to come by, and it was my pleasure to see that nobleman were shown our wares as they were being crafted.

"I was employed by the Duke, and within a span of some fourteen years rose to the position as chief artisan, and leader of our guild of potters and painters. I saw to the production of the finest in porcelain products to be found on the continent, and was a man content with my lot for years. But then the Duke's brother, Gregorio, became jealous, and sought to buy our services for his own needs. The Duke, however would not hear of it, and this led to his murder at the hands of one of Gregorio's men. We, as the guild, became the vassals of Gregorio, and were moved, en masse, to this mountain castle. The men became a dispirited company, and our pots became common by comparison, pleasing to the eye, but not the source of pride that we would sign our names to with true affection.

"It was now that a stranger appeared among us, a certain man, whose name was Drachma. His origins were mysterious, but he told us of a promise he made and, with our help, could now fulfill to a certain earl of Shepperton. What he proposed was a risky venture, but one that could reestablish our art to its great potential. He offered to free those of us that were willing from our bondage to Gregorio. He would arrange for an exodus, if you will, of our artisans, to go to this Isle of Shepperton, to leave on a boat at night. He would arrange for our passage, but could not guarantee its safety. And do you know what he asked of us? Only that we not speak of his exploits to anyone who could tell, and further, that I should adopt his love as my own daughter, and further, that I would become a nobleman and ambassador. As the former guild leader, then, to be known only to my men and to himself.

"And so it was that we set out in the dark of night, all of us, throwing our lots in with this mysterious man who offered us release from our stifling existence as pawns in the hands of a

tyrant, and toward a fate that we did not know, but which seemed fairer. It did, in fact, turn out much as Drachma said it would. The earl of Shepperton was very hospitable, and our work was very pleasing to all. But there was one thing that we learned as we started work, and that was the nature of our pots. It seems that something in the clay from which our pots were made bestowed upon their owners, by way of their drinking from the pots, a certain health and vitality. This fact was well known among the residents of the island, but now, apparently through Drachma's undertaking, it became known throughout the European lands and great houses.

"So, in the fullness of time, our small band of painters and potters became a nobility of sorts, and we did become wealthy and rightly proud of our works again. Each original painter or potter was head of a household, which then could bring in other workers (mainly from the old country), and would employ the local workers to bring in the clay from the mountains, tend the kilns, and see to obtaining the rare pigments needed four our paints. The pots of Shepperton became magnificent to look upon, as well as a boon to the health of their owners."

By now Marilyn was becoming quite wrapped up in this tale being spun by this old man who looked so out of place there in that hospital cafeteria, so obviously far removed from his home. She studied his clothing, noticed that it had the look of age, but not like anything worn around here, even by vagrants and by college-aged kids who frequented Salvation Army stores. His accent was one she could not identify, despite his having told her of his origins. It had a singsong quality to it, a little like a more modern Scandinavian accent.

"Excuse me, Mr. Vincente, would you like a cup of coffee or tea?" Marilyn couldn't help asking. "I'd like one myself and was wondering if you would like something."

"Most assuredly, madam. I shall have what you are having," Carlo Vincente said, with a slight twinkle in his eye.

"And how do you take it?"

"I shall have it like you, for I am not familiar with what you call coffee."

"Then I'd better get yours with a little sugar and cream." Marilyn got up and went into the cafeteria and sought out the coffee service. While up, she noticed that the two detectives were seated at the far end of the cafeteria and seemed to pay no attention to her. She got two cups of coffee and put some milk and sugar in one, and just milk in the other; then she paid for the cups and brought them out to where her strange companion was seated. She placed one of the Styrofoam cups down in front of Carlo Vincente then watched as he looked at the cup cautiously, turning it around, puzzled by its appearance. She then took a sip from her cup, laid it back down on the table, and said, "Better wait, it's a bit hot. Please do continue your story."

"Aye, well, as I had said, Drachma's love did agree to be my adopted daughter, though she was of age to marry, perhaps seventeen summers. Her name was Felicia, and a rare beauty she was. She was known thereafter by my surname, lady Felicia Vincente, a most extraordinary young woman. She brought life and light to our household, and she truly became as a daughter to me. When asked if she wanted to marry, she said she was married in spirit, and would not consider it. I knew that this involved the man, Drachma, and what had gone before, so I did not pursue this line of inquiry.

"Through the years, lady Felicia came to be loved and respected by all of Shepperton, and unofficially—as I came to find out that most everything important on our island was unofficial—she would become the confidant of the earl, and the men he trusted to govern his domain, which included a certain alchemist named Falma, his physician named Craycroft, and of course, Drachma himself. I was given the position of providing for and maintaining, the spirits of our group of potters and painters, as well I served the earl as ambassador to all of Europe, so, as you may readily see, I became vital to the island's well-being, a fact that I did cherish.

"One of the things I did find out through the years was that Drachma had written several books, but most notably was a book that he entrusted to Felicia, and which she kept in our library. Now there are many kinds of books, but none in reality like this one volume. It told of Drachma's travels in the East, and of his acquiring knowledge of events of power throughout history. It further discussed means by which people, who are stricken, can bring about aid in time of great need through changes in the fabric of time itself, which I did find intriguing.

"I should tell you that the book did contain in its preface a warning to any who did intend to read it, that merely reading the book would alter one's life in ways unimagined. So it was with some trepidation that I took occasion to read this book, with lady Felicia's knowledge, as it was she who read the book first and then gave it to me to read if I so chose. I looked again at the preface but then did read on. I did not, however, have any occasion to make use of any of its powers until this year, and that brings me to our current state of affairs. You see, along with my position as leader of our guild, I was also ambassador, and thereby in touch, shall we say, with the powerful families of Europe. There came to my knowledge a new threat that even Drachma knew nothing about. This one was one of deepest woe to me with my past. There was, it seems, an old acquaintance of mine, who had occasion to find one of our new Shepperton pots in the house of Marco Dimitrio, who lived in a castle some four hours from Genoa. He was astonished at its similarity to our previous work and began to inquire as to its origins.

"He was told by Count Dimitrio, that the pot was obtained by one of his nephews on a trip to the British Isles, and that this nephew had given it to the Count as a gift, having kept more of the pots in his own family. This old acquaintance, whose name was Vittorio Lonardi, came from a wealthy family, one of whose relatives worked in our guild. Now word of this pot's presence made it to Gregorio. Gregorio, never a man to take such a thing

lightly, then sent an envoy to the British Isles, and spoke with our English King, who owned quite a collection of these pots, and enthusiastically showed this young man his collection, and gave him a pot to take back to Count Gregorio.

"I am told that Gregorio, when he received his pot and noticed the signatures upon it, flew into a rage not unlike King Herod in the Bible. He then sent another envoy in search of Shepperton Island and in search of me and his missing guild of artisans. I was abroad at the time when I heard of this plot."

Marilyn, despite herself, sat transfixed at the old man's story. But she could not help but ask, "This is all really fascinating, but somehow this is going to involve Bob, and our time and place, isn't it?"

"Ah, but it does, indeed."

Marilyn took a sip of her coffee, and Carlo did as well.

"This is quite good," he said. "Not unlike a drink I once had in Asia. Though I am unable to recall what it was called. Quite good, madam, I thank you."

"My husband likes his coffee, and I've come to like it too," Marilyn said, a tear running down her cheek. She reached into her purse, and found a tissue, wiping away the tear.

Carlo Vincente said nothing, studying her intently.

"Can you at least tell me that he's all right? That much knowledge would help."

"What I am able to say is that I believe he is, or at least was, unharmed, but I am not certain. If I could tell you more, I would."

"Could you tell me where he is?"

"Ah, madam, it is purely conjecture on my part, but I do believe he is in Shepperton."

"You mean, across the Atlantic Ocean, in Britain? How would that happen? I don't believe he would have any way, even if he were to get on a plane—no, that's inconceivable."

"My dear madam, as you recall, I have asked that you suspend belief and judgment until you heard all my tale."

"Yes, of course. But you must know it's my husband you're talking about. He's not just some character in your tale."

"Very well, I shall remember, but as you shall see, he does play quite a role in our story."

"All right, then, go on."

Carlo Vincente took another sip of his coffee and then resumed his story.

"I had told you that Gregorio had sent an envoy toward Shepperton. I happened to hear of this while I was yet abroad. While I was abroad, I also learned, to my amazement, that Drachma's own father had been my tutor, and that before he died, he had written an epistle for me. So I went down to Genoa, and secretly sought out the house of Archepedes, where I found an old lady, who said that she knew me, and that, yes, she did have the letter for me. She asked that I not open it until I was safely away, and to bestow upon Drachma her best wishes.

"I did as she instructed, and when I was on the boat back to England, I opened the letter. It was written some eight years before the old man died. In the letter he explained that, for reason of security—he never did explain this—he had kept Drachma's identity hidden, even to me. He did explain that he had actually arranged for Drachma to come to our aid, and arranged the ship for our passage away. Further, he noted that Drachma had from time to time, written him and told him how our newly formed guild had grown and gotten famous and was again making porcelain that was the pride of Europe.

"He then mentioned in his letter that Gregorio had never forgotten and was certain to seek revenge and to be very wary of him, as he thought nothing of murdering those that got in the way of his plans. He also told of those within our ranks who might have gotten word to him by way of relatives still in the area around Genoa.

"Then he went on to say that Drachma had written a book, which told of powers beyond our control that could be called

upon in the case of dire need—this was the book I have already mentioned. He told me that I should seek out this book, that it might become necessary to use.

"A most unusual letter it was, having been written some years before, but now its foretelling appeared to be coming to pass. As I then came to England, I learned that Gregorio's man had been seeking an audience with the king of England to inquire of the king the particulars of the Shepperton pots and where he might obtain some for his liege lord. Fortunately for us, however, this man never reached Shepperton, as he appeared to have suffered a most unfortunate accident at sea—this was not my doing.

"When I got back to Shepperton, I did, in fact, find out that several of our painters and potters had sent word through letters to relatives of our doings, and of the wondrous pottery we were now producing. This was alarming to me, and I sought out Drachma when I was on the island, and mentioned his father, the letter written by his father, as well as the threat to our island. He listened intently but for a long while said nothing, just sat and stared. When he got up again, he said that now was the time, that we should invoke the powers beyond ourselves and our time, but that we should be careful as not to involve ourselves so deeply that we get caught up ourselves in the coming tumult.

"Then he bade me come to his place in Glen Oak Forest, where all would be made clear. When I got there a few days later—he had one of his trusted guides escort me there, as it was deep in the unmarked forest—we ate and drank like little kings, then his trusted aide, Angelica, escorted us to his personal study, and there while I was seated deep in a most comfortable chair, he said that I was to go to sleep, and that I would see visions of what was now and what was to be, and to tell him of what I saw, sparing no detail, no matter how seemingly insignificant.

"Well, as he said, I was soon sleepy with the good wine and filled belly, and he was chanting and plucking at some instrument by the fire, then all of a sudden, I was not there in that room, but

rather I was walking down a path in warm springtime with the earth fragrant and rich about me, the sun flitting through the leaves, and I could feel the pull of something impelling, as though I had not the will to refuse. I walked down the path and took a turn to the left, and there was before me a door, and powerless to resist, I opened the door and stepped into a tavern that looked familiar. Then I realized I was in the tavern of Barncuddy with the familiar warmth of companionship, with the ale flowing and laughter at the tables all about. Then I noticed at one of the tables was our physician, Master Craycroft, telling a tale of mystery, magic, and lore.

Although I was able to see and hear all that was happening, no one could see me. I tried to speak, but no words came. Then I noticed the stranger. He was seated at one of the tables in the rear. He was not dressed as we were, but rather his garments were like the garments worn by the people here in this hospital. He seemed entranced by the story Craycroft was telling, and, like the others in that tavern, took no notice of me. After the tale was told by Craycroft (and what a fine tale it was), the minstrel seated at Craycroft's table then took his harp, and began to play. But his playing was unlike anything I ever heard. The beauty of the sounds was truly rapturous and more like precious pearls than just the playing on strings in that old musty tavern.

"Then, as the music faded into memory, I was again outside, on the path in the woods, and again I felt that pulling at my soul that I could not resist. Again, as the path pulled me along, I came to a split in the path, this time I went to the right, down an embankment toward the sound of running water, and there was again a door, which I opened and stepped through, but this time I found myself here, in this room, with me again being able to see and hear all that was happening, but none noticed me, and again I was not able to utter a sound. Right where you are seated was the stranger, sitting down, weary, and drinking what I presume was coffee. Though there were others about, he seemed to take no

notice of them, as he was reading from a small book. Then of a sudden the device on his trousers make a screeching sound, that he seemed to acknowledge, and he went off to use what I came to find out was a telephone. As he turned to use the telephone, I was able to read that his name was emblazoned on his cloak, and it was Robert Gilsen, MD.

"Now, mind you, this was a most unexpected discovery, this man, in these two very different places. Then as I observed him to go off, as if in a hurry, to another part of the hospital building, I noticed the table over there was occupied by an elderly pair. They were discussing this Doctor Gilsen and how he had saved this elderly woman from certain death at the hands of another physician. How, by listening to her and providing medicines for her, he had wrought this miraculous cure. The woman was effusively praising this Doctor Gilsen."

"Oh, that does sound like Bob," said Marilyn wistfully. "I know that he truly believes in taking his time with patients, and his patients are always so especially grateful. It really is something of an embarrassment whenever we go out and come across one of his patients."

Carlo Vincente took another sip of his coffee then looked at Marilyn with very sincere, deep pity. He reached across the table and took her hand. She did not resist, rather finding his touch gentle and warming.

"Now, what I must tell you, you shall have to try to believe, for it is the truth. I did try to find where Dr. Gilsen went but could not. As I walked down the hallway, I could feel myself getting lighter, and the vision of this place faded away. Then I was back in Drachma's musty room, with the master leaning over me. He then asked me to tell him of my travels, about where I went, and whom I saw and to leave nothing out, and so I told him everything, as I have told you. He then pondered what I had told him, and then he said that this physician was exactly whom we needed, but that he would need my aid. Then he looked into my

eyes and asked me if this was what I wanted, and whether I was willing to sacrifice my own life for this venture.

"What I told him was that I had lived a long and full life and that if this was required to maintain our island's safety, then so be it. Now, mind you, I truly had no idea what all this would involve, but I felt an obligation to our island's, as well as our painters' and potters' safekeeping. He then said I should sleep, and upon waking, he would tell me of his plan."

"Now, his plan involved me in ways that are difficult to describe. Firstly, he said, we would find someone in this other time and place to contact, someone that could be both a foreteller and a companion to our healer. Then we must be able to convince our healer of our circumstances, as well as our need of his power to bring about resolution. Then thirdly, we must create circumstances on our island dire enough that even the king's men would fear to come ashore, as this was our real and true way to ensure the future of our venture. Now, I began to feel somewhat uneasy about all of this, as I only wanted to protect our guild and its ability to continue to produce pottery for the ages. It became obvious to me that Drachma had grander designs. Nevertheless, I did agree to his plans, at least until we could see how they were progressing.

"Now again, the next evening, we ate and drank heartily. Then afterwards, we went up to his study, where I again sat down in the same chair, he again chanted and made music of sorts on his little instrument, and I drifted off into a dreamlike state. This time, when I again found myself in the woods, with the path, I could feel the pull, as if the earth itself wanted me to go a certain way, but I resisted. I turned around, and behind me there was an old tree stump next to the path, and I sat and waited. Then came two people, walking down the path. One was Drachma himself; the other was a younger woman. The woman was distraught, but attentive, and she and Drachma were in conversation, though I could not make out the words. I simply watched as they went

by me. I got up and tried to follow, but the pull of this new world would not let me. Instead, I was impelled to go in another direction, down yet another fragrant path."

"I wandered down this path for some time, noting that the woods were ever deeper and greener, and then I again turned and came to a door. I could not help myself, the pull was too strong, and so I opened the door. This time I was back in your world, somewhere in this hospital, I believe, in a small, cluttered room, with considerable noise and commotion about. Again, it was Dr. Gilsen seated behind a table, eating something most unappealing, and drinking from a strange metal vessel. As the last time, he looked exceedingly tired, as if he were carrying some burden upon his back, when in walked the lady from the woods, but this time she smiled at Dr. Gilsen, said something I could not hear. Then she laid a hand upon his shoulder, and I could see the burden he was carrying lift just a little. He then got up, donned his coat and gloves, then left. I stayed and observed this woman, who tended to the ill and injured in that place. And I noticed the same thing occurred whenever she touched a person, that from each a burden was lifted.

"Then I turned back the way I had come, but could not find the way out, rather I was just walking about, unnoticed. And then I saw a most amazing thing. A youth was brought in, who was struggling to breathe. They brought him in on a conveyance with wheels; then the man and woman who brought him in were joined by others, including our lady from the forest. He was eased onto a table, then the people in that room were joined by others. Much was done to this youth, and it seemed like chaos. Eventually, though, he seemed to breathe more easily, and gradually, all left his side. Then he turned to me and bade me come to his side. I looked about, and saw that no one noticed my presence, so I approached his table. He then held out his hand to me, and I took it in mine. Then he said, 'Drachma sent you, did he not?' I could not help but answer him in the affirmative. Then he said,

'I thought so. I shall tell you two things. The first is to go and do what he asks of you, no matter the consequence. And the second is to tell Drachma that I shall warn Dr. Gilsen of his doings.' I tried to think of something to say, but as I did, he let go my hand, and he seemed to take no further notice of me."

"Just then, some women came up to the youth with a large machine, taking no notice of me, and sent me tumbling across the room, where I cut my leg on some object protruding into the room. I got up, with the blood oozing onto the floor and walked out, but this time I came to a door, opened it, and was out again into the forest. I then looked down at my leg, which was injured, but noticed that the bleeding had stopped, and there was no more pain. So then I walked on down the path but noticed there was no longer the pulling in any direction, just the quiet of the forest, the ripple of the stream, and the song of birds high above."

"I just walked down the path, toward the sound of running water, not caring where I was going."

Carlo paused, took another drink of his coffee. Marilyn just sat, absorbed in his story. When he resumed his tale, there was a note of resignation in his voice.

"What I did, then as I got to the river, may seem odd, but I did step into the river, and then I just laid myself down and let its current carry me downstream. The water was cool, but soothing, as I drifted with the current I could hear above me the commotion in the hospital. I could half see what they were doing to the young man. It seems as if they had him on a table in a large room, with lights all around, he was naked, with tubes inserted into his arms and some sort of tube in his mouth; then they covered him with green cloths, and they surrounded him, and then some woman, robed in green, with her head covered, as were the others in the room, cut open his chest, and worked inside his chest. There were others around the table, some of whom seemed to be assisting the woman, others walking about. Then after some time, Dr. Gilsen walked into the room, dressed as the others were, but still I knew

it to be him. He was obviously troubled about something, but I could not make out what he was saying. Then after a period of time, Dr. Gilsen left the room, but as this happened, I was back in Drachma's study again. Again, he asked me to tell him all that happened, and all whom I saw. I tried to explain all that happened, but I think I was too tired, and I drifted off to sleep before I could tell him of my visions in the river."

"The next day I woke to find that Drachma had gone off somewhere on some mission of great importance but had assigned me the task of writing a note to one of my workers named Garza, who had been one of the painters to have written to relatives back home of how we were now producing pots of great virtue, and whose note was received by none other than Gregorio. I penned him a note with heaviness in my heart, as I knew that he was not long for this world."

"Now I decided that I should go back to my own home. So I took the fateful note and gave it to Angelica, with instructions as to whom it should go. Then, as I was busying myself with preparation to go back on my journey, she turned to me and gave me this little box, with her instructions that I should give it to whoever I deemed most needed it, but that it sought out, of its own accord, with whom it stayed. I looked at her rather perplexed, but took the box, and looked inside it. On a velvet pillow of blue cloth was a small, silver coin, of ancient lineage. It was a Drachma. Now, as I prepare to leave all of you, I give you this."

Carlo Vincente took from under his cloak a small box, which he then handed to Marilyn. She took it with her hands shaking, opened it to find within it a small silver coin, obviously ancient, and obviously a Drachma.

"As to where your husband is at this time, I cannot say, but know ye that this token tells of his health, my lady. I do thank you for your time and for listening to this old man's tale."

With that he got up and walked away. Marilyn looked up, with her eyes brimming over with tears. She did not hear the detectives running up to her.

"Where is he?" Detective Bryant asked, "Did you see which way he went?"

"No, I didn't, Detective, and you know what? You'll never see him again." As she said this, she slipped the little box into her purse.

Chapter Ten

"Good morrow, Master Robert. The time is at hand. We must prepare for our day's journey." Martin's voice reached Bob as through a fog. "Will you not take some nourishment ere we begin?"

Bob sat up from his bed of blankets and straw. He couldn't remember ever feeling as stiff and sore as he did this morning. His back was knotted, his legs were like boards, his head throbbed, and his mouth felt like a baked riverbank. Somehow he managed to get to his feet and wander over toward the fire that had been dutifully kept alive by his guards. The warmth helped quite a bit, enough so that, after a few moments of rubbing and stretching, he was able to move over to the table and get a drink of water. Also on the table were some dried fruits and bread, which he sampled.

As he stepped outside the hut to relieve himself, he was startled by the glistening beauty around him. High above were the imposing mountain peaks, separated from the world below by a fog that had covered the bare trees and rocks with hoar frost. Except for the crunch of his own steps, all was silent. As he stared about him, he tried again to pull together what had happened to him in the last few days. The events themselves didn't make sense, but somehow his presence here did, in a strange secret sort of way which defied logic.

"Aye, 'tis a wondrous morning, is it not, Master Robert?"

Bob turned to see Stoneheft beside him.

"Yeah, it's beautiful all right. These mountains remind me of somewhere I've been before, a place there in the mountains. In the winter, we'd go up there to ski, and it was a lot like this…still, quiet, peaceful. We used to say that it was a place you could see yourself breathe and hear yourself think."

Stoneheft just nodded.

For a few minutes, the two just stood there, looking about. Strange thoughts again began tumbling about in Bob's mind, thoughts about the ill and dying, about hospital corridors, IVs and monitors, the sounds, sights and smells that had become so familiar over the years, but now seemed a distant, fading vision. Intermingled with these thoughts were those of a fragrant, deep green wood, of a path in springtime by a quiet stream, along with an almost palpable sense of yearning, pulsating like a heartbeat…

"Ah, Master Robert, it is good to see you up and out." Martin's voice startled him by its closeness. "Do you feel ready for another day's journey?"

"Well, to be perfectly honest, I am incredibly stiff and sore, but I really don't like the idea of just staying where we are, beautiful as it is. So, yeah, I guess I'm ready to go, even though I have no idea at all where we're going."

"Well said, Master, for I feel as you do, that we should continue our journey to the earl's castle. Your arrival there is eagerly awaited."

"Eagerly awaited? By whom?"

"By the earl himself, I should think, or so my instructions would have me believe."

"Hmm, well, I sure hope he knows what he's done. You see, I get the funny feeling that it's more than just your earl involved in all this. I know for certain that this fellow Drachma is somehow important in what ever is going on."

"Aye, Master Robert, that would seem very likely, indeed."

"What can you tell me about this Drachma? I know that he had a lot to do with my coming here, because…well, let's just say that I had heard of him before I ever got here, and when I asked about him earlier, no one would tell me anything. It was obvious, though, that they knew something about him, and that he had something to do with my being here."

"In truth, I am certain Drachma himself had a hand in your arrival upon this isle, but of that man himself, I am not so sure of what I may tell you. Indeed, he is a man of extraordinary power and influence here, yet he holds no title, nor is he a nobleman. He is more an advisor to the earl and the council, but, more than that, he is one who knows how to accomplish what he seems needful to be done, often by methods cryptic, else completely unknown. In years past, some have accused him of sorcery and black magic, but this has never been shown to be true, as the church fathers have attested on his behalf. I think it would be safe enough to say that any with power and influence on this isle owe much to Drachma.

"Yeah, what you're telling me fits with what I've run into so far. Oddly enough, though, I don't find myself all that eager to meet him in person."

"Ah, Master Robert, there are truly many on this island who have felt his influence greatly, yet have never seen the man."

"Have you met him?"

"Aye, I have, but of that I mustn't speak now."

"That figures, somehow."

"Well, then, why don't we get going? We might as well get this show on the road."

Martin cocked his head slightly, smiled. "As you wish, Master Robert."

As he was led into Craycroft's new quarters, Rust felt more ill at ease than he had in quite some time. The meeting of the council

had been near disaster from the beginning, and with most of the councilors seeming to side with Reordan against what Rust knew to be the earl's wishes, he now felt impelled to find the truth for himself, as dangerous as that might turn out to be. Representing what seemed to be a minority of the council determined to uphold their liege lord's wishes, it was imperative now to Rust that, regardless of his own leanings in the matter, which seemed ever more in accord with Craycroft's strange assumption of power, that the truth must be told and recorded.

What he saw, as he entered the chamber, surprised him. Craycroft was sitting in a large chair by the fire, obviously expecting the councilor, but this was hardly the same man he had gotten up from sleep not a week before in answer to lady Felicia's distress. There had been a transformation that was immediately apparent in the Master's eyes. Gone was the harried, unkempt, eccentric thinker. In his place now sat a man of power and confidence, changed by the fires of circumstance and loss.

Unconsciously, Rust bowed his head and averted his gaze.

"Good Councilor, welcome. Do me the honor of sitting here with my by the fire, and tell me of the council's doings. I can tell by your countenance that all is not well. I would be less than honest with you if I said that I was surprised. Pray, sit here and tell me what Reordan has said and done."

Rust sat in the chair offered him.

"As you have surmised, Councilor Reordan did convene the council to report on his meeting yesterday with the earl. Alas, what he reported to the council could not have been the truth, as it did not fit with what I already know of the earl's directive, and with what you have told us."

"What, then, did he tell the council?"

"What he told us was that he had come to the earl's chambers, but was only reluctantly allowed to see the earl, against your wishes, and that the earl was, in his words, ranting incoherently, and was clearly not in his right mind."

Craycroft glowered, said nothing for a moment then growled, "That serpent! I did suspect he would do such. I would assume, then, that he argued before the councilors that the earl could not have been in his right mind either when he wrote his directive to you and the council."

"Precisely. That is exactly what he told the council, and to my dismay, others either believe him or wish it so, and would side with him."

"Were you able, then, to speak of your own knowledge in the matter?"

"Aye, but against much turmoil and indignation…"

"Hmmm…are there any among the council who might see it your way?"

"There be two. I believe we can count upon the support of Councilor's Genet and Fitzgibbon, but of the others…"

"Well enough for now, I hope, as the earl still lives. But we must take care in this, for there is much at stake, besides our allegiance to our liege lord."

"Ah, but what shall we do now? For myself, I believe I know the verity of what the earl would have us do, but what can I say or do that would sway the doubting council members. For the present, it is merely my word against Reordan's."

"As for Reordan himself, there is nothing you can do, for it is obvious that the truth is not his concern, but rather power alone. As for others on the council, for whom the truth may have some value, and for whom allegiance may still have meaning, for them we must provide something from the earl himself that could sway their thinking."

"Here is what I would propose, that you would bring Councilor Genet hence, and possibly one other, and if the earl would be so disposed, have him sign and seal, in their presence, an order of state. Thereby, if any be opposed, then let them risk the accusation of treason. But I advise you, make haste, for the day is late, and I do not know how long the earl may survive or how frail his constitution may become."

"Master Craycroft, I shall do as you say. I depart anon."

As Rust got up to leave, a messenger arrived at the door. "Begging your pardon, m' lord," he uttered. "Master Kerlin has sent me in haste with a message. He said to tell you that a party has been seen, riding toward the castle, and that he believes he may know the riders, and that you should come at once, if I may be so bold."

"Aye, lad that may be news of great substance. I shall come at once if you will lead me to him."

"Master Craycroft," Rust interrupted, "do you know whom they might be?"

"Quite possibly I do, Councilor, and that would make your task all the more important. Pray, proceed as we discussed, and return here. I shall bring you news upon your return."

Rust bowed quickly then was gone.

Craycroft followed the servant through the hallways and up the winding stairways to the observation tower above the keep. There, Kerlin was waiting for him, eyes fixed toward the northwest, squinting into the stinging wind and fading light.

"There, m' lord, just beyond Garrity Bridge, you can see them. There be five riders, approaching out of the forest."

Craycroft looked in the direction Kerlin pointed. He could just make out the forms of riders, visible against the snowy fields.

"Aye, I am able to see riders, but my eyes are not so keen as yours, and I am unable to tell how many. I will believe you if you say there be five. Might they be the party dispatched by Drachma to bring the stranger?"

"None other, to my mind."

"That is well, indeed, then. Perhaps not to late…"

"Too late, m' lord? For what might they be too late?"

"Ah, I see they did not inform you of the nature of this stranger for whom the party was sent."

"No, indeed, nor did I inquire."

"Well, I am led to understand that his stranger is some mighty healer, possessing great powers. It is my vain hope that he will arrive in time to provide a cure for our earl."

"Indeed, then, time would be of the essence."

"True..."

"In that event, m' lord, may I request permission to send an envoy to greet the approaching party and hasten their arrival here?"

"Aye, you have my permission, and my blessing. Bring them to me quickly, but with all the courtesy due royalty."

"As you wish, m' lord."

As they left the lookout tower, heading back into the castle proper, Craycroft noticed how natural it seemed to Kerlin to refer to him as a lord, and also just how awkward it felt to be addressed in such a way, especially in light of the brewing conflagration in the council. As he headed toward the earl's chambers, the healer again fervently hoped it was not already too late.

Returning to the earl's chambers, Craycroft felt once more the overwhelming sense of loneliness and loss. He tried to bolster his spirits with hope of healing for the earl, but the huge uncertainty of it all, along with the knowledge of impending conflict with the council, and Felicia's recent death all weighed heavily on his spirits. To outward appearance, he was calm and controlled, but inside he was lost and afraid.

He walked in quietly, and asked the servant in attendance of the earl's condition.

"Resting fitfully, m' lord. When awake, he did ask of you, but bade us not to disturb you at this time."

"Very well, then, if he be awake, I'll talk with him, but if he sleeps, I shall let him be. Be advised, though, that I would not take offense if you were to come to me, whatever the hour, if you perceive that he needs anything at all of me. Do you understand, lad?"

"Aye, m'lord, I do."

The room was warm as he walked in, almost stifling. The curtains were drawn, and the only real light came from the doorway, the fireplace, and the few candles set about. After his eyes adjusted to the dimness, Craycroft could see that the earl did seem to be sleeping, though his eyes were only partly shut. His breathing was uneven, but not labored, and there remained the sickly sweet smell pervading the chamber.

Unable to think of anything better to do for the present, Craycroft decided to sit and wait. He found a stuffed chair close to the fireplace, poured himself a small portion of wine from a flask set on the table, and sat silently, awaiting nothing in particular but knowing well that this was where he needed to be. Oddly, in this time of turmoil, the place he felt most comfortable was at the side of the sick and dying.

As he sat and waited, it occurred to Craycroft that this recent spiral of events seemed to have taken on power and direction from the moment he set foot outside his chambers in search of Drachma's book. He wondered now if he would ever see the book again, or if he should even try to find it. There was a connection, he felt sure, and an odd sense of duty told him he should try again to locate the strange volume. Nevertheless, other matters were ever more pressing, and he could not envision a time soon when he would have the opportunity to seek it out without attracting undue attention.

He sipped his wine again, and as he did, he heard steps from the hallway, and muted voices. The page then stepped back into the chamber.

"M'lord, I fear to disturb you, but here come three councilors, and they told me you have sent for them, and that their business is urgent. Do you wish to see them?"

"Three did you say?"

The page nodded.

"And who might they be? Do you know them?"

"Aye, m'lord. There be Councilors Rust, Genet and Fitzgibbon."

"Well enough, lad. I shall see them, but first I must confer with our lord, the earl, if he is able. Have them wait. I shall be there anon."

"As you wish, m'lord."

The page bowed slightly, turned, and left the room.

With some trepidation, Craycroft approached the earl's bedside. Gently, he touched the old man's arm.

"M'lord, it is I, Craycroft. I am most sorry to disturb your rest."

The earl's eyes opened at his touch. He spoke in a voice just above a whisper.

"Ah, my friend…it is good to see you. What do you wish?"

"I should tell you, it is as we feared. Reordan has lied to the council, telling them that you were raving, and not of sound mind, and that your directive was therefore invalid."

The earl frowned, then spoke slowly, "Aye, it was as we… suspected…was it not? Tell me, what will you do?"

"M' lord, if you will, I have requested the presence of some of the council here. This so that they may witness the signing of your Order of State, with your seal, so that any that oppose it must do so risking accusation of treason."

"Of course, my friend, I shall do so…for you. But be advised…I know this man…he is evil, and …cunning. He will find a way to oppose…even this."

"Ah, yes, m' liege, I would expect so. My hope is not for Reordan, for he has played his hand. Rather, it is for the sake of others on the council, for whom truth, loyalty and honor may yet have meaning."

"Well said, Craycroft. Bring them hence…along with a scribe…and my seal."

"I shall m'lord, anon."

With that, Craycroft turned and went out into the hall, where the councilors were waiting.

"How is our lord, the earl?" Rust asked. "Is he able to meet with us?"

"Aye, that he is willing to do. He remains very ill, but for all our sakes, he will meet us and declare his wishes as an Order of State. You may proceed within. I shall send for a scribe and his seal."

"That is good, Master Craycroft." Councilor Genet spoke up. "I myself shall be glad to see truth prevail."

With a nod, Craycroft turned and went toward the main hallway, as the councilors entered the earl's chamber.

As he stepped into the hallway, Craycroft was met by the hurrying page.

"M' lord," he said breathlessly, "I have been sent urgently to tell you the riders have entered the castle. They be led by Master Dowdell, and approach anon."

"That is good, lad, but tell me, by which portal do they enter? I must attempt to greet our guests as they arrive."

"They have come in by the north gate, m' lord, and I should think, that after turning in their mounts, that they should come in by the main entryway."

"Very well, lad. I shall meet them there. And lad, I have a most urgent task for you myself."

"Pray, what is it, m' lord?"

"Go you at once and fetch the earl's scribe, have him bring the Seal of Shepperton to the earl's chamber. There he will meet three councilors, who will receive from the earl and Order of State, which he should scribe and give unto Councilor Genet. Tell them to proceed in haste without me, for I am needed elsewhere."

"Aye, m' lord. I shall do as you command, at once."

"Good, lad, go you hence."

The light snow had turned to a cold, stinging rain as Councilor Genet stepped outside the earl's chambers, heading back to his own home. His eyes were moist from more than the rain, as he checked the security of the sealed paper held within his cloak.

He recalled the shame he had felt about his own initial doubts as the earl, gravely ill, but very clear of mind and purpose, spelled out for the assembled few his reiteration of his wish to appointment of Master Craycroft as his immediate and future successor. The truth was now very clear, not only as to the earl's wishes, but of the unbridled treachery of Reordan and his supporters. There will be much for which they would be held accountable. Genet did not relish the thought of going up against his one time friend in this matter, but the truth was plain, and it spoke with all the authority of justice and right.

Thoughts of how to bring this all before the council tomorrow kept his mind occupied as he trudged ahead through the bone chilling wind and rain. He neither heard nor saw the figure in the shadows that followed close behind. As he stepped into the shelter of the archway, out of the rain, the club struck him with incredible force in the back of the head, knocking him instantly to the ground. He was only barely aware of being turned over, and having the paper seized from beneath his cloak, as he lapsed into oblivion.

No one saw the man run from the archway toward the stables in the fading light of evening.

Chapter Eleven

"My good lady, are you awake?"

The old man's voice, and his touch on her shoulder, brought Judy back from her dreaming. She was still sitting in the chair, slumped over onto the table, the tumbler of wine spilled onto the floor beside her.

"Oh, Mr. Falma, you're up. I'm sorry, I must have gone back to sleep."

"Aye, my lady, and in not a bed of much comfort, I fear."

"True enough, but anyway, I was talking to this Drachma fellow. He came here in the night, to check on us, I guess…"

"Drachma, he came here?"

"Oh, yeah, he was here while you were asleep. We didn't want to wake you. Anyway, he said he would have an escort for us to take us back to the earl's castle."

"An escort, you say? That is most interesting, most interesting."

"Yeah, there are supposed to be two of his guards outside, watching and keeping us safe until we travel. I must admit, though, that I haven't looked out to see for myself. Tell me though, what would he be protecting us from, do you know?"

"Ah, m' lady, I know not. I have heard much through many tales of these woods, but, in truth, I have traveled little beyond the castle walls in years."

"Well, anyway, we seem to have made it through the night safely enough. You think we should see if our escort is out there?"

"Aye, m' lady, that would seem wise, as the morn is upon us, and this would be the safest time to be making our journey."

"Tell me, do you have any idea how far we are from this castle?"

"If we be where I think, then we should be a full day's ride from the earl's castle. In truth, though, I am not certain."

"Then, I guess we better find out if the guards are out there, and ask them."

"As you wish, m' lady. Come, let us see."

With that, he took Judy's arm and led her toward the door of the hut.

Outside, as Drachma had said, were two young forest guards, alert, and obviously expecting their charges. They both bowed slightly.

"My good Master Falma," the older of the two said, "and m' lady, it is good to see you. I hope you are both well. My name is Cairn, and my companion here is Bernard. It is well you are up, for our journey to the castle may be long, and I am not at all certain we shall arrive yet today.

"Before we depart, though, we should feed you and make good our provisions. Would you then be ready anon?"

"I fear I am unable to speak for our lady, but for myself, I require very little this morning, for I am but an old man, and thin as a stick. A few bits of dry bread, a sip of water, and I shall be ready. But what of you, m' lady, are you hungry, and do you thirst?"

"Well, actually, I'm more stiff and sore than hungry, but I wouldn't mind a bite to eat before we get going."

"Come, then, m' lady," Cairn said, "We shall provide what we may for now, but be assured, when we get to the earl's castle, you shall be fed more fittingly."

With that, he bowed ever so slightly, and led the way back into the shelter, where he was able to put together a reasonable meal of bread, dried fruits and spiced meats. As Judy and Falma

ate in silence, their two guards readied provisions for the trip and prepared the horses, including a small mare for Judy to ride.

The trip from the hunting shelter took the small band over a high pass southeast of Croftus knob, which was hidden above them in the clouds. The air held a chill, but there was no breeze at this time, and the travel was not severe. With Cairn in front and Bernard at the rear of the company, they were able to wind over the rocky pathway then slowly back down into the forest. Conversation was nearly impossible, as they traveled single file, but Bernard was able to point out landmarks to Judy as they passed them. Judy, for her sake, did not pay much attention, as she was wrapped up in her own thoughts.

She remembered the end of her childhood. The mountains and snow brought her back to a time of decision and change. She was thirteen, and it was the first time she had been away from her own family for more than a weekend, and really the first time she had ever spent any time away from the city or suburbs. Her church youth group had raised money for a skiing trip to the mountains of Colorado, and this seemed to her parents a safe opportunity for Judy to get away for a while. In the last year she had become moody, alternately sullen, irritable or unpredictably ecstatic. Their previously cheerful and outgoing daughter had changed, and they no longer felt they knew her. Judy recalled the overwhelming surges of emotion that would come over her with no warning or reason. Things were happening inside her that made no sense, and she felt powerless. Other girls had started their periods that year with an almost eager sense of anticipation and accomplishment, but to Judy it was just one more thing that she had no control over, and happened to her without her consent. She, too, thought the chance to be away for a whole week would be great, yet part of her was terrified. Somehow, she knew a change was coming.

Judy recalled how being placed in charge of the "Babysitting Bureau" and the "Odd Jobs Corps" had given her a newfound sense of purpose and control, as she dutifully managed the funds

and kept the records of their growing account. By late February, with the money from their projects and some healthy donations, they had earned their much-anticipated trip to the mountains of faraway Colorado. The eagerness and energy were almost palpable in the group as they boarded the van after the Sunday service, and headed west. Their youthful exuberance turned to absolute awe a day and a half later as they began their climb into the rarified air of the majestic mountains. No one except Dave Spencer, the youth pastor, had ever seen anything like this before. Photographs they had seen could not do justice to the actual experience of riding up skyward surrounded by snow-enshrouded peaks. Adding to the experience was the fact that the girls in the group all had a terrible crush on Dave, and here he was, leading them on the biggest journey of their youthful lives. The boys' enthusiasm and crude humor seemed so immature by comparison, yet their boisterous companionship stirred feelings in her, too, that she hadn't known at school.

Thinking back, Judy realized she was emotionally primed for something big. It happened on Thursday afternoon. By now, the kids were remarkably confident, having mastered the beginners' slopes with the ease of youthful enthusiasm. They were ready for a bigger challenge, the intermediate slopes. The thrill that day was beyond description, racing freely like the wind down the mountainside, unfettered and so alive with all their senses, daring, yet invincible. Then in a heartbeat it all changed. Chris had gone down ahead of Judy, apparently without any problem, but suddenly she was there, in a heap, and there was no time to turn or stop. Judy's ski hit, and she was thrown airborne, another fifty feet, before landing, then sliding to a stop against a small pine tree. When she regained consciousness, she couldn't move or feel her legs. The rescue team arrived sometime later, Judy could not tell how long, and got her on a back board, then eased her down the rest of the slope to the waiting ambulance. When they lifted her in, she looked over and saw Chris, and stifled a scream.

There was almost no color in her friend's face, and a blood-soaked wrap surrounded her middle. The grave expressions on the faces of the two attendants only made the scene more terrifying. Judy tried to speak, but nothing came out. She wept silently all the way to the hospital.

The emergency room was dazzlingly bright, almost electric, as they wheeled the two girls in and placed them on stretchers side by side. Then her face appeared, silhouetted against the exam light.

"Judy, I'm Miss Potter. I'm your nurse. You're at St. Vincent's Hospital." Her voice was calm, confident, and serene. She gently touched Judy's face, brushed the hair out of her eyes. "Don't you worry, Judy, I'm not going to let anything happen to you, I'll be right here."

Judy could feel a warmth that spread like a healing balm emanate from where Miss Potter touched her face, and could sense her whole body relax, and surrender to the care of this wondrous person.

Judy was diagnosed with a spinal contusion, and remained in the hospital for most of a month. She did regain full use of her legs, though gradually. Chris suffered a broken leg and a ruptured spleen, but also recovered fully. Almost every day, Miss Potter made a point of coming up to see the girls, just to talk, tell jokes, and giggle or to listen. Seeing her was the highlight of each day, even more important, Judy realized later, than her parents' arrival.

From the moment she heard Miss Potter's voice and felt the touch of her hand, Judy realized that she could do nothing more important and powerful with her own life than to be that person for someone else in need. From then on, there was no question in Judy's mind about what she would be or do with her life. So many other areas of her life had been uncertain, turbulent, or self-destructive, but she defined herself in her own mind as an ER nurse, and that held fast and stable through the years.

Until now…

Now, it seemed, nothing of her previous thirty-five years meant anything. She was without bearings, without any sense of who she was, where she was, or what her role was.

Here she was, riding down a mountain pass, in the middle of winter, on some remote island, brought here somehow by a strange mystical sort of person called Drachma, for purposes that seemed obscure at best, and in the company of a frail, old, gentle fellow named Falma, and these two guards escorting her to the castle of some earl.

Another mile or so down the path they reentered the forest, and here the trees were all evergreens, growing ever taller and denser as they silently followed the narrow way that the guards seemed to know as they would know their own yards.

As the small band turned south and then east again, they could hear the sound of running water coming from somewhere below then, to the right. The forest became deeper, and the path more steep as they descended toward the sound of the water.

"That would be St. Sebastian's Rill, m' lady," Bernard said, as he rode closer. "The way is a little steep, I fear, but you seem to be riding with some ease. You should be safe, I feel, but I shall stay close by, m' lady."

"Thank you Bernard," Judy said, rousing from her reverie. "I'm fine, really."

"Ah, yes, and the way should prove easier once we cross the water. It is not far."

Abruptly, the company stopped, as Cairn held up his right hand. All was silent as he looked; listened, tried to sense something of what had caught his attention. Bernard listened too, and reached quietly for his blade, scanning the area to the rear, as Cairn did the fore. Judy tensed, her heart suddenly pounding in her chest, not even knowing what to fear. Only Falma seemed perfectly at ease, serene on his slender mount.

Then Cairn gave the motion, and they eased silently forward again, but with heightened vigilance fore and aft. Judy's horse

dislodged a rock with her hoof, sending the stone clattering down the slope. All held still once more, and then hearing nothing further, the small group pressed on.

They arrived at the rill, and Cairn halted, then led the way across the water, looking both ways as the company made its way through the stream toward the far side. The forest across the stream was even thicker, and the way narrower, with tall fir trees and shorter cedars defining the path. As they climbed up from the water's edge, turning left around a large rise, Judy heard something off the right, and turned to look, when Bernard suddenly let out a yell. When she turned toward him, he was clutching at his chest where the arrow pierced through his leather vest. Then the arrows suddenly flew like vicious raindrops. When she turned again, Falma was down from his horse, grabbing at Judy.

"Come, m' lady. I must protect you."

His grip was strong, sure, as he held her down, covering her with his thin frame, waiting out the rain of arrows.

Judy heard scuffling, could see movement of men, as Falma held her down.

"You, there, stand up. You will not be harmed."

The voice belonged to a large, pale man, standing over the two figures. Behind him stood six or seven men, some with bows, with arrows pointed at Falma and Judy, others with drawn swords.

Falma stood up, keeping Judy behind him.

"Ah, Master Finch, we meet again," Falma said with utmost calm. "Can I be certain that no harm will come to m' lady, here?"

In answer, the man turned to his henchmen, made a sign with his arm, and the men promptly put away their bows, and put up their swords.

Chapter Twelve

To Bob, the way had become arduous. The wind had shifted and was now blowing from the west, and stinging rain soaked through his cloak, and the light was now fading rapidly. He was relieved to see the castle off in the distance.

"That, I assume, is the earl's castle up ahead."

"Aye, that it is," replied Martin. "A welcome sight to me. This rain is colder than the snow up yonder. A fire within the walls would be most welcome to me."

"And me." Bob agreed.

In the distance, it stood out from the muddied fields, scattered huts, and thin copses of evergreens, as a sanctuary on the hilltop. The road up to the castle was little more than a path of mud, but it was at least wide enough for two to ride abreast. Unlike most castles of the time, this was not built primarily as a fortress, and there were actually two main entrances, one on the north, with the main road on which they traveled, the other southwest, with a road that led down to the little port on the sea.

As they climbed the hill toward the castle the group picked up the pace, and it seemed as though the horses knew their ride was coming to an end, and began to trot, a gait Bob was not familiar with, and which hurt his tailbone mercilessly. However he didn't complain, as he could see and feel the end of his journey.

What is this I've gotten into? he wondered again. *And who is this earl, and what has this to do with me? This is so far removed from anything I've ever seen and done. And this horse…I've got to get off this thing soon, before I bust a gut. I sure hope they've got a fire and some warm, dry clothes.*

The little band moved on up toward the castle, albeit slowly. Then they caught sight of a rider coming in their direction. The rider moved quickly, and soon came even with their little group.

"Ah, Master Dowdell, you have come, and that is good, but, pray tell, why such haste?" Martin spoke with the others gathered round.

"Pray, let us get inside the walls, then you shall hear, as there is much to tell. Suffice it to say, Master Craycroft is expecting you most eagerly."

"Craycroft?" Martin asked.

"Aye, acting on behalf of the earl. Now come, make haste."

With that the little company, now six, headed off toward the castle, with Bob noticing that his horse was now cantering, which he found a much more bearable gain than the last. He felt something of a surge of anticipation, as they sped through the last village, turned toward the broader road that led through the huge gate into the castle. The company, following Dowdell's lead slowed to a walk as they made their way over the moat and into the great courtyard. They were led leftward toward the great stables. There they were met by groomsmen who held the horses steady. Bob made it to the ground without too large a display of ineptitude, and was thoroughly glad to be touching the ground with his two feet. He looked around him, and was astonished at the size of the castle inside the walls. The rain was still falling, but out of the wind, he felt he could at least breathe, and though the light was dim, he could follow Dowdell and the company, as they entered a sheltered walkway that led into the interior of the castle. The company then entered a doorway, into a great hall, with massive pillars, and torches lighting the central open area.

"You should wait in here," said Dowdell. "I shall let Master Craycroft know of your arrival."

Bob looked around him. He was in a great hall filled with mighty purpose, with high, narrow windows and rich tapestries and rugs. In the middle of the room was a large fireplace. The cold riders all huddled toward the fireplace, warming their frozen hands and faces. No one said anything for a time. Then Stoneheft finally broke the silence.

"Well, then Master Robert of Ewe Ass, here ye be at the castle of the earl of Shepperton. What think ye of it? How does it feel to be here?"

"First of all, I'm very glad to be off that horse and out of the cold wind and rain, here where there is a warm fire. As to the castle, even though it's obviously dark outside, I can see that this is one spectacular building. I guess we're expected, and that's probably a good thing."

"Aye, Master Robert, that you are, indeed."

Bob turned around to look toward the sound.

"Allow me to introduce myself," he said with a courteous bow. "I am Craycroft, and I represent our lord the earl, as this is his domain. I do bid you welcome into his house."

Bob was taken aback; as this was the first truly courteous greeting he had received since coming to this place. The speaker was a man, who was of indeterminate age, of great bearing. There was something strangely familiar about him, but Bob could not place him. The others in his company suddenly seemed to sense that their riding companion may have been more than he appeared, and backed away.

"I am honored by your presence here, and I bring greetings from the earl himself. It is my hope that your arrival on our island was a peaceful one, and that you were shown due courtesy, though I should doubt that your companions knew of your true worth." Craycroft glared silently at the ragged band of guards and

noticed that no one held his head up. Craycroft, though, could not help but smile, as he noted Tom among the group.

"I'm sorry Mr. Craycroft. But I myself don't know of this 'worth' you speak about. You see, I don't even know how I got to your island in the first place. I don't know what is expected of me. All I really know is that I've come a long way, and I've trudged through snow, rain, mud, and misery. I know that I'm tired, sore, wet, and hungry. But here I am, and, I guess, at your service."

"Very well, Master Robert, I shall have one of the earl's servants escort you to your quarters, where there be a warm fire and dry clothes for you. Then we shall send for you, and you will be fed and given drink with me, and I shall explain what I may of our present circumstances. Unfortunately, I know not how you did arrive, but I can tell you some of the why, as I understand it."

"That would definitely be good," said Bob. "I especially like the idea of some dry, warm clothes, and a good meal."

"Very well, then, you shall be shown to your rooms by this page, named Hermes, whom I have instructed to be at your call at all times. Should you need anything, simply say the word and Hermes will obtain it, if it be possible. Now, Master Robert, do you need anything else?"

"It seems that I had several things that were taken from me when I arrived. It would be really nice if I could have them back now."

"Martin, do you have knowledge of such things of which Master Robert speaks?"

"Aye, m' lord. Stoneheft has these things in a satchel."

Stoneheft rather sheepishly pulled out of his larger bag a smaller bag that he handed to Bob. "Here, I'm quite certain that ye will make better use of these than I shall. I only hope that ye will find everything in order."

"My thanks. I have a feeling that if anything is missing, it'll come back to me somehow," Bob said, rather sardonically. He took the bag and opened it, finding several pens, tongue depressors,

his various papers and cards, his reflex hammer, his beeper, and finally his stethoscope. "Yes, I think it's all here." He then put all the stuff back into the bag. "Okay then, I think I'm ready. You may lead the way," he said, turning toward the young page, who had been staring at Bob's stuff with absolute fascination.

"I guess I'll see you later," said Bob to Craycroft. Then he turned to Hermes. "Lead the way young man. I'm cold, wet, and hungry, and I smell like a wet horse."

"This way, Master Robert."

The two of them went off in the direction of the extensive guest quarters of the castle, as Craycroft stayed and spoke with Martin and the others, gathering what information he could of his new guest and how he got where he was. He expressed his rather severe displeasure over the treatment Bob had received, and explained to them that Bob was not just a guest, but was a healer of great power, and that he should be treated with the utmost respect, and further that he had come to them by way of Drachma, the elder, and that any further sign of disrespect would be dealt with severely.

He then turned to his page and said, "Now, Aaron, we must be off, for I have to send a message to Drachma this evening, explaining that Master Robert has arrived safely." Finally, he turned his attention to young Tom, who smiled rather shyly when asked about his role in all this. Tom explained that he was dispatched by Drachma himself, to accompany this healer, and to make a full reporting of events back to Drachma, and that he should hurry back with his report.

Craycroft then seemed to ponder this, then told Tom to come back with him, as he had some important work for the young page. He then dispatched the others to their quarters, explaining that they should meet again after their evening meal, and that they would be in charge of seeing to the safety of their new master in the future.

Bob and his page wound through the corridors and labyrinthine passageways of the castle before arriving at his rooms. He was pleasantly surprised to find that someone had built a nice, warm fire in the main room, and there was, on the table, some bread and dried fruit, as well as a tumbler of brown liquid that had a pleasing aroma. Hermes showed him where there was a large bowl of water for washing, as well as dry cloths for drying himself. Then he showed him where there were clothes for him to wear, that were dry, but seemed to Bob like the costumes worn by actors in some play by Shakespeare.

Bob couldn't help but chuckle, and commented, "In some ways, this looks and feels like you've brought me to some fine resort, where I'm supposed to tip the bell boy, but I have no cash, and I am cold and smelly, and it's apparent that I have no idea where I am and barely speak the language."

"Most sorry, Master, is anything amiss?"

"Ah, no, Hermes. It's just that I'm not native to your island, and have no idea about your customs."

"Our customs…?"

"Well, for one thing, these clothes," he said, picking out a pair of leotards, "These are not exactly what I typically wear…"

"And what ye have on, is that more typical?" Hermes could barely avoid chuckling himself.

Bob looked at what he had on. He got out of his cloak, and below that he had on his formerly white lab coat, over his scrubs, with his brown socks and loafers, all wet, muddy and clinging to his skin, which felt like a wet, infested swamp. Then all he could do was laugh, at his own predicament, his obviously foolish appearance, his current state of rather extreme exhaustion.

Hermes laughed along with his master.

"Well, I might as well get started. Even if I look ridiculous, these clothes are dry and don't smell like horse." He then got

out of his clothes; washed up as well as he could, found some of the clothing that looked a little less garish. There was a little mirror in which he could see himself, and what stared back at him was hardly recognizable. He had grown a few days worth of stubble, and his visage had a new quality he did not recognize. He looked around, and he could see nothing to suggest toothpaste or toothbrush. Seeing nothing like a comb, he ran his hand through his dark, matted hair.

"Master, if it be all right with ye, I'll have these clothes cleaned, dried and returned to ye on the morrow. Now, if ye wish, ye may sit here by the fire. I am quite sure this bread is fairly fresh, and the drink is one from Barncuddy, and should be pleasing to ye, at least that be what I am told."

"Thank you, Hermes, I think I'll do just that." Having said that, Bob sat down in the comfort of the old chair by the fireplace, while Hermes gathered up Bob's clothes, placed them in a sack, and stepped out, indicating that he would be back to tell Bob when Master Craycroft would want to see him.

The bread was, indeed, fresh, and still somewhat warm, tasted like what was served in fine Italian restaurants back home. The drink was unlike anything Bob had ever tasted. It had an aroma that was of cardamom, cinnamon, and just a whiff of something else. Its taste was just a little sweet and just a touch bitter. It went down easily, and spread warmth through his chest. He sat back with a sigh, and then thought about his circumstances once more, this time thinking about his wife, and that there was no way on earth he would be able to contact her to tell her that he was alive, and amazingly, quite well.

He wondered about how the people "back home" would handle his disappearance. What were they thinking? How could a well-respected cardiologist just disappear? He wondered if anyone saw him. Then he realized that he himself did not know how he got here, in this place and time, with all these strange people, with their strange names, weird clothes, and ancient

dress. And who was this Drachma, and what did he want? Then another thought struck him. Where was his wallet, with all his personal identification?

"Shoot, I must have left it in my scrubs when I changed into these loud leotards."

He took another draught of his drink, felt the warmth flow through him, felt himself slip seemingly deeper into the cushions of his seat. Exhaustion began to overtake him, and he drifted into a deep, dreamless slumber.

"Master Robert, Master Robert, it is time. Master Craycroft has summoned you to join him for the evening meal."

Bob was awakened from his slumber by Hermes, his page, gently shaking him. It took a few minutes for Bob to get his bearings, test the reality of his current situation, and to realize where he was.

"All right, I am ready." Bob stood up from his chair, and immediately sat down again. "Oh, man, I'm stiff and sore. That ride here was more than I am used to. Just a minute, let me get my bearings." He then got up more slowly and stiffly, as if he were some old rheumatic. Hermes just looked bemused, offered to help.

"No, I'm all right. Just give me a minute. By the way, that was some potent, but wonderful drink, there. I'll have to ask about getting some more of that stuff. All right, then let's be off, young man."

Hermes held out Bob's cloak for him. "Here, Master, ye may need this. The weather has not improved outside, and it is a fair walk to the earl's quarters."

They headed out the door, and immediately Bob could tell that Hermes was right. The weather was not any better at all, the rain was now mixed with icy particulate matter that was whipped by the wind, and stung his face as he tried to keep up with his

youthful page. The walk across the courtyard was particularly brutal. Neither one spoke while they walked. Then Hermes turned down a long corridor, then into a building, by a side door. Once inside, they paused, stamped their feet, rubbed some feeling back into their faces.

"Pardon, Master, but I have taken you inside by way of the servants' entrance, as it was faster, and out of this hideous weather. Now we may go down yonder hallway, and enter by way of the main entryway.

"Thanks, Hermes. I appreciate that more than I can tell you. And it is good to come in out of that awful weather out there. I'll take the servants' entrance any day."

"Ah, we pages know where there are ways and byways through this castle."

The two of them headed down the dimly lit hallway toward the main entryway. There they turned into another grand room, similar to the great room they had seen earlier, complete with a big fireplace, with innumerable torches all around. Hermes led the way toward the back of the great hall, where a door led into a smaller room. It was brightly lit, pleasantly warm, with a large table in the center. On the table was a sumptuous array of foods, including breads, fish, meat, fruit, vegetables, with pies and cakes. Craycroft stood up from a seat at the table, and greeted Bob with unexpected warmth.

"Welcome, good Master! It is my most sincere hope that your arrival at our earl's castle has been comfortable. Though I do understand that your arrival on our island was something less than one would have hoped for. Pray, sit you here at this table, and enjoy what food and drink you would like. As you can see, we have food for all tastes, and drink to soothe."

"Why thank you, Master Craycroft. This is truly the finest feast I have seen in some time. And I should say that my rooms aren't bad either. Like I was telling young Hermes, here, it's like a luxury hotel. I'm just not too sure about these clothes, and whether I've got them on right or not."

"Ah, you do indeed. You do look, in fact, splendid, though I must say that my own sensibilities do no run along those lines. Why not sit here and tell us of what food you will partake. I'm quite sure we can accommodate your wishes."

Bob sat down and surveyed the feast before him. There was some fish that looked particularly good to him, as well as a roast that looked like pork, some fine vegetables, and some warm aromatic bread. Not knowing, he said he would like to try some of most of the foods.

"Splendid! Why not a little of everything, then? And some wine? This is some of the earl's best from last year."

Bob's plate was then piled with great helpings of things from the table. He looked around, and did not see any utensils at his place, but as hungry as he was, he looked to Craycroft for clues, and seeing that his host was "digging in," he did the same. This was truly a feast for the famished, and Bob enjoyed every morsel. The wine was just a little too sweet, but it went down easily. Not much was said during the meal, as it was apparent to all that Master Robert was famished, and seemed to be thoroughly enjoying himself.

After eating himself almost into a stupor, Bob pushed his way back from his seat, washed his hands in a bowl set there for that purpose, and dried his hands on a cloth at this side.

"My goodness, that was some meal. Tell me you don't eat that way all the time. It was magnificent."

"Ah, but no, this is a truly rare meal, as your arrival here would warrant such a celebration."

"There you go again. I'm really no one special, just a cardiologist from the Midwest, who got onto your island by some method unknown, at least to me…"

"Are you not a healer?"

"Well, I guess I am that."

"Then we must have much to discuss. Come, let us then retire to one of the sitting rooms, with a good fire."

With that they both got up, Bob still a bit stiff, and the very full and slightly tipsy Dr. Robert Gilsen followed Craycroft out yet another door, down a hallway, reasonably well lit by torches, then they turned into a room that was obviously set apart as a study, with many shelves full of books, several comfortable padded chairs, and a fireplace that glowed warmly. Craycroft turned to young Tom, mumbled a few words about something to drink, and then offered Bob a seat.

"Very well, then Master Robert, let me begin by telling you a little about myself, as I am sure you know very little about me."

"That's for sure…"

"I am a native of this island, which is called Shepperton Island. I was born to parents of the working poor, my father was a metal smith, and my mother was a maid and cook. Not being adept enough to follow in my father's trade, I was given the opportunity, in my youth, to become a page for the earl's house, from which position I then rose to apprentice for Master Cartho, who was a healer, and may I say, a great one. It is from him that I learned of the art of healing, and also the art of record keeping. It was this love of my art that caught the attention of the earl, and I have been in his employ for nigh unto fifty years. Tell me, have you ever heard of Master Cartho?"

"No, I can't say that I have. His name isn't one I recognize, though I must admit, I am not much of a medical historian."

"Ah, well then I must show you some of his writings. They must mean more to you than the others of this age.

"As it came to pass, my employment, and my friendship with the earl provided me opportunity beyond the healing arts, and, as such, I have become his closest ally. Though I have no official role as such, I have come to act as advisor to the earl, and he has recognized this fact. But now the earl is himself quite ill, and this comes very shortly after the death of one of our beloved ladies, lady Felicia Vincente…"

That name struck out of the blue, like a flash of memory. He was taken back to his meeting with Judy in the ER, when she told him it was Carlo Vincente who had given her the little box with the Drachma inside.

"Vincente, did you say, Vincente?"

"Why, yes. Does that name mean something to you?"

"Indeed it does. Before I came here, I was given a little box by one of my colleagues, who was told to give it to me by someone with that name, a Carlo Vincente, who later died in our emergency room."

With the mention of that name, Craycroft's eyes widened, but he did not say anything immediately.

"And do you know what was in that box? It was a drachma."

Craycroft was stunned. This was no mere coincidence. "You say it was a drachma? A coin of ancient Greece?"

"The same. It was the start of multiple odd things that I thought at first were merely coincidences. And I understand that it was someone named Drachma who is somehow responsible for my being here."

"That is most odd, indeed," Craycroft said thoughtfully, "and what do you know of this Carlo Vincente, and of Drachma?"

"Well, of Carlo Vincente I only know that one of my colleagues said that about a week ago—or so…it's hard now to keep track—a very old man came to the Emergency Ward at our hospital for an infected dog bite, and when there was no one else in the room, he took her aside and asked if she knew a doctor of hearts named Gilsen—that would be me—and he gave her the box, which she then gave to me per his instructions, with the drachma inside. Now where that box is, or the coin for that matter, I have no idea. Anyway, this guy, Drachma, also sent her a note—how, I have no idea—telling her to find someone skilled in the arts of healing, and tell him that somewhere there were people in great need, and that he should be prepared to make a journey unlike any before. And then, a very old man, named

Carlo Vincente, with a large mane of flaming white hair, a hawk like nose, and a certain regal manner came to our emergency room, desperately ill, and told them he was a patient of mine, and then before he died, he turned to me and told me that it was the day. Anyway, later that day, as I was cardioverting one my patients, something happened, I really don't know what, and that is how I came to your island, as far as I can tell."

"Most remarkable, Master Robert, most remarkable. Now, before I tell you of our tale, I would ask what you would desire to drink, as our page has returned."

"Well now that you mention it, I am a bit thirsty. You know, some of that magnificent brown stuff that was waiting for me in my room would really be nice."

"Ah, yes, Carlisle's brew, I feel certain that our good page has some of that available, am I right, Tom?"

"Of course, Master Craycroft, here it is, with Barncuddy's compliments."

"Many thanks, my good page. Now remind me, Master Robert, to show you Barncuddy's Ale House, a place unlike any other, with good ale, excellent food and music unlike any you may have heard."

Bob suddenly remembered the dream he had, with the inn, the tables, the ale, the harp music, and then it dawned on him— there was Craycroft! For the life of him, though, he could not remember the tale that Craycroft told, nor could he remember the actual music, though he could remember how it made him feel—the powerful, inexpressible longing, all conveyed through that incredible music.

"Master Craycroft, would it be harp music…a very special sort?"

"Aye, that it would, but not like any other music to my ears. But it would be from the magical fingers of an angel. Then it is settled—we should go someday soon. Ah, here ye be—a flagon of Carlisle's brew."

"Ah, thank you."

Bob drank in the fragrant, warm brew, letting its warm, gentle fingers reach him through his throat and chest. "Sometime, too, I'll have to get the recipe for this most marvelous drink."

"That if only Barncuddy would reveal its making. I am quite certain that he keeps such secrets well hidden."

"Well, for now I'll just have to sit and enjoy it. Now, Master Craycroft, you were going to tell me your tale, and I'm anxious to hear it. Then I should tell you my story as time allows."

"Indeed, Master Robert, that would seem fair." Craycroft smiled, winked knowingly at Tom then began his tale. "Now you have already heard part of my story, but that is not the tale of what brought you here. That would be the real story, it would seem, that you should like to hear. Is it not so?"

"Ah, yes, it would be nice."

"Well the, let us start with the story of our pots."

Bob's expression was one of surprise.

"Aye, that would be right, our pots. For there are none finer and more rewarding, both to the owners and to the island. Ever since William Fitzgibbon first discovered the source, here on our island, our Shepperton pots have been a boon to our people, and to the wealthy households throughout Europe, and have shaped our lives as nothing ever could. You see, our pots impart a certain vitality to their owners, that, it would seem comes from the clay from whence they are made, a clay only found upon this island. It is clay that comes from the base of Croftus Knob. You may remember passing by there on you way here."

"As it happens then, our little thriving economy here on our island became centered on the manufacture and sale of our pots. Then something went awry. Last springtime, one of our esteemed potters took ill and died, and then another, then our painters also. Then later our Carlo Vincente (of whom you know), then his daughter, our beloved lady Felicia have taken ill and have died, and now our earl, who has taken ill, but, thank the Lord, has not yet died. What all this had done has stirred havoc among our

people, and the manufacture of our pots has come to naught. And there is talk of witchcraft and murder, some of which might be more true than one would suppose."

"All right, now let me get this straight. You have this thriving little community on your island, that makes its living selling these magical little pots to wealthy noble houses all over Europe, then quite mysteriously, the potters and painters necessary to the production of these pots are suddenly dying off. Then the nobility on your island have also start to succumb. Is that about right?"

"Aye, that would appear to be an accurate, though a little crass, summary of events thus far."

"Now, then, you've got to tell me a little more. First, about this illness that afflicted these painters, potters, and nobility. Second, what do you expect from me, and what do you suppose I can do that might be helpful. And lastly, but most importantly, how did this Drachma fellow get involved, and how and why, in heaven's name, did he pluck me out of thin air, and another time and place, to get involved in your crisis."

"Ah, I can see that you are most perplexed. As to the how and why of Drachma's behaviors, that I cannot hazard a guess, or to why he would pick you and the lady Judy Morrison…"

"Now wait just a minute. Did you say Judy…Judy Morrison is here too?"

"Aye, that would be true. Do you know this Judy Morrison?"

"Ah, yes. You could say that."

Just then a messenger appeared at the doorway. "Master Craycroft, a matter most urgent. It is Councilor Genet. He has been injured. We have him in yonder room. He asks for you."

"Councilor Genet? Ah, this cannot be good. Master Robert, if you would be so kind as to accompany me. This may shed a bit of light on our travails."

Bob could feel the tug of fate pulling him along, as he got up, and joined Craycroft. He found Hermes, just outside the door and

said, "listen I've got my things in a little bag in our room. Could you please go find them and bring them where we're going?"

"Aye, Master Robert, I shall bring them anon." Bob could not see the eager look on Hermes's face as they departed.

Chapter Thirteen

Judy had to admire Falma. Here was a man, old enough to be her grandfather, yet who felt it right to protect her from dangers, real and imagined, and thought nothing of it. He was willing to give his life for someone he just met. And yet, there was something extraordinarily powerful in his persona, a certainty that he was here to serve his purpose, and there was nothing on this earth that could touch him. And there he sat on his mount, as calm as any man could be, while Judy just shook uncontrollably after what she had observed.

As an ER nurse, she was used to seeing the effects of violence, usually on those brought in on stretchers, and to react calmly and efficiently to their needs. But what she just went through was beyond anything she had ever seen, or experienced. Outwardly she was calm, as she tended to the wounded Cairn and the rapidly dying Bernard. What she lacked in help and resources, she made up for with her nurse's empathy and caring. The fact that Finch and his henchman were standing over her did not seem to deter her, especially with Falma standing between her and what appeared to be very real trouble.

She was able to help Cairn, with two arrows in his arm and flank. It was obvious to her that the arrow in his arm did not go

through any major vessels, and the arrow in his flank, though very painful, did not seem to have hit any vital organs. She was able to calm his nerves, and get him to relax. She did what she could to assure him that they were there with him, that he should just breathe slowly, and that would ease his discomfort. She was even able to get one of the men to cut off the tip of the arrow that went through his arm and to cut the arrow in his flank, a few inches from the skin. She then was able to talk the henchmen into carefully picking him up and getting him back on his horse, where one of them guarded him.

Bernard, on the other hand, was rapidly dying from the time she was able to reach him. His color was ashen, his pulse was rapid and thready, and he was bleeding profusely, both internally, and externally. Before he lapsed into coma Judy reassured him that she was with him, then in minutes, he was dead.

Not knowing quite what to do, she turned to Falma and asked, "What do we do now, with one guard dead, the other injured, and these men about to take us who knows where?"

Falma calmly, but forcefully told Finch that they represented no threat to him or his men, and that he would appreciate it if his men could bring Bernard's body along with them so a proper burial could take place. Furthermore, he explained that Judy was a woman of some worth, and that they would be held accountable if any harm should come to her.

To Judy's amazement, Finch seemed to accept Falma's authority, and had his men do as instructed. Then, when the men had gotten Bernard's body loaded on his horse, they set off, back into the forest. They went up a steep path, away from the river, and toward Croftus Knob. Judy did not say anything, as she knew she was a prisoner, but did manage to mouth the words "thank you." Falma just smiled at her, a truly beatific utterance.

What a man, thought Judy. *Here we are, beset by these thugs, in the middle of winter, out in the forest, and he acts like this was nothing out of the ordinary, with no fear or weakness, and not backing down*

at all. Maybe Drachma was right, he might just be the right man for this now perilous undertaking, whatever it is.

Falma, for his part, remained erect in his saddle, alert, but calm, staying close to Judy's horse, but every now and then checking on Cairn, and assuring himself that the guard was still doing all right.

It had started to snow, at first a light dusting, then more seriously, and with a stiff wind, blowing in their faces. Judy tried to shield herself from the onslaught, but found herself still shivering. As they climbed, the weather became truly unbearable, and when the path turned around a huge stone, Finch halted.

He said something to his men in a dialect unknown to either Judy or Falma, then dismounted and came back to Falma's horse. "Well, Master Falma, I think it best we wait a bit here in this lee before proceeding. My men have some blankets for ye."

"Thank you that would be nice, but make sure your injured prisoner has a blanket as well, for he surely shall need it more than I."

The blankets were brought out and the three prisoners huddled together beneath them. The snow continued, but the little band had hunched down in a sort of make shift lean-to, between their horses and the stone cliff behind them. They lost track of time, and could not hear what was going on outside.

As well as she was able, Judy tended to Cairn's needs, which he minimized. She was able to determine that he had stopped bleeding, and did not look particularly pale, as nearly as she could see in the dim light, and his pulse was reassuringly strong, and not too rapid. Either he was not in too much discomfort, or he was able to mask his pain. In any event, she had no morphine to give him. The arrow in his arm could wait until better circumstances would allow her to properly inspect, and possibly remove it altogether. The one in his flank posed another problem altogether. With its tip embedded deep inside him that would take a certain amount of care and a dose of good luck to remove.

And besides, there were no surgeons she knew or trusted to be found in these woods.

Having reassured herself that Cairn was reasonably likely to make it, at least for a while, she turned her attention to Falma. "Let me ask you, Mr. Falma, you seemed to know at least the leader of the men out there. What does this all mean? Are we in danger?"

"Well, m' lady, I would say that you would certainly be more valuable alive and well, than injured or dead. And aye, I do know Finch, and know of his alliances. Let us just say that his services may be bought, but dearly. As to whom he is working for at this time, I know not. Though I have some suspicions. You see, there are, on this island, those who would, for themselves, and not for the earl, seek power, and would try to wield it in ways most unseemly. I shall wait and see to whom this man, Finch, would bow. Of that, I feel fairly certain that we should find out in good order."

"And what about you? Aren't you afraid?"

"Ah, but nay, m' lady, I do not fear for myself. I am protected as long as I am in your service, of that I am sure."

"Protected? By what or by whom?"

"It is well that you do ask, but I cannot say at present. It shall become apparent to you in time, though."

"I seem to be hearing that sort of thing quite regularly. It makes me wonder if you guys are in some kind of conspiracy, to keep us foreign types from figuring out what it is we're doing here."

"Conspiracy, m' lady? I should think not, But here, among these ruffians who answer to someone I do not trust, I think some things are better not discussed openly."

"Mr. Falma, I don't mean to sound ungrateful, for I really am most appreciative, and I do admire you. Here you are risking your life and limb for a total stranger."

"Ah, m' lady you are no stranger to me, for I do know of you and your doings, for Drachma has made his decisions with care..."

"What do you mean? How is it possible to know me? I'm from many miles and many more years away. I bet you don't even know where Ohio is."

"You are right about that, but I do know of your decision to become, what would you call it, a nurse. And I know of your struggles with the ill and injured, and how you were not able to deny those feelings even here in this foreign time and place. Now when you were young and injured yourself, was it not the touch of another nurse that gave you the will and courage to seek out the healing professions? And was it not also your contact with the Master Gilsen that we made happen, that really made your decision to come here a reality?"

"What do you mean, you made happen? How…"

"Does the name Carlo Vincente mean anything to you?"

"Why, yes." She was unable to keep the surprise out of her voice. "He was a very old man who told me to find Dr. Gilsen (I think he called him a doctor of hearts), and to tell him that he would be going on a journey, unlike any that he had been on. Oh, boy, if this is what he meant…"

"Ah, m' lady, then you do know of this man, Lord Vincente. He was one of our own. He was dying here, which was partly his own doing. Then on his deathbed, he sent for me (of all people), and told me his extraordinary tale, which I cannot speak of now. However, he asked me if he could do anything to help toward the healing of this misery he had wrought. I told him that there was a way…"

"A way? Do you mean sending him to us was his way out of his dilemma? If he were able to send back a couple of 'modern' health care types to salvage this mess that he helped create. Then what? All could be forgiven?" Judy tried to keep exasperation out of her voice. "I'm sorry, Mr. Falma, but without our modern technology, I'm not sure at all that we can be of much help."

"My good lady, I fear you do not know of your own powers, nor those of Master Gilsen. As they have not truly been tested

except here in the wild, among these ruffians. You may not realize, but I was witness to your truly remarkable healing touch. Just ask Cairn, here, if I speak not truthfully. What say you, Cairn?"

"Aye, m'lady he does speak truthfully. Your touch is one unlike I have ever felt. It was like unto a most precious balm."

Judy did not know what to think or say. Here she felt out of her element, but still felt a nurse's obligation to her charges who suffered. Perhaps it was really true, what they said about the placebo effect, that it was a significant part of what she did, and that she was able to use it unconsciously. But perhaps there was more.

"I'm glad I was able to help you, Cairn. It was as much out of gratitude as anything else."

They heard a rustling; then Finch's voice broke through.

"Well, it would appear that it is time, as the snow has let up, enough to travel where we need to go."

"If you say so, Master Finch. We shall move out. Come, m' lady, may I take your hand."

"Now wait, just a minute. What about Cairn? We should help him get up on his horse. Come on, then, sir, can you get up?" With the help of Judy and Falma, Cairn was able to get up on his feet, though slowly and with a certain stiffness. When he was upright, he looked pale and a bit shaky, but was able to get along side his horse. One of the men then helped him into his saddle. Judy and Falma then followed suit, and the band was ready to move on. The weather having eased up, they returned to their positions and made their way deeper into the forest, with each rider left to his own thoughts.

With the newly fallen snow it was intensely quiet as they wound around the edge of the mountain. Even the horses were quiet as the forest grew ever deeper and darker. After another half hour of steady riding, they turned abruptly left, then the way led downwards again. The light was fading, and it was all Judy could do to make out the form of the rider in front and back of her.

Then she thought she heard it again. From nowhere in particular, came a sibilant noise that sounded to her like a person whispering. It seemed no one else heard it. Then it was more distinct.

"Judy, Judy," the voice said, "Do not fear. This message is for you alone, though you are not alone. You shall be safe. I know this to be true. Falma can be trusted in all things. Listen to him. He shall provide guidance when you will need such."

Judy listened to the voice, turned around to see that no one else was hearting it. Then with just a hint of a breeze, the voice was gone. She knew what the voice had said, and knew it was a message just for her, but where was it coming from? She couldn't help but feel some sense of relief, however, as the group moved steadily through the forest. They forded streams, went down and up again, all the while the forest darkened. Then they turned again and saw up ahead some flickering lights.

"That would certainly be our camp for this night," said Falma to Judy.

"Aye, it be that old man," said one of the men at the rear. "But I would venture to say that ye know not where we have come."

"Aye, you speak the truth, young man, for we have come by ways truly mysterious, and with the darkness, and my poor eyesight, I fear we are in your hands completely."

Judy thought to herself that there was just a hint of irony in Falma's voice, as if the old man knew more of this forest than the young man behind them could ever know. Then when she caught up to Falma, he turned and gave her an impish grin.

Oh, you sly old devil, she thought. *I can be sure that you are plotting something even as we arrive as prisoners.*

They arrived at the camp, with its simple huts, arranged in a large semicircle, got off their horses, and were led toward one of the huts.

"Here is where ye'll be staying 'till morning," said Finch. "My men shall see to yer horses. Inside ye'll find some food and drink.

And we'll be taking care of the dead man. Now don't ye fret. He'll receive a right, good Christian burial. Now the door will be locked, and there will be a guard outside. There's a fireplace inside, with some wood, so ye can make yerselves warm. 'tis a chilly night, it is."

With that, the three of them entered the small hut. There was a small lamp on the table, which was lit. There was some food, consisting of old bread, dried fruits and meats on the table as well, but Judy noticed, it did not look or smell too appealing. In addition, there was a jug with some vile liquid on the table, which she assumed was to drink. She turned to Falma and said, "if this is food and drink, I think I'll go without for tonight. I'm not hungry or thirsty anyway."

"You would be wise not to partake of this prisoner food, methinks," said Falma. Then busied himself making a fire. With the little light of the lamp, Judy then inspected Cairn's wounds.

"I think, until we have more light, we'd better leave your wounds alone for tonight anyway. How much pain are you having right now?"

"M' lady, I think it bearable for now, but made even more bearable by the fact that you are here, for by your hand is my pain lessened."

Judy wasn't sure if Cairn was being serious, or flirting with her. Here she didn't know the rules of conduct.

"M' lady," said Falma, as if sensing her uncertainty, "he speaks the truth. What he says is from the heart."

It was good that the light was dim, for Judy was blushing.

She got back up and looked around at the surroundings. The room, though dimly seen with the light from her lamp, was very spare. There were five cots around the outside, a table in the center, with four simple chairs set around the table. She then sat down in one of the chairs, put her head down on her arms. Pretty soon the day's emotions caught up with her, and she began crying, silently, deeply felt emotions tumbling out of her, down her cheeks onto the rough wooden table.

Chapter Fourteen

After the evening's hectic doings, Jeanne was finally able to sit down with Frieda in her mistress's house and have a quiet meal. She had invited Councilor Rust over, after lady Felicia's funeral, to see to some of her lady's unfinished business. The councilor had told her that he would be over later, after he met with the council in yet another emergency session. She knew that Craycroft was too busy with the earl, and though she knew that he would certainly have made the effort to come over, she also understood that his grief was very private, and that time would allow a better opportunity later to discuss matters of some importance to them both, including the things in her mistress's notebook.

So now, she was able to just sit and have a meal with her trusted friend. She was famished, and realized she had not eaten that whole day, as it had been too chaotic and too emotional. The two friends sat down and quietly ate their meal, hardly speaking. Then Jeanne finally looked up at Frieda and sighed.

"My friend, what shall we do? We have no official rank to hold us here, and all this," she made a sweeping gesture with her arm, "does not belong to us, or to anyone that I know. With Master Vincente's death and now our lady…"

"Aye, it would seem just that there be an heir, but none are here that we know of, and I know of none that Master Vincente

talked of from the old country. She did talk of her brother but he was not of this house, and I know not if he would be entitled to any of this."

"Nay, I also know of none. I would like to confer with Master Craycroft, and with Councilor Rust. Perhaps they might have some knowledge. Oh, Frieda, this is all such a burden. All this sadness is too much for me to bear. Would that we could find someone to help us, as we do need an ally."

"Aye, it would seem that all of Shepperton is in dismay, yet none to help us in our hour of greatest need."

It was then a page appeared at their door, and announced that Councilor Rust was here, and would like to speak with Jeanne. Jeanne told the page to let the councilor in, and to inquire whether he would like something to eat. She then asked Frieda to accompany her to one of the sitting rooms, to better talk with Councilor Rust.

The councilor was shown in, and looked every bit as ragged as Jeanne felt.

"My thanks to you, Jeanne. For I am weary of these councilors, and of their machinations. It would seem that they are all afraid of their own shadows, and none know what is really at stake here on our island."

"Please, good councilor, have a seat, and tell us what you may of our island's peril, for I am certain that it does involve our lady and her father as well."

"Ah, my good lady, what can I say? There is much talk of land holdings and great wealth, but none to claim them, and none to oversee to their safekeeping. I should like to speak to the earl, or in his stead, to Craycroft about all this."

Jeanne raised an eyebrow when he mentioned Craycroft.

"Ah, I am certain that you have not heard, but the earl himself has appointed Craycroft to be his immediate and future successor. Though I must also tell you that not all of the council are in accord with his decision in this matter."

"But the earl has spoken. Is that not enough?"

"It should be, but as you know, the doings on this isle are often not according to the king's edicts. You see there are those, upon the council, who see Master Craycroft as an intruder, and do not desire to follow his direction."

"By that, you would mean that Councilors Reordan and Silvo were not in agreement, and would like to have it their way, is that not right?"

"My dear lady, you are most perceptive, and it would appear that you did much talking to our good lady, Felicia, before her untimely demise."

"Aye, that I did, and much of late. What is it, dear friend, that you would have us know, as things about this place are in disarray, and I know not whom I can trust, or what to do."

"Well, I am not expert at many things, but what I tell you is not to trust anyone who says that he speaks for the council, for as you know the council has no such voice. Further, I would tell you to speak with good Master Craycroft, as he has the ear of our earl, if anyone does, and you know as well as any that the earl was always supportive of your good lady. You may be certain that whatever advice Craycroft would give would be in accord with the earl's wishes."

"Now you do have, in your possession, do you not, a certain notebook from our lady for Master Craycroft? I would start by trying to get that notebook to him. I would try to get it to him yet this very eve, if that be possible. Now do you have knowledge of what that notebook contains?"

"Nay, Master Rust I do not. I only know that it does deal with matters most private, and I was instructed to trust no one but Master Craycroft with it."

"Hmm, I wonder, it would seem that your lady did have some knowledge, then of Master Craycroft's possible rise to power."

"Nay, I think not, Councilor, rather, it seems that m'lady and Master Craycroft did share some private knowledge, and this

notebook was but to clarify some of what she knew or thought, and also what would be of importance to Craycroft. But then, I truly know not, as I have not read what is in the notebook."

"Well, then I would try to get it to Master Craycroft soon, as it would appear that your lady did deem it important enough to mention it on her deathbed."

"Aye, then I shall. Now you have wisdom and experience in matters before the council. What do you consider we should do, that is Frieda and I, with all this?" Again, she indicated with a sweeping gesture. "You see, we are not wise in the ways of commerce, and there are those among us who would take advantage of our trusting nature."

"Indeed, there most certainly are, I fear, but I do feel that their attentions may be diverted elsewhere, so it would seem wise to act with some haste, as they that would have no opportunity for plunder—if that be the right word. What would you be needing, then, my good woman?"

"It would appear that we need someone trustworthy, who does know of our needs and yet would be loyal, truthful, and above all, someone who is not seen to gain unseemly from our association with him."

"Hmm, well, I think it would be best to steer clear of any on the council, as they are a notorious lot of bloodsucking scoundrels. Perhaps Father Henri could recommend one of his own." Rust thought for a moment, and said, "I know there is an apprentice of Falma's who might just be the man you would need. His name is Melchior, and, as I am told, he did study law and letters, but is now studying under Falma, and is one whom none can say would seek to gain by his association with you in any way. Yes, I do think Melchior is your man. And if it be all right with you, I shall seek him out upon the morrow, and see if he would be available for your assistance. What say you?"

"Thank you Councilor Rust, he does sound to be a man most appropriate for our needs. By all means, go, seek out this

Melchior, and tell him we shall meet with him anon. But tell me, as I have never heard of him, what sort of man is he?"

"Well, he is a man, originally from Tarrington, raised in obscurity, but found by Drachma when he was studying law at the University in England. He had completed his period of study, and was seeking apprenticeship with one of the lawyers in the city, when in walked Drachma, bought him a drink at the local pub, told him about Falma, then the two of them came over on the next boat, and Falma had an apprentice."

"He sounds interesting, but then why haven't I seen or heard of him? I have certainly had occasion to seek out Falma's aid on occasion, but I have never seen anyone but Falma in his shop."

"Ah, that is because Melchior is extremely shy, and tends to hide whenever anyone does come by, and he prefers dealing with books and chemicals, than with people. You are most certainly not alone in never having seen this man, and that is partly why he would be such a help to you in this endeavor. You see, none of the council truly know of this man."

"And you do feel that he would help us, as shy as he is?"

"I do believe that he would, especially if he hears that Craycroft is your friend in this, something I would tell him. But I would recommend that you see what Craycroft thinks of this plan. Then, if you need an ally in this, Craycroft would simply say the word, and Melchior would be your man, I know this much is true."

"Well, then, I think that we should seek out this Melchior fellow. What think you, Frieda?"

"I think he sounds perfect. If anyone can keep our affairs secret, it would one such as he. Now I do know a little about this fellow, as I have had occasion to deal with some of Falma's requests for books, herbs, ground pigments and such."

"Oh? You did never mention such to me."

"Nay, I thought naught of it at the time, as he was so unassuming. I only perceived that an apprentice to Master Falma,

that's a special one there. One that can take all the darkness and odd smells. Now you just give me the word, though, and I'll seek out this Melchior, and I'll make certain that he comes to see us about this business, and all."

"Well, then, Frieda, I do believe that's settled, then. I shall go to Master Craycroft, for his advice, and to take him the notebook. Then upon the morrow, you go to try to find this Melchior person and have him pay us a visit. Now Councilor, would you consider having something to eat. Frieda and I have eaten, but there is food aplenty available, and my good woman, Frieda, can keep you company, while I search for Craycroft."

"Why, thank you, my good lady, I think I shall accept your hospitable offer. I am rather hungry, and in this house there is at least peace."

With that, Jeanne rose up and left Frieda with the councilor. She got up and searched briefly in her room, and found the notebook, and tucking it safely away in a sack, she then got her overcoat, headed down the stairs, and out into the bitter weather.

Jeanne arrived at the earl's abode, where she knew Craycroft was staying. She entered through the main portal, and was a little surprised to find it unguarded. Looking down the main hallway, she noticed some activity, and walked toward that. What she found was a group of servants, and a guardsman, engaged in animated conversation. When she got closer, she could tell that they were discussing some rare events occurring in the castle.

"Well, I've never seen anything to match him. How old do ye think he is?"

"Nigh unto thirty summers, I'd say. But ye can't really tell, as he is definitely foreign, and you know them foreign types. Some looks older than their years, some younger, so I'd wager, at least he'd be younger than forty."

The guardsman then turned to Jeanne, and asked, rather officiously, "Now, me lass, what brings ye out on a night such as this?"

"I have something for Master Craycroft, and him alone. And I need to speak to him."

"Ah, do ye now, m' dear? Well I can tell ye that the master is busy now, and may not be disturbed."

"Then could you please tell me where I may wait, as my business cannot wait 'til the morrow."

"That I know not, lassie, for the master has not said, and he does keep strange hours."

"If I may be of some help, m' lady…"

Jeanne turned toward the voice. It belonged to a page that she knew, named Aaron.

"Oh, hello, Aaron. Yes you could truly be of help to me. I need to see Master Craycroft. Tonight, if possible."

"And what may I tell him brings you here tonight?"

"Well, m' lady, before she died, did keep a notebook, which she told me I should give to Craycroft, and to him alone, and I have that notebook with me tonight."

"Then come with me, and I'll show ye where it would be permissible to wait. I fear that tonight may not be a good night, as it seems that he is occupied with a very important guest."

"A guest? Who might that be?"

"Some great healer from afar."

Jeanne and Aaron then headed down the long hallway toward the earl's private rooms.

"Tell me, Aaron, how is Master Craycroft? I have not seen him since that fateful day when my mistress died. I do know that her death was one that none of us were prepared for, and it was particularly hard on Craycroft."

"Ah, madam, it was truly hard on the good master, I know, because he himself talked to me about it. That my sound strange, that a master would be talking to a page about such things, but

as he, himself said, he was once a page himself, and now to be in his position…"

"That I did not know, though I did hear that his origins were somewhat humble."

"Indeed, madam, he was a page for a while, but was such a page, I am told, that he was sought out by Master Cartho, who then taught him of the healing arts. But Master Craycroft, as great a man as he is, did not forget his humble origins."

"I do believe that, young man, for Craycroft is not like others of the nobility. He seems, instead, to be quite at home with those of us who are of common arising."

"Indeed, he has told me of yer mistress, and of ye."

"And what, pray tell, did he tell you of me?"

"Only that ye are but a most extraordinary woman, and that I should make every effort to bring ye around to him, if I do get the chance." He said this with a distinct twinkle in his eye. "And so I am doing what he did ask of me."

"Well, then, Aaron, what can you tell me of this healer who has the ear of Master Craycroft now?"

"Only that he arrived today in the company of the forest guard, as well as one page, named Tom."

"Tom, did you say a page called Tom?"

"Aye, that I did."

"Well, now that is very interesting indeed."

"Oh, and why is that interesting to ye?"

"In the same sense that you would speak of Craycroft as a page. For I do believe that Tom is also marked for greatness. There is something about that lad that speaks deeply to one's heart. Of this even Frieda has spoken."

"Hmm, well then we shall see, for here is Tom ahead of us.

"Ho, Tom, here is a lady to see ye."

Tom turned, and when he saw Jeanne, his face beamed in recognition. Then he hurried over to her. Jeanne embraced the youth as one of her own.

"Oh, Tom, it is good to see you. Are you well?"

"Of course, Jeanne, I am well, indeed."

"And where have you been? And what can you tell me about this powerful healer that is here? I understand that you did accompany him here."

"Aye, that is true enough. But I cannot say much about him, other than he was dressed in strange garb, that he speaks strangely, and that his instruments of trade seem wondrously made. But come hither, I do know that Craycroft would be most certain to receive you. Then you may see for yourself what this stranger is like, for he is presently with Master Craycroft."

Tom led the way, with Aaron and Jeanne close behind. They went down the hallways toward the back of the earl's abode. There they took a turn toward one of the rooms. Tom hesitated at the doorway, knocked. It was answered by Hermes, who looked out to see the most unlikely trio.

Tom mumbled something to Hermes, who then disappeared into the room. He then reappeared with Craycroft, who looked out at Jeanne, and smiled, the look on his face was one of relief.

Jeanne, for her part, looked startled, for this was hardly the same man she had seen last week, attending to her sick mistress. The man who stood before her looked like he had been through torment and come out on top.

"It is with utmost respect that I welcome you, Jeanne, to the earl's house, and thank you for coming."

"Oh, Jeanne, please, I am not of the habit of having ladies curtsy before me. And you, of all people should know me by now. Please, do come in. I shall introduce you to our guest, a healer from far away."

Jeanne stepped inside shyly then managed to say, "Master Craycroft, I do have something for you from my mistress. Here it is, a notebook that she wanted to be sure you received."

"Why, thank you, Jeanne. I am very appreciative of your efforts to get that notebook to me. I shall read it carefully. Now

come, my dear, over here, and observe as our healer prepares to deal with one of our own who needs help."

Meanwhile, Bob was over at the bedside of the injured Councilor Genet, taking no notice of the intrusion.

Damn, he thought, *I would really like to have a CT scanner available right now.*

Before him was a man in his twenties or early thirties, who had suffered a blow to the back of the head. There was little, if any, external bleeding, but there was blood oozing from his left ear. He was only semi coherent, muttering something about the fact that they took something from him. His pupils were pinpoint, but his eye movements were conjugate. His sensorium was a bit clouded, but he was able to move all extremities and had normal reflexes. His heart and lungs were fine, and there was no evidence of trauma elsewhere on his body.

Hermes was helping Bob with his examination, and was absolutely rapt in attention. He had never seen anything like this in his life.

"All right, Hermes, we've done what we can initially. Just keep him lying here as quietly as possible. Now, Mr. Craycroft, oh, there you are. What we've got here is this fellow who suffered a blow to the back of his head, and has what I assume is a basilar skull fracture. There's little, if any additional trauma that I can find. Without a CT scan there is no real way to tell if he's had any intracranial bleeding, and I certainly hope not. The best I can suggest is to keep him quiet, and to check on him in a couple of hours. He does look to be otherwise in good health."

Craycroft heard what Bob was saying, but only understood about half of what came out of his mouth. "Ah, we shall do as you would instruct. For it would seem you do have knowledge that surpasses ours. We should 'check him' again, as you say, in two hours. I shall have one of our servants here to observe him.

"Now, Master Robert, may I introduce you to this fine lady, whose name is Jeanne. She was attending to my close friend,

lady Felicia Vincente, who recently died and left our island a much sadder place. I have asked that Jeanne work with me as my personal aide, though I doubt whether she knows it, nor has she had the opportunity to respond."

"Indeed, Master Craycroft, I was unaware of this, your request. I am indeed honored and humbled by such a request. I do not know what to say…"

"There is no need to say anything yet, as I have only just made it known to the earl. Now, I would request that we should get to the earl's side, Master Robert, Jeanne, and you, Tom, for he did request that we should all come, as he has some important business he wants all of us to hear. And Hermes, you should come along as well."

With arrangements made for Councilor Genet's observation, and Aaron left to run any messages, the little group then headed out toward the earl's private quarters; with Bob all the more certain that he was walking into something still bigger and more mysterious than anything he had so far experienced.

Chapter Fifteen

Judy woke to find that Falma was up and was tending to the fire. She looked about her and realized she was lying on a cot in a room that she only vaguely remembered. She noted that it was fairly dark outside, and there was a person sleeping on the cot in the corner, then remembered that Cairn must be the man on the cot. Then she sat straight up. As she regained her memories and composure, she got up and walked over toward the fire.

"Oh, Mister Falma you are up, and taking care of our fire. Tell me, could you not sleep either?"

"Nay, m'lady, I could not sleep, but I do see that our companion has, at long last, fallen asleep. That, I believe is good."

"Yes, I think so. That arrow still in him has got to hurt, and, if we don't get it out of him, it will get infected."

"In fected? What do you mean?"

"Well, the bacteria on it will set up an infection."

"The back terria? Whatever do you mean?"

Judy then paused, stopped to realize that to people of this time and place, the idea of microorganisms even existing, let alone causing disease, was about as far-fetched as nuclear arms, and space travel.

She started again. "Well, you see, where—and when—I come from, we think of many illnesses as arising from little, tiny organisms that get under the skin, where they don't belong, where they multiply, and live off the tissue around them, and then the body tries to fight them off, produces pus, and infection sets in."

Falma thought for a minute, then with a flash of insight said, "Are you saying that illness may be caused by very small creatures, such as maggots?"

"Hmmm, well you got the right idea but bacteria are much, much smaller than maggots. But you've got the concept."

"And you have seen these back terria?"

"Oh, yes, when I was in nursing school, we'd look at all sorts of bacteria with microscopes."

"And that word…micros…is that some instrument to view these little creatures?"

"Why yes, a microscope is a device that lets you see very tiny creatures."

"Hmm, well I shall have to tell the good Master Craycroft about all of this. Then he shall know that all of his heretical thoughts may have some veracity. And I should have my apprentice begin working on building a, what do you call it, a micros…"

"A microscope."

"Ah, aye, that is the word."

"Oh, Mr. Falma, you're so, so much like one of my old professors. You seem to think a lot like professor Turnbaugh. He was such a great teacher, but more than that, he was a man you could just talk to, and he wouldn't seem to find what you said childish, but he would find something useful in almost anything you said."

"Ah, then I should take that as a compliment, eh?"

"But of course. Now you mentioned someone named Craycroft. Is this someone important I should know more about?"

"I am certain that you should, and most assuredly shall after we get through this business of you being a prisoner."

"Somehow, I get the feeling that you have been plotting something. Am I right?"

"Ah, my lady. As usual, you have guessed correctly, for it was that that prevented my sleeping, though I see that you did sleep some, as well as our faithful guard, Cairn. Aye, it is something that I have been concerning myself with."

"Then I don't need to be concerned about that, right?"

"Nay, m' lady, you do not need to be concerned. I only hope that I am right about these guards, and their loyalties. Ah, but look who awakens."

She looked, and Cairn was stirring on his cot. She hurried to his side. She felt his forehead, noting it was not unusually warm, then checked his pulse, just a bit rapid, but not alarmingly so, and noticed that his pulse was still strong and steady.

"Well, I'm glad to see you are still doing reasonably well. When it gets lighter I should try to remove that arrow from your side and your arm. Unfortunately there is nothing I can give you to ease the pain, but that arrow's got to come out, or you're liable to get an infection."

Cairn looked at Judy, then asked, "Infection, what is that?"

"That's where the wound gets all festered up, and you get pus oozing out, and it gets all red, sore and swollen."

"Ah, I see. And you can prevent this from happening?"

"Well, I don't really know, but what I do know is that the longer that arrow stays in your side, the greater the risk of infection, and any infection in this age before antibiotics is serious business."

"Then I would say let us proceed with what you would suggest, as I am in your hands, my good lady."

Judy felt both honored and humbled by Cairn's trust in her, which she knew was sadly misplaced. But here, in this time and place, none of the old rules seemed to apply. It was all new to her. What should she do now? It was still a bit too dark, but something told her that it might be better to try something, anything, before the daylight returned.

"All right, Cairn, I'm going to try to take the arrows out of you. Can you come over here where at least we have a little light?"

Cairn got himself up, and, Judy could tell, with some effort, and came over toward the table and the one lamp. Judy then examined his wound in the dim light. There was dark, purple discoloration on his flank, below where the arrow entered. The whole flank was swollen, and very tender to touch. Where the arrow entered, the tissue had sealed itself off with a clot. The arrow in his arm looked better. She was able to get it out without significant bleeding. But the other arrow presented problems.

"Mr. Falma, I'm going to need your assistance in this." Falma came over to her side. "Now, you see, I'm going to need you to pull the arrow quickly and very firmly just like this." She indicated with her arms the direction and technique. "While you pull, I'll apply pressure. I'm not sure, but I think there may be some bleeding associated with this, I'm just not sure how much we're going to have, because there's no telling what vessels are there along its path. I'm going to try to keep it to a minimum with my pressure. Now, do we have some kind of clean rag?"

She and Falma rummaged around, and found an old rag in a pile of discarded cloths in a corner of their little building. It was a bit oily, and smelled of something Judy couldn't name, but it was fairly soft, and was the right size. It would have to do. She came over to Cairn's side, and pressed gently with the rag, then she had Falma grab hold of the arrow firmly.

"Now, on three, you pull firmly up and away. I'm so sorry, Cairn, I know this is going to hurt."

Cairn simply nodded, gritted his teeth.

"All right, now...one...two...three!"

Falma pulled, and at first nothing, then the arrow gave way. Cairn cried out, but meekly. There was a gush of old, dark blood from the wound. Judy pressed firmly on his flank. Then Cairn became lightheaded, as Judy laid him down on the floor, keeping pressure on his side.

Falma was examining the tip of the arrow, and noted wryly that it was an arrow meant to do real harm. Judy just kept pressure on Cairn's wound, then she checked his pulse. It was rapid, but not thready, so he was at least maintaining his blood pressure, and his side, though oozing, was not bleeding profusely.

"My lady, how is good Cairn? I know, looking at this arrow, that it was quite painful."

"Well, I think that for the moment, he will be all right, though I don't know what his blood pressure is, and I have no way of knowing. I'm going to hold pressure on his flank for a little bit."

"Cairn, how are you doing? Are you in much pain?"

"Nay, m' lady, not much for now, at least it seems bearable."

"Try to hold on, for I'm not sure of how they're going to treat you, so you might as well just concentrate on breathing slowly. I'm going to hold some pressure on your side for a while. I know it's uncomfortable, but you've done amazingly well so far."

"Mr. Falma, is there some potable water, or something Cairn here can drink? I'm sure that he's lost quite a bit of fluid, and some water would be good for him to drink."

"Ah, m' lady, I shall look. There is this water that they left us last night. Whether it is drinkable or not I am unable to say, but it is here at least."

Falma poured some of the water into a cup that was on the table. After sitting all night, the sediment had gone down and the water was actually quite clear. "Here, m' lad, here is some water for you. I hope that it shall be acceptable. Our good lady said that you should drink."

Cairn was able to take in a cup of the liquid, somewhat awkwardly, then muttered some thanks, and settled back down.

Their ministrations were interrupted by the abrupt appearance at the door of a very large, unfriendly man. He brought with him a gust of cold air. Falma immediately took charge of the situation.

"Now, my good man," he said. "I see that you have come in upon the orders of master Finch. Tell me, then what would you

have us do? You see, it is still dark outside, and quite cold, I might add. And could you please tell me, what have they done with the body of our fallen comrade? We should dearly like to know, as his body does deserve a proper burial."

The large man in the doorway just stared, as if this were some apparition. He was left speechless by Falma's little monologue, so much so that he didn't take note of Judy and Cairn. Judy had him sit up again, and noticed that Cairn did so with relative ease, a fact that was not missed by Falma.

"Nay, my orders come from someone of rank higher then Finch," he was finally able to say, "so ye'd best be comin' with me. We've got mounts fer ye outside. And as to yer dead friend, I know nothing about that."

"We are not going anywhere until we hear of our dead friend's body. For what then do I tell his wife and family–that he was just murdered, and his body left to rot? Nay, my good man you must find out what they have done with Bernard before we go anywhere with you and your men."

Falma spoke with absolute conviction, and not as prisoner. It was as if he was in control of forces that he would not hesitate to bring down upon any that stood in his way. The guard was again taken aback with the forthright attitude of the old man in the hut, and immediately acquiesced.

"Now, I shall go find out about your dead comrade," he said, then left the hut, slamming the door.

"Well, that was some show of force," Judy commented. "You acted as if we had some army to back us up."

"Ah, m' lady, if you only knew. You see, I do know for a fact that Drachma himself, and his men, have surrounded this encampment, and you shall be safe."

"Oh, is that what you meant when you said that you could not sleep?"

"Aye, you have discerned correctly, m' lady. For while you were yet sleeping, I heard a soft sound as if a whippoorwill were

outside our little hut, a most unusual thing at this hour. So I went over to the window to investigate. There was outside the window a messenger from Drachma, who gave me this." He then reached into his cloak and pulled out a small piece of paper, which he then brought over to the lamp. Judy looked at the paper. On it was the same handwriting that she now recognized, with the same backward slant.

My Dear Friend,
Know ye that I am well aware of your circumstances.
My men and I are now preparing to rescue you
and the lady Judy.
Just stay where you are, and if any try to move you,
do what you must to stall
D

Kerlin caught up with Tom on his way from the earl's rooms.

"Ah, Kerlin, we meet again, but this time the circumstances foreshadow even more than before. Could you tell me of Falma?"

"Ah, Tom, my young friend, that I shall, though his exact whereabouts I cannot say. But come with me, as there is much that I need to say to you. I have had occasion to speak to the earl, and he said that you and I should speak. He does know of you and your connection to Drachma, and thinks that we should exploit this for the benefit of our island."

"Ah, you have spoken to the earl…"

"Aye, and it does grieve me to see him in such a sorry state."

"Well, then, my friend, where do you suggest we go?"

"Why, Barncuddy's. My throat is a little parched, and he can provide a little enclave off the main floor where we can talk freely."

"Then, Barncuddy's it shall be."

So Tom and Kerlin set out for Barncuddy's Ale House. Tom had visited it earlier, and noticed that, at that time it was its

usual noisy, boisterous self. Barncuddy had been in a fine mood, especially when he heard that a stranger was with Craycroft, and it was for them that Tom was there. Barncuddy had asked that young Tom would bring him news of this stranger, and the Carlisle's Brew would this time be on the house.

When the pair arrived back at the Ale House, Barncuddy looked up from behind the counter, grinned in greeting.

"How now, me young lad, and ye bring a forest guard with ye, too. Well what can ye tell of this stranger now?"

"Why there is much to tell, my good brewster, but first, can ye get us a table off from the rabble, for this Forest Guard, Kerlin by name, and I have matters of serious import to discuss. But I promise thee, there is much to tell."

"Very well, then, me young lad, how about me little meeting room upstairs, very private, ye know, and fit for such a meetin' as ye'd want?"

"Very well, good Brewster, ye lead the way."

As Barncuddy led the two upstairs, Kerlin looked around the Ale House, and noticed among the usual rabble, a person he recognized from his years as a Forest Guard, seated at one of the backbenches. Through he couldn't recall exactly, he knew the person was one of those that he had arrested some ten or more years ago, and it was one of those faces that he would always remember. He stared back at Kerlin with a look of intense malice, then smiled as if to note that here was prey, just walking in unexpectedly.

I'll have to watch my back, thought Kerlin, as he went upstairs behind Barncuddy and Tom.

When they were shown to their table, and Barncuddy had taken their orders, Kerlin turned to Tom and said with an intensity that took Tom off guard. "Now, I do not mean to frighten you, but there is a man downstairs I would advise you to be very wary of. I know that I did arrest him some years ago, and he is a man most evil. And he did recognize me, and I mean to tell you that

his smile was that of pure malice. When Barncuddy comes back with our drinks, I should ask him if he knows of that man."

Tom was a bit unnerved by Kerlin's attitude. He then asked where the man was seated, as Tom knew many of the patrons of Barncuddy's. When Kerlin told him, though, he couldn't think of anyone that struck him as unusual.

"Anyway, what did you and the earl talk of? As you can well imagine, my life is turned on its end right now. Just last week I was only a page, working here in the castle, but now, it seems as if I am the grandson of the most powerful man on this isle, not sure of whether I am in danger or not, nor even what my role shall be in the coming events."

"Ah, Tom, so it would seem, for I too have seen my role change very dramatically. I have been given the added responsibility, by none other than your grandfather, of the safekeeping of persons who it seems shall have more to do with the future of this isle than they do know of. I speak of Craycroft, Master Robert, whom you have met, the lady Judy, also from the same place as Master Robert, and you."

"Me?"

"Aye, that's correct. And for what reason, I am not at all certain. For on my last assignment, I did manage to lose both you and Master Falma, and came back to the castle without either of you, thinking that I would at the very least be demoted, but nay, Drachma and the earl, as well as Craycroft chose to see things differently."

"And what, pray tell, can you tell me of Falma?"

"Well, lad, as you know, I was with Master Falma when we lost you, but as I later found out, you were taken by Drachma's own men. Then, as I returned to the path, Falma was not there, and neither was his horse. I searched frantically, but then had to turn around, as the weather was becoming truly terrible, and any chance of finding him vanished with the oncoming blizzard. So, it was with a very heavy heart that I turned back toward the

castle, as miserable a man as you could ever hope to see. I was then traveling along as cold and miserable as I was, I was certain that the earl would tell me that I was demoted, but surely I would go and tell the earl myself what had happened.

"When I did come back to the castle, I found to my dismay, that the earl was ill, but when I spoke to his servants, I found out that the earl himself had appointed Master Craycroft to rule in his stead, which, you may well imagine, I found heartening. So then I sought the counsel of Craycroft, who told me that the earl, though ill, was still of sound mind, and that it would be permissible to see him, but as Craycroft had assumed his new role, I spoke with Master Craycroft. Then I told him all that transpired, and to my surprise, he was not upset with me at all, but he calmly told me that Drachma himself had set up all that was to occur. This was apparently grievous to him as well. He did express his dismay over sending Master Falma and you into that horrible winter weather, and was most assuredly relieved by later news that you were safe in Drachma's keeping. And to find you safe once more here in the castle was heartening to us all. He did express his concern over Falma's safety, which, I am told, the earl shares."

It was then that Barncuddy came clattering up the stairs with their flagons of ale.

"Here ye be, my good Master guardsman, and commandant as well, and Master Tom," he said with a wink. "For tonight your tab is on the house, as I heard, from someone who should know, that ye have been appointed to high positions."

"It would be better, my good man, if that information were kept between us for now," Kerlin said, thinking of the man downstairs. "It is not yet public knowledge." Then the name struck him. "LeGace! Of course, the man downstairs is Antoine LeGace."

"Tell me, my good man, that man in the back, did he give you his name? For I know him. His name is Antoine LeGace."

"Nay, he did not give me his name, nor tell me of his business."

A look of worry clouded Kerlin's otherwise stoic countenance. Tom looked at Kerlin with a note of apprehension. "What is it, Kerlin?" Tom asked, "I have never seen you this way. What do you remember of that man?"

"Tom, when I was younger, I worked as a forest guard under the direction of one named Malcolm, a stout and steadfast man, whose authority came from none other than the earl himself. You were too young at the time, but there came to be a band of brigands that were stealing from the people of the far western parts of our isle. When the village elders did complain to the earl about it, he sent Malcolm, along with me, and Stoneheft's brother, Cleaver, in search of this band of brigands. Well, the earl had decided that they should be caught, and brought to the castle, rather than killed. Catching the brigands, as it turned out was not much trouble, but one of the men, this fellow, LeGace, decided to make it difficult for the others, before fleeing, and slit the throats of the others. But as it happened, one of the men was not yet dead and told us of LeGace's plans to kill the earl. He indicated that LeGace would take his time, and later, when we were not expecting anything, he would strike, in a way that would be memorable."

Now Kerlin turned his attention to Barncuddy, and asked if he could go back down the stairs, and to see if he could determine what, if anything this man was doing here and now, but to do so without attracting undue attention to himself. Barncuddy readily agreed, and disappeared down the steps.

Kerlin then turned his attention back to Tom, and continued his narrative.

"Now, Tom, his presence here is most disquieting to me. I have been given explicit instruction by Craycroft to take you back to Drachma's forest home, yet I feel that I should stay and guard the earl and his house."

"Is there anyone else who could take me? I am quite sure that your work here is important enough…"

"Nay, Tom, I do feel responsible for you, especially after our last adventure. And I am quite certain that Craycroft and the earl feel likewise. I should simply tell Craycroft, and take you without delay. What say you? Are you ready for yet another winter ride?"

"Aye, just as soon as we've eaten, then let us go leave word with Craycroft, and head out." Tom was still young, and adventure was as important to him as anything.

"Ah, here comes good Barncuddy now. Well, what news, my good man?"

The portly innkeeper brought their steaming bowls of stew, some yeast bread, and some sweets, laid their meal down in front of the two. Finally, he turned to Kerlin and said, "I am afraid that our master LeGace has left our establishment (without paying I might add). But before he left, one of the patrons heard him say that one in this place now knew that he was back, and to beware.

"Ah, that I did expect, my good man. Now, Tom, you be sure and eat hearty, for we have a journey to make ere morning light."

Chapter Sixteen

Deep in Glen Oak Forest, there was a deeply hidden encampment, where Drachma lived and worked. Finding it was nearly impossible, unless one knew the trees and their "language." Tending the fire in Drachma's forest home was an old woman named Angelica. One could tell she was old, very old, but no one spoke of her years. What was noticed about her was her sharp tongue, and sharper wit. What her relationship was to Drachma and his band of close followers was hidden in time and lore. It was said that nothing could surprise Angelica, but she most certainly could surprise the unwary herself, and was justly proud of the fact.

"So, Master Tom, have ye had yer fill? It would seem a good thing to me that ye're still a growing weed, and now planted in Drachma's garden, eh?"

"Is that what I am, then, a weed?"

"Aye, well look at ye. All thin, green, and gangly. Aye that's what I'd call ye—a weed."

"Very well, then, Angelica, a weed I be. But then what have I to do with this garden that Drachma has planted? What else has he planted, and do I have anything to fear?"

"Ah, so many questions, young man. Well, let me tell ye that ye be truly blessed, to be tended by one such as that. Many's the man who would be in yer position. But, in truth, ye have much to fear, for Drachma has many enemies, who now would be enemies of thine as well."

"Enemies? Who might they be?"

"Well, young man, does the name Reordan mean anything to ye?"

"Aye, it does, of course. He is one of the council, not well liked I might add. And it would seem that Master Craycroft and he are not friendly."

"Of that I can believe, for Craycroft is a man of true worth, mind ye. I would not be disappointed to see Master Craycroft named the earl's successor, but that be not my place to say (e'en though I'll be offering my opinion to ye). Anyway, as to Councilor Reardon, I'd be very wary of that one, mind ye. A true serpent, he is, with venom as powerful as any, as I'm told. He wishes to rule the council, and he will not stop at anything, even murder, to get what he wants. Be mindful of that one, I tell ye."

"That I shall," said Tom firmly. "It would be most careless of me to get anywhere near him. Who else would be among the enemies?"

"Well, let us see. Do ye know a fellow named Gilbert? There's a man to be avoided as well, and not too friendly a man is he."

"Is that the guardian of the village of Champour? I have heard of him, but have never had any occasion to get close to him."

"And that be good thing, if ye ask me. Now, he and Councilor Reordan go back years in their knavery. And do ye know of one called Finch? Now there's a truly lawless one that, and can be bought, that one. Aye, I'd be wary of such as him."

"Nay, him I know not."

"Well, I can tell ye that he is one rogue I would not trust to carry out my kitchen scraps. He is one that I've seen often through my many years. He's a big lout, he is, and not a very

bright one to my mind. But as long as ye be the one paying him, he'll do whatever ye ask. But ye never know if yer the one paying him that week, if ye know what I mean."

"Aye, that I understand," Tom said, though he did not.

"Do you know of one that is called LeGace," Tom asked. "Now I am told that he is one that I should be wary of as well."

"Antoine LeGace? My that is one terrible name I have not heard in years."

Angelica paused, thinking. "If he is now back upon this Isle, than ye have much more to fear than I thought. Ah, laddie he is one that I would not want to meet without good Master Kerlin at yer side, that is my opinion."

"And what has Drachma told you of me?" said Tom, quickly changing the subject. "Has he told you anything about me at all?"

"Aye he has, indeed, m' lad. He even told me that ye be his grandson. And that ye be the son of his own, dear Maggie, of Killiburn."

"You mean, she was real? I thought that she was just a story, made up by the peasants. You mean to tell me that Maggie o'Killiburn was a real person…"

"Not only that but yer own mother as well."

Tom sat in silence, not sure what to believe any more. Finally, he turned back to Angelica, and asked, "What then of the wolves, and her horse, is that also true?"

"Well, now young Drachma, I can see there be a tale worth telling, Now come with me, and we'll sit down in yonder room, and I'll tell ye the tale of yer own mother."

She led young Tom to the sitting room, with the low chairs and stuffed down cushions. The old woman tended the fireplace in the sitting room, and threw on another log before she turned and sat down herself.

"Now, lad, this tale begins with your grandfather, and his love, the lady Vincente. Now, I can see by your face that ye know some of this tale already."

"Aye, I was told of such by Master Falma, but do go on, as I have not heard beyond that fact that lady Vincente bore my true mother."

"Ah, that dear old man, Falma. How I miss seeing him. Does he still dodder about in that alchemist's shop in the castle?"

"Aye, and that is where I heard this tale only days ago."

"Well, then let us begin and I'll tell ye the tale of Maggie o'Killiburn. As ye know, Drachma had fathered this love child before he was sent away, and lady Felicia, herself pregnant, was sent to live with me in the village of Killiburn. At the time I was a widow, and when I heard of the chance to see to the caring for a daughter of any ambassador, in secret, I was very willing, as I was also a midwife. Now mind ye this fine young lady was a handful, full of vinegar and all, and she would like to go on walks and such, and thought nothing of her condition, which was becoming more obvious. The young men of Killiburn, who took notice of young Felicia, when she arrived in the village, began to shun her, as it was more obvious that she was with child, and they did not want to be seen with a woman of ill repute—little did they know—and be accused of being the father. But that did not deter Felicia, and she spoke to one and all the same. There was young Willie, though, who did, in fact, form a sly friendship with the young woman, and who did promise to be there if she should need anything when the babe was born."

"Well, it did come time for her deliver, and Willie was mulling about our place, and asked if there was anything at all that he could do for Felicia, if she needed anything at all. Well, I finally told him that this was the daughter of Ambassador Gianni, in the earl's castle. Now ye could have knocked him over, he was so shocked. But anyway, I told him, as the babe was born, he could take the message back to the earl's castle, find Ambassador Gianni, and to tell the Ambassador that he was the grandfather of a fine young girl, and ask what was to be done with the child and her mother. But for the moment, all were well, and in my keeping."

"That very day, Willie packed his pony, and set off toward the castle. Once he did arrive at the castle, he set about to find the ambassador's residence, only to be told that the ambassador was off the island, but was expected back, perhaps within a fortnight. He then sought out the earl, and was told that he would see him on the morrow. Not knowing where he could stay, he found the old Ale House (now Barncuddy's establishment), and asked if he could stay the night, in exchange for whatever services would be needed."

"What can ye do?" asked the proprietor. "Well, sir," Willie replied. "If ye but have an old fiddle or harp, I can make music for yer patrons."

Well the proprietor happened to have an old harp that belonged to a minstrel who died some years before. He then went to the upper room and brought down the harp. Seeing that instrument took young Willie's breath away, for it was none other than a clarsach that had been made in Ireland by James McFeeny, from county Down. Now ye may never have heard of any of this, but I'm sure ye know Willie Minstrel who plays at Barncuddy's"

"Aye, of course. Willie is a regular at Barncuddy's, plays there most every Friday and Saturday. But I did not know his story. I only know that he is a most magical musician, and can spin tunes out of his harp that bring grown men to tears."

"Aye, and that I only found out later, as ye shall hear. Anyway, the proprietor was so impressed with this young man's ability that he asked him to stay on, as his playing brought around patrons. Now it turns out that young Willie was able to get an audience with the earl, not the next day as he had been told, but within the week, and so this young man came before the earl with the news that Ambassador Gianni had a new grandchild, a girl, and that mother and daughter were in Killiburn."

"Well, the old earl knew of lady Felicia, and why she had been sent away. The earl pondered this news, then told young Willie that he should go back to Killiburn, and tell lady Felicia

and whoever was caring for her (that would be me), that upon his return from his journey off the island, the ambassador would be informed of this news, and for the present time to keep things as they were. Then the earl went and got things to send with Willie back to the lady and me, including bedclothes and some silver. Then the earl surprised Willie with a request. He asked him to give a concert before leaving for Killiburn, for the earl had heard of Willie's playing on his harp, and wanted to hear for himself some of this young man's music."

"Well before Willie left the next day, he borrowed the harp from the old proprietor, and gave a concert, the likes of which the earl had never heard. He was so taken with the young man's music that the earl offered to buy the harp for him, with the proviso that, should on any occasion that Willie be in town, and the earl should see fit, that he would grace the earl's halls with a concert. Willie readily agreed, and to this day, if the present earl should need his services, Willie would go play in the great music hall at the castle. But what Willie dearly loved was to play at the Ale House for all the nightly rabble, as he'll tell ye."

"Well then, back to our tale. Anyway Willie did, in fact, come back to Killiburn, with the presents from the earl and the news. However, before returning to his new employment in the castle he gave a very special concert on his new harp for Felicia, her child and me. And I'll tell ye it was music like I've never heard, before or since. I was moved to tears by his strumming, seemingly simple, but profound. I heard the sound of the great and small of the woods, the running of steams and the flight of birds overhead. Ah, if ye could have been there…"

"Then things in our merry little house went on, as we waited for news of the ambassador. Weeks turned into months, still nothing. Willie had returned to the castle, to his new employment. Felicia and the babe seemed a most happy, contented couple, and life in Killiburn also returned to a state that could be called tranquil."

"Then one day Willie returned, in the middle of the night, with the word that Felicia's family, including her mother, father and younger brother had died on the seas, that their boat came ashore in pieces, with none having survived. Felicia was shocked and saddened by the report, as well as by her newly orphaned state, and spent the next fortnight grieving. When I asked her if she should like to return to the castle, she just looked at me and said no, she would prefer to stay where she was and raise her daughter, but then she told me something extraordinary. She said that, if there was some way to let Drachma know of her plight, he should be informed, and would know what to do."

"Well, I did not know what to tell her about how to contact her man, but I suggested that she write a letter, and that maybe we could find a way to get it to Drachma. So she wrote him a long epistle, and sealed it with wax. Then we told one of the earl's guards as he passed by that we had a message to send to Willie (as the only one we knew we could trust), and that if he could tell him, we would like to speak to him. The guard promised to do so, and that he would love to visit the Ale House anyway, the next time he was at the castle."

"Again weeks passed by with no word, but then again, in the night, came Willie. He and young Felicia stayed up and played with the infant, Maggie, and Felicia told Willie all about Drachma, and how she was truly sorry, but no man could ever take his place for her. Willie, to his credit, took the news like a true gentleman, and said that he would, upon his honor, take the message back to the castle, and the to the earl, with the letter that she would like delivered, if at all possible, to Drachma, wherever he may be. Then I remember she did a most unusual thing. Before he left, she bade him come, and she kissed young Willie, full on the lips, and said that if ever there was a man most worthy, it was he, and that she thanked him with all her heart. Poor Willie was speechless, with tears overflowing his eyes. He took the letter, placed it safely in his vest, then was gone."

Angelica then stood up, and played with the fire, drank a swallow from her cup. When she could speak again, she sat back down.

"My, how those memories stirred my heart. You must forgive this old lady for it has been a long time since I visited that bygone era."

"Well," said Tom, "That would explain why to this day, Willie has never married, though I understand that many a young maiden has tried to catch his eye."

"Aye, if ye had only seen Felicia in her prime. Your grandmother though she was, was a rare and beauteous gem."

"That I can believe, as even later in years, she was an extraordinarily beautiful lady." Tom suddenly thought of the book, and felt shame at having taken it away. Then he wondered if he should ever see it again.

Angelica noticed the far away look in the eyes of young Tom.

"Well then, back to our tale."

"Ah, aye. Do go on, for your tale is one that needs telling."

"Indeed 'tis one that you most certainly need to hear. Now, after that we rarely saw Willie, as he became quite busy traveling about, and giving concerts, playing in the fairs and markets and all. And at home we watched little Maggie grow up first as a hearty, healthy infant, then a little girl, all curious and fearless, and charming."

"Then, again at night, who should appear at our door, but Drachma himself, all grown up, strong, swarthy, and smelling of the sea and far winds. It was all too much for Felicia, who ran to him, all teary-eyed and blubbering. She held onto him, not wanting to let go. They kissed and held each other for seemingly an hour, then the little one, Maggie came up to them, pulled at her mother's dress, asking who was this man. Felicia explained as best she could that this was her father. Little Maggie then looked up at Drachma, and asked to be picked up. She then examined his face and features, and kissed him, and put her little arms

about his neck. A tear fell from Drachma's eye, which the little one kissed away."

"Then the two of them went back to the lady's room, and I busied myself with Maggie, and preparing something for him to eat. When they appeared from the back room (methinks the smells from my kitchen made him come out at last), they were smiling and she was glowing radiantly. She asked about Maggie, and I told her she was asleep."

"When we sat down to eat, Drachma told us of his plans for us. He said he did receive Felicia's letter, naught but four months ago, then began to work his scheme. One of his father's trusted friends, Carlo Vincente, who was then master of the guild of potters in their province had come with him back to our island, along with nine of their finest potters, and five painters, all ready to work with our earl in the craft of pottery for which we were becoming known throughout Europe, but Carlo himself would be appointed ambassador, and Felicia would become his daughter, by adoption, and live within the safety of the castle. Thus he was able to secure for the island a line of excellent guildsmen, keeping his promise he had made to the earl before he left the isle. He was also able to provide for Felicia's well-being."

"As for their daughter, Maggie, they both decided that she should stay with me here in Killiburn. Grievous though their parting would be, they knew their daughter would be cared for and brought up rightly. Furthermore, Felicia did agree to send me silver every month or so to keep her daughter fed and clothed, but not so well that she would stand out from the others in the village."

"Now it fell to me to bring up young Maggie, and to tell her of her parents when she came of age. Maggie, though, clearly stood out from the other children of the village. She was never fearful of anyone or anything, ever the first one to venture forth and the last to return. She grew into a tall, graceful child, well mannered, but very hardheaded that one. She had no true friends among the

other children of Killiburn, and was prone to wandering off in the fields and forests. Many was the time she would come back to supper, late, and saying she was out with her friends, but when ask which ones, she would get that certain look in her eyes, shrug her shoulders, and say nothing."

"Maggie was then of an age when I could speak to her of her mother and father, so I told her of them and their lives. She would sit and ponder what I told her, say nothing, then go about her business again, and told me that I was her real mother and father."

"I would get letters from Felicia—now lady Vincente—asking after her daughter. I would always send her back some token of what Maggie was doing, such as her little drawings, always of forest creatures, or to tell of her antics. There was one time I remember that Maggie was about six years old, and had disappeared as usual in the afternoon, then she came back hours later with a wolf cub in her arms. She implored me to keep it, but I said no, we had to return it to the forest, but it being late, we did keep it that night, and all through the night we could hear its mother howling. She returned it to the forest where she had found it on the morrow, but she named it Greyling, and ever after, it would visit us for an hour or so in the evenings, then scamper back to its forest home."

"As she grew, I told her mother what a bright and unusual child she was becoming, and I asked her if she though that any schooling might be appropriate for her daughter. Her mother wrote back to say that she would see to getting her an education. Then two months later, who should appear at my door, but Drachma himself. Maggie recognized him instantly, and came running, then leaped into his arms."

"Drachma as it turns out was back on our island, and apparently for to stay, and since he was lady Felicia's tutor in her younger years, so it would seem that he was a natural choice to do the same for his daughter. The only problem was where he would

provide the tutoring. It turns out that Killiburn was too exposed a place for Drachma. He then suggested that he could take her to his place in Glen Oak Forest, but she would need someone to care for her, especially at times that he would be gone, which could be weeks or even months. So I agreed to go with him into the forest, and it is where I have been since that time, at first caring for my dear Maggie, and then caring for Drachma and his men, and tending his little garden of weeds."

"Ah, I see, then that is what you meant," said Tom, with a new piece of understanding.

Angelica continued, "Mind ye that it was with some care that gardener worked these many years. All the men that have come through here and all. There have been thorny ones and good ones. And as Maggie was getting her education, she would love them all, the knaves, as well as the saintly ones. She was becoming a winsome lass that one, but also a wild one, untamable as that wolf she kept company with. She would go with Greyling on long excursions, especially with Drachma gone so much of the time."

"Now she was getting well educated, mind ye, and was becoming a fine writer herself. She could read and write in Latin and Greek, and she would sit and discuss topics well into the night with Drachma, as well as some of his men. And she could ride like the wind. Any horse would do, but her favorite was a stallion named Bacchus. He was a horse with fire in his eyes and temperament. It was said that none could ride him, save Maggie. It becomes a sport with her, to ride bareback into the village of Killiburn in the evenings, to challenge the young men to race, then to outrun them all, and to disappear into the forest."

"So that is how some of the stories of Maggie o'Killiburn got their start, how in the evenings in summer, this waif of a girl with the wind in her hair, and a wolf by her side, would appear out of the forest, and say that whoever caught her could have her, then away in a flash she would go, back into the woods. Many was the

young man who sought to catch and to tame her, but still to no avail. She was a rare girl, educated, intelligent, but still wild…"

"Tell me, Angelica, I heard stories of her even in our village of how she would arrive at dusk, there in the village, her clothes like breezes of silk, her hair flaming red as the evening sun, bewitching the young men of the villages to try and race her into the forest. Then upon her black steed, with wolves as escort, dash away back to the woods, never to be caught. It was quite a fairytale as I remember it."

"Aye, in many ways her life was a fairytale. How I was pleased to be with her, we would sit and talk, then she would go back to her room by herself and she would read and write, but what she would write, I never knew. Then she would be up with the dawn, flitting about just like a fairy princess. How Drachma and his men would light up whene'er she was about. Then she would study with Drachma until afternoon. How charming it all was."

"Then one summer it all changed. She came back from one of her evenings away, bedraggled, forlorn, and with her dress torn asunder. 'How did this, happen, child?' I asked, 'and who was it did this to ye?' She was weeping, and I ne'er did find out who it was that did this thing. Then later, she told me that she was late with her womanly flow—I don't expect ye to know about that—and sure enough, the lass was pregnant."

"Then later, we heard that one of the woodsmen had been beset by a pack of wolves, was torn apart, with his heart eaten out. Drachma did not say a word about his, though it was a thing well known in these parts, and I often wonder…anyway, his mood changed, and he became sullen. Maggie remained cheerful, though some of her vitality was gone from her.

"She tried to bring cheer, even now, to our little band. Though it became harder for her to ride, she would still get on Bacchus and they would walk the paths she had once taken so joyously, and with such high spirits. Then it became winter, and she gave up riding, and just helped me about the place. There were still

moments of great joy that winter, as our little lass blossomed out, not knowing or caring about things in the wide world. She would make great apple fritters for the men around here, and she would sing tunes that she had learned from Willie, whom Drachma would bring by every now and again."

"When springtime came around, it was time for our lass to deliver. By now she was bloated, and stiff, and her heart would beat so fast that I became alarmed, and her breath became like she was running. There was naught I could do but keep her at rest, and hope for the best."

"Well, the night finally came for her to deliver, and what an awful night it was. The weather outside was terrible, and the poor lass was in misery. She did push out a large baby boy, but as she did so, she breathed her last. Oh, it pains me so to tell you."

Angelica got up again, fooled with the fire, took another few swallows, then sat back down. Tom sat still, didn't move.

"Angelica" he said at last, "the child, I assume was me."

"Indeed, it was, m' laddie. That was how ye came to be. Well, and then, as there was not a wet nurse anywhere near abouts, Drachma took ye quickly to the village, where he was able to procure the services of a wet nurse for ye, and then made arrangements for yer mother to be, as it was not expedient for me to care for ye. But he did make certain that yer mother and father were paid a sum for caring for ye, and he left them with instructions, that when the time came, ye should become a page in the castle. And so, here ye be, three fourths grown, tall and gangly, and now ye do know where and how ye got here."

"Many thanks, good woman. I do owe you a debt of gratitude, for you have been a marvel of caring. For it would seem that your fortitude has served us all."

"Most eloquently said, young Drachma. I only now know that my time on this earth has been in some measure fulfilled. Now, come with me. I have a few things to show ye."

With that, she got up, took Tom by the hand, and led him down the hallway, to a room he had never seen. She unlatched the door, and led him inside.

Inside was a most extraordinary room. There was a small bed in the center, with a table and a chair. On the table was a quill, and an ink bottle. Around the room were bookcases, filled with books of all kinds.

"This was Maggie's room," said the old woman, "a truly remarkable room it is. For what years she was among us, I know not whether there could have been a more learned person, man or woman, nor one of such beauty and wildness, a true flower of the forest. Now it would be fitting if it were thine, so here ye be, Master Tom. Oh, and one more thing.' She reached for one of the top shelves, and pulled down a small linen bag. "I was told that this was thine as well."

Tom instantly recognized the bag, and his hand shook as he took it. Inside were the drawings, papers, and the book. The little box with the Drachma, however, was missing.

"Now, I'll leave ye be. Just come on out if ye need anything."

Chapter Seventeen

It was quite late when the shrouded man arrived at the gate to the property at the end of Yarborough Lane, outside the Castle, and set apart from the village. There he met the guard, exchanged pleasantries, a few coins, and was let in. He proceeded to walk on up to the mansion, where he rapped on the heavy door. After what seemed an eternity, the servant opened the oak doorway to let the man in.

"I shall assume that your master is in, and may be expecting me."

"Aye, he is, and is in his study. Come this way with me."

The interior of the building was furnished with great and expensive rugs, chandeliers, and tapestries and the hallways were lit with torches. The servant led the man down a long hallway, into a very large and opulent study.

"Master, here is the gentleman you were expecting."

Councilor Reordan turned, and greeted the stranger, who took off his hat and shawl.

"Have a seat, Master LeGace. I take it, then, that you do have something for me, and the councilor was dispatched as directed?"

"Most assuredly, good councilor." He reached into his cloak, and pulled out the paper with the red seal, handed it to Reordan. "As to the councilor, I cannot say with certainty that he is dead,

but was most assuredly not conscious when I left him. It was too dangerous to stay and make certain."

"Well, let us hope that he shall not recover." The councilor looked at the envelope in his hand, examined the seal carefully, then turned toward the fireplace and tossed the paper into the fire. For the next minute the two of them were silent, watching the earl's dispatch burn.

"Very well, then here is your payment." The councilor handed the strange man a bag. The man looked into the bag, assured himself that the payment was correct, then placed the bag securely within his tunic.

"Now, as to the other matter before us, what did you discern?"

"I have it from reliable sources that Kerlin has been placed in charge of security for the earl (which should not matter), for Craycroft, for the young fellow, Tom (apparently Drachma's grandson), for the castle as a whole, and for some lady named Judy, who is not here."

"That may prove to also be nothing of consequence," said Reordan, with a hint of a smile "For now, as we speak, this Judy is, in fact, our prisoner, along with master Falma, or so I am led to believe, on another part of the island. But what concerns me in all of this is that Drachma seems to be more actively involved in all these doings. For years he was just in the forest occasionally advising the earl, traveling about, and being a nuisance, but now, it seems, he is much more actively involved in affairs of running the island, and he has brought more people to this island, such as Falma's apprentice, Melchior, as well as these two new persons, one of whom, I am told, is some kind of healer with great powers. What I shall want from you is your eyes and ears. The payments shall be commensurate with the risks you take, but believe me, you shall be well paid. But you must work alone, and let none know of your doings. What say you to this?"

"I believe that I can do what you ask, but I did want to let you know that Kerlin has seen me, so he is on guard, but as to

the others, you may be certain that they know nothing, and suspect nothing."

"Well, I would be very wary of Kerlin, for I do know of his prowess and skill."

"That I know all too well, myself, as we did meet many years ago, before I fled the isle."

"Then you know what to watch for, and whom you may trust, I take it?"

"But of course."

"And you are aware of the importance of secrecy, for if you are caught, I shall not, in my present capacity, be able to help you out."

"But then I do hope your circumstances shall change in the future."

"That they most assuredly shall, but I know not when. However, when they do I shall certainly notify you."

"Well, then, I do believe we have an understanding, and I shall report back within a fortnight."

"Do that, and about this same time."

With that, the meeting was ended, and LeGace was shown out into the night, but not before he had a chance to survey his surroundings, and to decide that he did, in fact like this house and its location, but the owner would not be all that easy to dislodge. He smiled to himself as the servant showed him out.

"Here ye be, matey, I'll give ye this one fer what ye've got in yer hand. Do we have a deal?"

Antoine LeGace moved through the marketplace, ignoring the peddlers and shoving aside those that tried to talk to him out of the way. This particular peddler, though got more than just a rough push, for he got the pointed end of LeGace's cane thrust roughly into his upper abdomen. He collapsed into a heap at the man's feet. The taller stranger then put his foot on the peddler's

midsection, pulled out his pointed stick, watched briefly as the old man writhed in agony, his blood staining his old, grey cloak, then spreading out in a dark pool out onto the mud. Satisfied that he had made the necessary statement, he then strode purposefully through the crowd, as they parted the way for him. A small crowd gathered around the old peddler. One woman cradled his head as another one softly held pressure on his abdomen with her scarf.

"You there, boy, go fetch one of the guards, there back by the gate. Tell him there's been trouble, now hurry."

The boy ran toward the gate, he came breathlessly up to the guards.

"Pardon me, sir, there's been some trouble down in the marketplace. An old man has been hurt."

"All right, son, now where is he?"

"Down yonder, where there's a crowd." The youth pointed toward the direction from where he'd just run. The guard stepped down, then he and the boy hurried back toward the cluster of people gathered around the fallen man.

When the guard arrived, he could see that it was an old peddler, and there were two women attending to his needs. The guard could tell that the old peddler was still alive, so he bent down to him and asked, "Tell me, old man, who did this to ye? Was it anyone that ye know?"

"Nay, I know him not, but it was a devil, I tell ye, a devil, as sure as I'm here. And if I should recover, he'll suffer for this, I tell ye."

The guard then got up, and asked the crowd if any could tell him what happened. No one answered him. They all looked away, or down at their feet. Finally, the youth sent after the guard spoke up.

"Er, Master," he said rather hesitantly, for he knew better than to interfere in the affairs of adults, "I can tell ye what happened, but I cannot tell ye who that man was. He was a stranger. But he was in the castle last night, then came out when it was late. I did

see him go toward the mansion up the hill. Then, when I saw him again today, I followed him into the crowd. He was very severe man, that I could tell, and seemed well—off. I kept my distance, though, so as not to attract his attention, for like I told ye, he seemed a very severe man, that one. He just kept walking through the village, into the marketplace, pushing his way through the crowd. Then this peddler stopped and said some thing to him. Then I saw the man take his walking stick, and he just thrust it into the peddler's stomach, I tell ye, I've never seen aught like it."

"Tell me son, what be yer name? And who be yer parents?"

"Me name's Eustace, sir, named fer that famous man. Me mum's Diane, and she's a maid at Barncuddy's. I don't know me father. Leastwise, I've never seen him around these parts."

"Well, then Eustace, why don't ye come with me? I'm quite certain that yer story would be of interest to me captain."

He then conscripted a couple of the younger men in the crowd to carry the peddler toward the guardhouse. He had evidently stopped bleeding, but was lapsing toward unconsciousness. The men hurried toward their appointed task, as they definitely did not want the fate of poor Eustace, having to face the captain of the guards. When they arrived at the guardhouse, they laid the old man out on the floor, and fled the premises. When the guard came in with Eustace, he found the other guard attending to the old man.

"And what have ye brought me now, Cayman? It appears that this old man is dying here on our floor."

"And what would have had me do, McGill, just leave the old man out in the snow and mud, in the market? Nay, it's better this way. Now Eustace, if ye would summon the captain, tell him that Cayman and McGill need his assistance here in the guardhouse. Here, take this with ye, that way he knows ye mean business. Ye'll probably find him in the castle, in the main constabulary."

Cayman reached into his belt, and handed Eustace a large, bronze coin, with an eagle on it. "Mind ye," he said, "I'll be needin' that back."

Aye, sir, ye know ye'll have it back when I come with the captain."

Eustace then hurried out the door, and headed toward the castle proper.

McGill turned toward Cayman and said, "Now what kind of fool thing was that to do, give that child yer work token? Do ye know what that could bring, out on the street, and what sort of trouble ye'd be in if he sold it?"

"Ah, me good man, I can see that ye're not much of a judge of character, and besides, do ye know who his mother is? It's Diane and Barncuddy's"

"Oh, ye sly devil. For shame!" McGill said with a wink.

Eustace looked at the coin he had been handed by the guard. On it was an eagle, and some writing, which he could not read. The coin was made of bronze, was heavy, and obviously worth something. *Why did he give to me?* he wondered. *Ah well, I'd better do as he said with it.*

He arrived within the castle, turned to the left, went down toward the stables, then found the constabulary, and entered. There was a large man within and he asked if he could speak to the captain.

"The captain? Ye? Why don't ye tell me what's on yer mind, laddie?"

"Well, sir I was told by a guardsman called Cayman that I should fetch the captain, for there's been trouble in the village.

"And can ye tell me why he sent ye to fetch the captain, and did not come himself?"

"Well, sir, there's a man badly injured in the marketplace, and I'm afeared that he may be dying, so he sent me."

"Oh, he did, did he? And what of this man who is injured, is he a knight or nobleman, or is he just one of you?"

"Please, sir can I speak with the captain?"

"Oh, all right, I shall see if he'll speak with ye." The guard then disappeared into the back hallway. A few minutes later, he came out, along with the captain of the guards, who did not look too pleased at this intrusion.

"And is this the laddie then? Well, what did ye need to tell me, lad?"

"I'm most sorry, sir, but there's been trouble in the marketplace. I was sent by one of the guards, named Cayman, told to fetch ye, sir. And here, sir he told me to show ye this."

Eustace reached into his tunic, and pulled out the coin. The captain looked at the token then turned to the other guard and said, "Well, it looks if Cayman's truly serious this time, Blodwen. He must really think this needs higher attention. Ye're in charge 'til I return, d'ye understand?"

"Aye, sir, that I do."

"So, m' lad, while we go, ye can tell me what ye know of the circumstances. Let us be off, then."

Eustace put the coin back into his tunic, then the two of them headed out, and off toward the village, a most unlikely pair, indeed.

"So, tell me, laddie, why this hurry? I know that if Cayman sent his work token with a stranger, let alone a mere lad, that he thinks something must be of significance, fer ye see, it is a signal of the highest order of business."

"Well, sir, I'll tell ye what I know. See, it began last night at Barncuddy's. Me mums' a maid there, and I was deliverin' a parcel to her, of some flour and onions, which I had obtained in the market. Now this was fairly late, but it was before closing time. Anyway, as I was leavin', I noticed this stranger was also leavin', and after I'd gotten a look at him, I followed him, from a distance, so's he'd not notice me. And then I saw where the stranger was headed. He was going up toward the mansion of Councilor Reordan. And when he got there, I saw that the guard let him in the gate. I then went home to the village. But this

morning, I saw him again, striding toward the marketplace with a look on his face as if he meant to do someone harm, if ye know what I mean. Well, when he got into the marketplace, there was a crowd, and I could tell that this got him upset, then when one of the old peddlers tried to talk to him, well, he took his walkin' stick, and he used it like a sword, and thrust it into the old man's belly. And now I think he maybe dying."

"And do ye know the old peddler, son, is he someone who Cayman thinks is significant?"

"I know only that we call him Old Leroy. Some say that he was once a man of some renown, from somewhere off this island, but of that I could not swear."

"Well, m' lad, ye've given me quite a story there. And let me tell ye that ye may have to tell it again to my commandant. For, if all ye've told me is true, then we may be looking at an investigation that we'll have to try to keep on this isle, and not let it get out to the king's men, for ye know what that would mean?"

"Aye, that I do understand. It would seem most prudent not to let any of the king's men hear of it."

"Very well, then, ye seem a most extraordinary lad, indeed. Tell me, what do yer parents have planned for ye? Are you going to be apprenticed to anyone in particular?"

"Nay, me mum's not said what she would have me do, and me father's not anywhere in these parts. I know him not."

"Now, m' lad, maybe we can take care of that little problem, for ye and yer mum."

The two of them then turned down the lane toward the village. There was a small crowd gathered around the guardhouse, which dispersed quickly when they saw the approaching captain and his young companion. The two of them entered, and happened on the scene of the two guards attending to the needs of Old Leroy, who was awake, but not fully coherent. He was lying still, in obvious pain on the floor of the guardhouse. He was covered with blankets. Cayman, upon seeing his captain, rose and greeted him.

"Ah, good, Captain Proust, I'm glad you have come. This matter is of some urgency, I fear."

"It seems you gave me little choice. I was about to send off this young fellow, when he produced your work token. So, what can ye tell me of our situation now? Bear in mind, I have gotten this lad's full and accurate telling of events."

"Well sir, we are now facing the very real possibility that this old man may die before he is able to tell his story, that is my fear."

"Aye, that would seem to be a very real concern. What have ye gotten from the old man?"

"Only that he was in the crowd, and saw what he thought to be a gentleman, and when he tried to talk to him, that he was assaulted with the man's walking stick."

"That much I did hear. Now can he talk?"

"Talking seems to be difficult for him."

"Well, then let me try." Captain Proust then knelt down beside the old man.

"Listen, Leroy, I'm Captain Proust of the guard. What can ye tell me of what happened to ye?"

The old man's eyes opened, and he mouthed some words that were not understandable. Then he tried again to speak, and the words came out jumbled. Then the captain placed his hand on his head, and said reassuringly, "No matter, Leroy, we shall find this fiend who did this to ye, mark my words, and when we do, he shall hang."

Then he abruptly got back up, turned toward Cayman and said, "Get this man to the castle, get him a room in the sick bay, and notify the castle guards that they should find a physician for him. And ye, McGill, I want ye to interrogate as many of the crowd as ye can, and before noon, then report back to me anything ye find out. I shall set the guards about the castle to be on the lookout."

"And ye," turning toward Eustace, "shall stay with Cayman; I shall meet both of ye at Barncuddy's this afternoon, at three bells. Now yer mother is working there, is she not, today?"

"Aye, that she is."

"And what, pray tell, is yer name, me good lad?"

"Eustace, sir, named for that famous man."

"Ah, aye, and fitting, too, I might be adding. Now are we are all clear as to what we're to be doing?"

Everyone nodded in agreement.

"Well then I'll be seeing you again, I reckon."

With that the captain strode out of the room and was off. Eustace fumbled in his tunic, and brought out the bronze coin, and handed it to Cayman, who took it with a smile, the first of many, then he and his new companion set out to arrange for Old Leroy to be brought to the castle.

Kerlin's ride back toward the castle turned out to be rather a nice change from the past week. He had managed to drop young Tom at the three mirrors lake, where two of Drachma's men were waiting for him, as he was told they would be. After saying farewell to his newfound friend, Kerlin then turned and almost galloped back to the castle not stopping on the way, and arriving around midday, which, if anyone had been recording such things, would have been in record time.

As he alit once again from his horse, and turned him over to his favorite groom, he paused, thinking back on what an extraordinary journey he had made in the last week. When the week began, he had been a captain of his guard unit, doing the usual things of his time, chasing minor thieves, catching the occasional poacher or counterfeiter, always reporting back to his own commandant. But now he was coming back to the castle to perform new duties, and to have to report only to Craycroft. He had been made special commandant by the earl himself, and now he needed to establish just where the measure of his responsibility would take him, and to determine who would be under him. He

needed to set up a meeting with his men, at least those directly under him.

But first and foremost, he needed nourishment, so he stepped into the main constabulary, where he knew there would be something for him to eat and drink.

"Why, look who just blew in from the cold, our new special commandant," said Blodwen, with a slight chuckle. "Who would have thought that ye'd have such a day startin' off? Now I don't mean to be pushy, but the captain's in the back, and he's got something fer ye that he said could not wait."

"Oh, hello, Blodwen, and good to see you, too. Now whatever he's got for me I know shall have to wait until I find yer privy, and relieve my bladder, which is screaming at me. Also, I have got to get something to eat and drink before I pass out from hunger and thirst. So, if you'd be so kind as to raid your cupboards and bring it round to the back room, where I shall meet with your captain, that I would appreciate."

"Aye, sir. That I shall."

When Kerlin entered the back room of the constabulary, he found Captain Proust busy with his men, giving them orders in regard to their new duties, and filling them in on what had happened earlier in the day.

"My good friend and now my commandant, Kerlin. It is most good of ye to come. Here, m' lads is your new commandant, Master Kerlin, formerly of the Forest Guard. I was just giving these fellows their orders for today, then I shall tell ye of events that have occurred here, of which ye need to be told."

"Very well, Captain, carry on, while I sit down to enjoy some food and drink."

What Blodwen had brought him was some bread, some dried meats, and some cheese. In an old wineskin was some wine. To Kerlin right now, it looked more than inviting, and he sat down and ate like a starving man. Then, as he was pouring some of the wine form the skin into a cup, Captain Proust sat down.

"My good friend, when I heard that they made you special commandant, nothing could have made me happier. Here, let us drink to your advancement." He poured himself a cup of the wine, then the two of them raised their cups. Kerlin then poured another. For a while the two old friends just sat. Finally, Proust said, "If ye don't mind me sayin' so, I'd say that ye look beat, like ye haven't seen the fair side of a pair of clean sheets in a week. Am I not correct?"

"Aye, my friend you are more than correct, and I'll tell you, if one were to say to me right now, 'here's a clean bed for ye,' you would have to fight me to keep me out of it."

"Ah, so I thought. Anyway, what has happened here today, ye do need to hear, but rest ye well, as I'm takin' care of matters for today anyway."

"Well we've had an attempted murder, as ye know, of one of our councilors, who is at this time doing rather well, under the supervision of this new healer brought in by Drachma. But then, just today, in broad daylight, one of our poor peddlers was assaulted by some man in the marketplace, in some unprovoked attack. Now his assailant has been described, by the peddler, as the devil, and by a witness, as being a very severe man. The peddler, I fear may not be doing as well as our councilor, but is now also where our healer can take care of him. I have taken the liberty of advising our forces within and around the castle to be on the most high alert for any signs of this stranger."

Kerlin acknowledged his friend wordlessly, while continuing to munch on his bread and cheese. After another swallow of wine, he then spoke again. "And does anyone have a description of this provocateur, I mean, besides being the devil and very severe?"

"Nay, not yet, but we shall have, of that I am quite certain."

"I'll tell you, my good friend, that I think I know who this assailant is, but let me ask you, was the attack in the marketplace done with a walking stick, but with an injury that should have been brought on by a long knife?"

"Why, aye that is precisely what happened."

"Well, then the identity of our assailant is none other that Antoine LeGace."

"That is what ye think?"

"Nay, my friend, that is what I now know. That I did suspect, but now it is a certainty."

"You know? How?"

"If you must know, I did once apprehend this LeGace fellow a number of years ago, but he did escape, and cut the throats of his companions before escaping, then he fled this isle. For a while I did attempt to pursue him on the mainland, for he did flee to Ireland, and I have a brother over there, but all we got were snippets of stories, most of which were much like what you told me today. Then I tell you, last evening while I dined at Barncuddy's, there he was, in the flesh. I must admit, it took me a while to remember, but it was he. Then when I asked Barncuddy to investigate further, the man was gone."

"That is very interesting, for there was this youth, who told us this tale which, I must say, fits in with what you said."

"A youth?"

"Aye, and quite a lad he is, and observant too. I shall be meeting with one of my trusted men and his young lad again today at three bells at Barncuddy's."

"Might I give you a suggestion my good captain?"

"An order, if ye prefer, my commandant." He managed to say, with the utmost sincerity.

"Well, then, an order it is. You shall keep that lad protected at all times, for I'll tell you this—his life is now in danger, my friend. And be most wary yourself, for this is an enemy most vile, and most cunning."

"Aye, my commandant. Ye have my word upon this matter."

"Very well, for now I must find a place to rest. Be sure that I am awakened when you are to go to your meeting."

"Oh, that ye shall, my friend. There is the bunk in the back of this building, that would suit ye, I'm quite certain."

"Thanks, I'll go there, now."

With that, Kerlin got up and headed down the hall toward the back room.

Chapter Eighteen

Frieda rapped on the door of the alchemist's shop, then waited. She rapped again, and again waited. She then rapped a third time, then as she was about to turn back, she saw a light inside, coming toward the door.

The latch clicked inside, and the door opened. Inside was the unmistakable form of Melchior. Though he stood well over six feet tall, his constant stoop and effusive manner made him the least intimidating of men. His voice, as well, was a bit raspy, and was not the voice one associated with self-confidence. But his smile, one of unabashed pleasure, made him one of Frieda's favorites.

"Oh, my dear Frieda, it is you indeed. My master is not in at the moment, and I know not when he shall return."

"Aye, I know that Master Melchior, it is not yer master that I seek."

"Not Master Falma?"

"Nay, it is but thee alone that I seek, but not here in this cold. Might I come in?"

"Oh, Frieda, of course, do come in."

Frieda came inside, closed the door firmly, glad to be in from the cold.

"Madame, why not come in to my small rooms in the back? I have a nice warm fire, and you may tell me what you need from me."

The two of them walked down the dimly lit, odd smelling hallway, with a number of little rooms on either side, to the very back, then turned into another room, remarkably bright and warm, and oddly cheerful. Melchior cleared off one of the two chairs for Frieda to sit in, then sat down himself at the other side of the cluttered desk.

"Now, my good lady, can you tell me what I may do for you? You know that I shall do anything for friends of Falma."

"And I do thank ye for that," said Frieda, "well, as ye know, me mistress, the lady Vincente, did recently die, God rest her soul."

Melchior nodded.

"As it happens, Lord Vincente, who also did die recently, left everything to m' lady, as it seems that his family from the old country and he had separated their ways. But now she has left no one to inherit her things, and, to make matters more complicated, there seems to be no one to come and protect her things from the vultures. Now Jeanne and I are still at the home, with no official roles, and no one we can turn to as protector of our mistress' estate. Mind ye we're not trying to get anything for ourselves, but it would be such a shame to see it go to Councilors Reordan, Silvo, and that brood of vipers."

"Vultures you say, and brood of vipers? I couldn't agree with you more. But m' lady, what can I possibly do for you? I am no person of power or authority."

"But ye do know the law, do ye not?"

"Aye, that I do, but how did you know that?"

"Councilor Rust, he told us."

"Ah, well, he is truly a good man, and he is a true friend of Master Falma."

"Well then, will ye not do this thing for Master Falma and for Councilor Rust, and also for Master Craycroft."

"Ah, for them I shall do what even I am able, and for thee as well."

"Good, then, why not come by this evening, and we shall have a good meal for ye, and we'll cover what things we shall need. Can ye come over at half past six bells?"

"Aye, that I can, as I have no other plans this evening."

"Very well, we shall see ye then for dinner. I shall tell Jeanne to be expecting ye."

"My good lady, shall I bring anything?"

"Ye might bring something to record notes upon. For there is much to see and to discuss."

"I shall do just that." He hesitated just a moment, then said, "now, m' lady, I must ask, as a friend, and not wishing to pry, but I have heard that lady Felicia did, in fact have a daughter, who did die in her prime, but that this daughter did have a son who walks among us. Is this true? And if so, would he be an heir to her things?"

"Why, aye. I do believe that, but it is not well known among the people of this isle, and I think that Jeanne would be better able to tell ye of the details. But I do believe ye're correct in what ye've been told."

"Well, that may make matters a bit more interesting, and more complicated, especially with the council certain to be involved."

"My, my, I had not thought of that."

"It is definitely better to know this now, though, than to be surprised later."

"Agreed."

Frieda then got up, thanked her host. The two of them then made their way back out the corridor, with its odd smells, out to the front door.

"Now we'll be seein' ye for dinner, good Master Melchior. And I would recommend not bein' late, for I am certain that it shall be as fine a meal as ye've eaten in many a day."

"Be certain that I shall be there, my good woman."

Bob woke from his silent, intense slumber, looked about him, disoriented. He could see that he was in a large room, in an unusually comfortable bed. The details were hard to see, but he could tell that the room was cool, had a very tall ceiling, and had tall windows. He could tell that there was a fireplace, with the fire dying, and he tried to decide whether it was worth getting out from under his warm covers to stoke the fire. Then it hit him—he was in the castle, here in this old place and time, with all the chaos, all the weird expectations, and all of the weird people. He found himself wondering what happened. What had he done? What could he have done differently? And then was there anything he could do to return to his own time and place? He could hear nothing, and what he could see was only the dim shapes in his strange room.

Eventually, Bob decided to get up and stoke the fire. He found the small lamp on the table, adjusted the flame then went over to the fireplace. He found a couple of logs, found the fireplace tools, and got the fire flaming brighter and warmer. He stood over the flame, enjoying the warmth, still trying to find answers, but getting none. All he found again was loneliness. Then he remembered his conversation with Craycroft, and the incredible realization that Judy was here as well. Somewhere on this island, or so Craycroft thought.

I've got to do something to find her, he thought. *It is not inconceivable that she may have gotten hurt, or be in some kind of trouble. Where might she be? Perhaps, if I can contact this Drachma person, I can get some answers.* All these thoughts started tumbling out of his subconscious. He looked around the room, and noticed there were none of the gadgets around that he was used to reaching for on those rare nights when he had trouble sleeping. There was no television, nor radio, no magazines, not even books. This room, though nicely furnished, and with a very comfortable

bed did not even have electric lights, let alone a TV set. It felt like camping out, but in all the times he had been camping, there had been people all around him, playing cards or just talking, and there was not this sick feeling in the pit of his stomach that told him that this was probably permanent. Again, he felt the urge to scream at his surroundings, but did not. Instead, he headed back to his bed, got under the covers.

For a while, he tossed in the bed, trying to quiet the thoughts racing in his mind. He tried different positions, all to no avail. He remembered the previous evening, the very strange encounter with the injured councilor brought in with the basilar skull fracture. He remembered that he had diagnosed his condition, without the benefit of X-rays or CT scans, how the others, including Craycroft had been so thoroughly impressed. And then there was the encounter with the earl, whom he had finally met. But what a meeting it was.

The earl himself was a strikingly handsome man of middle age, whose commanding presence was still palpable, even in his weakened state. He remembered how he had been so thoroughly impressed with the apparatus that Craycroft had constructed to provide the earl with breathing treatments, and just how sick the earl actually was. It was obvious that the earl had some form of pneumonia, and it was equally obvious just how powerless Bob now felt, with no antibiotics, no IV fluids, no supplemental oxygen, no cardiac monitors, nothing but a diagnosis, and it appeared that Craycroft was doing all that was possible for his earl. He remembered, too, that strange odor that came from the earl's breathing, that sickly sweet sort of odor that he had never encountered before. He remembered that strange and fascinating woman, Jeanne, who was somehow tied in with all of these folks. And there was talk of the council, and of this Councilor Reordan and his cronies. It was too much for him in one evening. And the notebook that Jeanne had brought Craycroft—what was that all about? Evidently, it was of some significance to Craycroft,

as he seemed to treasure it. And what was the relationship of this Lady Vincente to Craycroft, and to Drachma. Now here he was, suddenly immersed in this quagmire of relationships past and present.

Bob realized very quickly just what an extraordinary healer Craycroft was. And this man, Cartho, who taught Craycroft, must have been some kind of wonder as well. Bob was going to have to see what Cartho had written down. Here was a healer, who by powers of observation alone, long before it became common knowledge, had figured out that the blood in the body circulated through pipes, and that disruption of this circulation led to clotting. He also determined that many illnesses were the result of transmission of some mysterious agent, through the air, or through contact, and were not the result of unbalanced bodily humors. This, Bob realized, was an astounding conclusion, and, he felt sure, that here was a treasure trove of incredibly astute observations by a master heretofore unknown.

Finally, Bob decided that sleep was not going to happen, so he got up, put on his weird pants and top. He then put on his old brown loafers, and then his cloak. He decided to head on out the door and try to explore this little area of the castle. But outside the door, he found Hermes, sleeping on a bed of blankets. Hermes was instantly awake, and at the ready to assist his new master.

"I'm sorry, Hermes, I didn't mean to waken you. I was just lying in my bed, not sleeping, and decided to explore this part of the castle. But since you're awake, maybe you could show me around a little."

"Show you around? In the middle of the night? Well, if ye must, I'd best get us a torch, so we can at the very least see the walls around us. Just wait here, I shall be back anon."

While Hermes disappeared, Bob realized what a foolish thing this might be, trying to see anything at this hour. He just wasn't used to not having electricity, and all that came with it, such as light and sound and music. All he could really see in this

light was the vague shape of things such as the walls that formed the corridors of this labyrinthine part of the castle. There were not even windows here in the hallway, just the faint light from some torches on the walls. Then a thought struck him, and he went back inside his room, and found his sack, and took out the penlight. He then placed the little light in his cloak, and walked out into the corridor once more, as Hermes was coming down one of the corridors, carrying a torch.

"Well, Master, I have the light of this torch to guide us. Whither shall we go? I shall try to keep ye informed of where it is we're going."

"What I'm really looking for is to find my way back to the sick bay where we've got our poor councilor with the skull fracture. But I need to find a way that I can remember, because, if I can find that, then I figure I can proceed to at least start to become useful around here."

"Very well, Master. Come with me down this corridor."

Bob noted that Hermes took him down the hallway to the right.

"Now we are going down the main guest corridor. Ye'll notice that it is paved with dark slate, and the walls are of our usual grey stone, but there is a different pattern that is unique to the guest section of the castle. If ye'll pay attention, that is a good way to know ye're in the right place. Now here, we'll turn leftward, and go down this corridor. They both turned and headed down a long and very dark corridor. There was a door at the end of this corridor that led into a stairway going down into the darkness.

"I don't remember coming up these stairs before," said Bob.

"Nay, I didn't bring ye this way before, because we were, if ye remember, talking with Master Craycroft, then going back to his new place of abode. That was on the east side."

"Ah, yes."

They came down the stairway, carefully, and then out the heavy door into the weather outside. The night was now clear,

and there was a bright moon that shone down upon the castle interior. There was a glistening stillness to everything touched by the moonlight, from the towering battlements to the now gleaming ruts in the muddy streets below. To Bob it was an awesome sight, especially now, with no one walking about, and with no sounds, except their own steps.

"Tell me, Hermes, does no one walk about at this hour of the night? Are we the only crazy ones about tonight?"

"Aye. I do believe we are the only persons madly walking about this night, Here, now turn around. From here ye can see whence we came out of the guest quarters. Then over yonder is the building we'll be going to. That'd be the building where we should find our councilor, now come along with me, and we'll go over to that building."

Bob hesitated, raised his hand.

"Shh. Do you hear it too? There, if you listen very closely, you'll hear it."

"What, master? I hear nothing."

"Now, listen. It's real quiet, but there, do you hear it now?"

They both listened intently. There was not doubt about it. Just above the incredible stillness of the night it was there – a very soft strumming. The source of the sound was not obvious at first, but as they went toward the other side of the courtyard, it became clearer. It was emanating from a small alcove that was walled off from the main corridor. For a minute they both just stood and listened to the quiet music of the harp that was reaching them from behind the grey stone walls. The tones fell out into the still night, as if adding jewelry to the evening, making this moment memorable. Bob had no trouble recognizing the playing, for there was none like it.

"Now I know that playing. It's Willie Minstrel, isn't it?"

Hermes looked over at the stranger with a look of incredulity.

"Master, that is Willie Minstrel, without a doubt, but how would ye have known that?"

"Hermes, before I ever came to this island, I had a dream, and it was unlike any I've had before. The dream was so real, that I felt the touch of the tables and chairs, and I could smell and taste the food and drink. And there at the table next to mine was Craycroft, who was telling a most remarkable tale—though to this day I can't remember any of it—and also at the table was Willie Minstrel. He was playing his harp, and such incredible playing, too, that it took me to a place even farther off, in the warmth of late springtime, in the woods. Well, when I met Craycroft in the flesh the dream came back to me. And we talked of this place where Willie plays, I believe its called Barncuddy's, and of his harp playing that goes beyond simply music. And now, in the middle of the night, in this place and time, I hear this music, and it brings me a sense that I do belong, in someone's strange logic, right here at this time."

Hermes could think of nothing to say. So the two of them just stood there, drinking in the music that flowed out to the courtyard from that little building, alone in that winter night, thinking nothing of the cold or of the dark. Finally, Bob turned to Hermes, and with a note of resignation in his voice said, "Come my young friend, show me how to get to the sick bay from here, then maybe I can get some sleep, now that this night has been blessed by this magical music."

So Hermes showed Bob the way across the courtyard, and down the corridor of arches, through the interior hallway, into the sick bay. It was quiet inside, and there was enough light from the burning torches, that they could easily find their way back to the bed with Councilor Genet. His attendant rose in greeting.

"My good Master Robert, whatever are ye doing at this hour? I should think that ye would be sleeping."

"That's just it, my good man. I couldn't sleep, so I thought I'd check on my patient here, isn't that right, Hermes?"

Hermes caught the sly wink from Bob, and nodded in agreement.

Then Bob got into proper doctor mode and began reexamining the councilor. He found that his patient remained dazed, but was able to recall a few things, namely that he had just left the earl's side, with some paper. He kept asking about the paper. Then he remembered nothing, until waking up in the sick bay, with Master Craycroft, Bob, and others in attendance. Then he asked about the paper again, said it was sealed with the earl's seal upon it. Bob could tell that there were no focal neurological signs developing, and that the councilor appeared to be doing somewhat better. The bleeding from his ear had stopped, and there was no cerebrospinal fluid leaking out, as near as he could tell with just his penlight, the use of which caused murmurings from Hermes and the attendant.

Satisfied that all was going about as well as could be expected, Bob turned again to Hermes and said, "Well, then young man, I've seen about as much now as I'd hoped. Let's get back to my room, and perhaps now I can sleep."

"Very well, Master Robert, let us be on our way."

Bob then left with Hermes carrying the torch. He made his way back with surprising ease, then upon arriving at his own door, he thanked Hermes for a most delightful evening stroll. Hermes just chuckled and bade Bob goodnight.

When he stepped back into his room, he found that someone had kept the fire tended, and there was a flagon of ale on the table. He sat down after taking off his cloak. Not giving it a second thought, he drank half the ale, then crawled into bed, pulled up the covers, and was asleep before he could even contemplate what had happened.

Chapter Nineteen

To Drachma's men this was a wondrous chance, as they were primed and ready to deal with the likes of these ruffians, who did plunder and loot the forest and surrounding villages with seemingly no concern for the common folk. And now they had crossed the threshold, had not only captured a lady, but had killed one of their own. As he had explained to them their mission, it was to be as quiet and bloodless as possible, and that there was a lady involved, one from another place, who was a lady of some power and beauty, and who was important to their own welfare. And further, that Loremaster Falma was also involved, which as they all knew made the matter even more significant. The lady and Falma were to be rescued, with as little fanfare as possible, and to be quickly taken toward safety. But what really got the men emotionally charged was that these ruffians had killed one of their own, and wounded yet another of their brave brethren and for that crime alone, death was too light a sentence to be passed. To a man, each was eager to get going, and to make this a most memorable rout.

Drachma's plan was not elaborate, rather simple, actually. It involved surrounding the camp, getting the message to Falma, who knew the secret code from years before. Then, before the guards had time to react, spring the trap, while the lady, Falma, and their companion were to be whisked away, and taken to the earl's castle. The remainder of Drachma's guard would capture Finch, and of the remaining men, find who would talk, who would bolt, and who would be otherwise useful in their cause. There were no major preparations, as the men knew their own duties, with years of training and experience, though done quietly, and with nothing recorded, except in their memories.

This operation was what the men were ready for, as over the years they had, in many ways, protected the island from incursions by the king's forces. There had been many previous operations, always done without fanfare, and with only the earl and Falma, as well as the men involved, knowing anything about them. This was, as Falma understood well, why he had been chosen for this particular mission.

After he made final inspection, and assured himself that everyone was ready, Drachma gave the signal to proceed. After making sure that there were no more than two guards in or around Falma's hut, who were quickly dispatched. Drachma himself, with two guards then appeared at the hut. One guard kept lookout while Drachma and Johnny quickly took care of the lock, then quietly appeared in the door.

"Well, as I live and breathe," said Falma, "my old friend, it is you. I do not believe that I have ever been so happy to see you."

"Oh, Mr. Drachma! What a surprise. You really do get around, don't you?" Judy could not keep the thrill of surprise out of her voice.

"Ah, my friends, it was the least I could do to come here and greet you in person. Alas, it shames me that you were put through such as this, and to have lost one of my own men. Ah, my good fellow, Cairn, I see you are wounded, yet are upright. Are you in much pain?"

"Nay, m' lord. Thanks be to this lady, who I feel has kept me alive."

"Ah. It was she and her powers that did it, no doubt." Drachma flashed Judy a sly smile.

Judy just quietly blushed.

"Well, friends, it would appear that time is of the essence, and you should escape now, or risk more peril. There are mounts for you all outside and guards who shall escort you this time to the earl's castle. It is my hope that your journey this time shall be less trying for you all. So hie you hence my friends, and may it be that the next time we shall meet again, it be under less strenuous circumstances."

"Before we go, my dear friend," said Falma, "might I have just a word with you?"

"But of course, maybe as we ready your departure. For you see, I have other conflicts that I feel I need to oversee. Come then. We must make haste."

He saw that Judy was properly seated upon her horse, and that Cairn was also able to be seated as well. Then Drachma and Falma conferred in hushed voices. Their conversation was intense, and obviously animated. Then with a word to his guards, the party set off at a gallop. They could tell there was turmoil behind them as they left, but none turned around to see. They just rode hard until the guards slowed the pace. Then they came to a river that looked somewhat familiar, and slowed to a walk as they crossed the river. This time, however, there was no ambush waiting for them on the bank.

The pace seemed to tell of the guards' comfort level with the surroundings. The one in the lead then led the group to a clearing. There he stopped and addressed the others.

"My good people," he said, "we can thank the good Lord that we have come thus far safely. Now me name's Johnny, and this one's called Blackfist, and the one in back is Malcolm. Now, we'll be taking you back to the earl's castle by another route, as I think there may be sentries still along the old road, and we don't need to be meeting any more of them, I think ye'd agree. This

way may be somewhat harder, but it will be safer, of that I'm certain. Now, we may have to go single file for a while, but the path should not be too rigorous. I'll lead, then Master Falma and Cairn, then Blackfist, then the lady, Judy, with Malcolm in the rear. Are we agreed then?" He saw that no one disagreed. "Well, then, let us go."

They then followed the river for about a mile, then turned sharply left, across a rocky stretch, the back abruptly in to the forest. The air this morning was crisp and clear as the sun made it over the horizon, when they could catch glimpses of it through the thick growth of evergreens. Unlike her companions, Judy finally felt as though she could begin to relax.

Back at the camp, Drachma's plan was unfolding, with proficiency and sharpness that the men under Finch came to realize too late. They were surrounded and separated before any even had time to draw their swords and ready their bows, and the few who tried regretted it very quickly and painfully, as Drachma's men moved ever so swiftly to make sure that the others knew of the penalty for drawing weapons against them. These were men of the forest, and it was their domain that these intruders had molested.

Finch had been one of the first to be captured. He stood by stoically silent, and watched his men being tied up, or worse, having their right hands cut off in the event that any of them drew swords against Drachma's men. Finch stood there, saying nothing, and giving nothing away, and listening to the wail of his men seemed to do nothing to his demeanor.

Then Drachma arrived, and quite suddenly there was a change in the whole scene. A hush fell on the men; both the captured and the maimed sensed a new, more powerful presence among them. He looked about and frowned. Then he noticed Finch.

"How now, then, Master Finch? I see that you've assembled this band of ruffians, and have killed and injured my men. What say you to that? And under whose authority have you acted thus?"

Finch remained mute.

Drachma then made a subtle sign with his hand, and the two men on either side of Finch twisted his restraints, sending a burning pain from his arms to his shoulders. Finch moaned, but said nothing. The men then pulled out their knives and at Drachma's sign began cutting his skin, first the exposed skin of his arms, then cutting away his clothing, and beginning on his chest.

"Now, Master Finch, I have got plenty of time to make this as painful as I need, but you could make it easier for yourself by answering my questions. In particular, I should like to know who paid you, and why. And I do think it would be better if you answered, because things could certainly get worse for you."

"I shall not give you that satisfaction." Finch finally answered.

"Oh, we shall see."

The men then started rubbing salt into the wounds they had created. Finch was now in exquisite agony, but still would not talk. Then Drachma went to the fireplace and plunged the end of the tool into the fire, making certain that his captive saw him do it.

"Now, while we wait for this rod to redden with heat, I shall ask you once more, who paid you, how much and why?"

There were now beads of perspiration forming on Finch's forehead, running down his temples. Still, he did not talk. Drachma, then, checked his fire iron, found that it was glowing red. He then picked it up and took it over to Finch.

"Now, hold his head steady, m'lads. There, just like that. Now, Master Finch, I'll give you one more chance to talk, before I poke this into your eye. If you value your eyesight, you shall answer my questions." He then brought the hot poker close to his face, close enough that Finch could feel the intense heat from the iron.

"Enough! I'll talk," he said. There was a palpable sigh that emanated from the others caught, and held prisoner. Drachma then pulled the poker away from Finch's face, and placed it back into the smoldering fire.

"It was Reordan who hired me. He paid me in silver, said that there would be more after I did capture and bring to him the lady. I did not know that Falma was to be part of the bargain, but I did figure that was to become his problem, not mine. As to why, he did not tell me. This is the truth, I swear on my mother's grave."

"Ah, that is all very interesting, Master Finch. Now, I must ask you, and I would have you remember that the fire iron is still in the heat of the flame, what do you know of Antoine LeGace, and what role he is playing in all this?"

At the mention of LeGace's name, the color drained rapidly from Finch's face, and his pupils dilated, as if in terrible fear.

"Antoine LeGace? Is he here? My God, that is a name I have not heard in years, and thankfully so."

"Ah, so there exists, even among the killers for pay, certain, shall we say, levels of malice?"

"There is none like LeGace. He is the very devil incarnate."

"Very well, I do believe you. Now, I must ask you, Master Finch, what do you say to the slaying of one of my men, and the injury to a second? You should know, by now, that I do not take such action lightly, nor do my men. What do I tell Bernard's widow?"

"I was merely doing the work I was paid to perform. They were both men-at-arms as well, and that is the risk, as we all know." There was a murmuring among the others in the building, and one could feel the rising animosity among the men.

Drachma moved swiftly, took his small dagger, thrust it suddenly into Finch's upper abdomen, with its tip up into his chest. Finch gasped, then slumped forward. He was dead within minutes, but before he died, he heard Drachma say, "You should have been more careful about whom you chose to attack, for attacking my men is also attacking me."

"Now," he said, addressing all within the small hut, "you have seen what comes of an attack upon my men. Remember this, at your own peril, for Drachma the Elder, of the Forest has spoken." He then took the poker with the red hot tip from the fire, brandished it above his head, and then thrust it like a spear into the floor of the small hut with a deep reverberant crash that left an unforgettable message. He then carefully wiped off his blade, spoke to his men about what to do next, and walked out of the hut.

The captives all within the hut were now primed for Drachma's men to carefully interrogate them, and to determine, as he had said, which men would be useful to them in the future, and also which needed to be brought before the earl's court, for swift justice. Having just witnessed Drachma's version of swift justice, and seeing how easily his plans went off, it was just possible that some of the men might wish to serve another leader, but there would need to be care taken to insure their loyalties, and of course, there was no room among Drachma's men for any who were not seasoned.

Craycroft rose early, and went out into his hallway, where he found Aaron sleeping.

"Come, Aaron," he said, "let us get ready for the day's doings. I do believe that this day shall be full of surprises for all. I should like some food and drink, then a bath. And could you also see if Hermes needs anything for Master Robert? I should like to meet with Master Robert this morning, as well as our new commandant, Master Kerlin. See if he could come by this morning."

"Aye, m' lord. Would ye like Gerald to get ready yer bath?"

"Aye, that would be good, lad."

He then went back into his suite, stoked the fire. Though the light was faint, he was able to sit in a chair by the window, as he took up the notebook left him by Jeanne, which was a fairly small, grey volume, and he opened it up, and read the first page.

My dearest Will,

Forgive me, but this is my entreaty to thee. Ye have been my rock through the years, but in this time, which I know shall be difficult thou shalt have my heart in thy hands. It is with some degree of sadness that I must tell thee of my past, of which thou might know some, but it was with one thou dost know. Drachma, in a life that I so now recall with some sadness, and I did have a dalliance, and from this youthful flame we did produce one child, whose story is one of immense sorrow and woe, and is but known to only a few. From this flower of youth, from her short time on this earth, there did come one, known to thee by now, as Tom, or Drachma. It is my wish then, that thou would provide for young Tom that which I was not able to provide, namely a home, and all the comforts and advantages of a home, with thee as parent, and tutor.

Now, I have asked the earl if this should be reasonable to accomplish, and he did indicate to me that it shall be done, but that thou would need to see to the particulars, especially as the council of Lords shall be in opposition to this entreaty, as thou dost know.

Please, then, dear Will, if thou would but see to accomplishing that which I have been unable to provide for my own grandson, I shall truly rest in peace.

With all my love,
Felicia

Craycroft was stunned, not by the revelations, of which he was now becoming familiar, but by the request, as well as the implied actions. Had lady Felicia had gone to the earl, with the request that the earl provide for Tom, albeit indirectly, and that Craycroft should be the one to do it? Also, he wondered about whether his recent change in status was made at the request of Felicia. Did she know she was dying? If so, when? And what of the earl? Was his decision made before he knew he was ill, and dying? These matters he would have to take up with the earl in

private, but he still feared that the earl might die, despite the presence of Robert, and his powers.

Then he wondered about Drachma, and what of his wishes for Tom. Would he not be a better choice as parent? And was Drachma not already assuming that role?

Ah, well, he thought, *maybe the lady's notebook might provide some answers.*

And this would certainly change the nature of his meeting with Jeanne, Frieda, and Melchior, which he had set up for this evening, after dinner. If only Falma were here. He would know much of what happened, he was sure, and what should be done. Then he turned the page, to read on.

"Master Craycroft." It was Gerald, who came with two large buckets of steaming water.

"Pardon, m' lord, but Aaron did say that ye would like yer bath this morning. Shall I set ye up for yer bath?"

"Ah, most certainly, my good man. I should like a bath now."

Craycroft put the notebook down, got up, and went over to the bathing room. While Gerald poured the large buckets of steaming water into the tub, then got more water from the large urn, and mixed it with the hot water in the tub, Craycroft got out of his clothes, then stepped into the tub. Gerald then placed a few drops of rose oil into the water. As Craycroft leaned back in the tub, Gerald got out a new set of clothes for his master. "Here ye be, then m' lord, here's freshly washed clothes fer ye."

"My thanks, good man. Never have I felt the need for a bath as I do now."

Gerald then got one of the smooth, round stones, and started scrubbing his master's back, as Craycroft relaxed, thoroughly enjoying this moment of indulgence.

Bob was awakened by the birds chirping outside his window. He had been asleep at long last until then. He woke to find a roaring

fire in the fireplace, and a table set, with spiced cider, bread, some dried fruits, and meats waiting for him.

Hermes was there, as well, with Bob's own clothes, washed and dried.

"Well, good morrow, my master. I do see that ye have slept well. Now I can ready yer bath, while ye eat and drink here."

"A bath? My that does sound like a good idea." Bob knew that he must really smell ripe, by now.

"Well, then, I shall be back with some hot water for yer bath. Here, then is some food and drink fer ye. And the maids did find this among yer clothes. Now ye'll have to explain these things to me, I imagine after yer bath."

Hermes handed Bob his wallet. Bob took the wallet with some relief, but then came to realize that there would be nothing of real usefulness in it. Not here, not now.

"Thanks, Hermes, yeah, my wallet. Sure, I'll explain some of the things in it. But, as you say, first things first."

Bob sat down, ate, and drank, while Hermes rushed around, getting his bath ready. When he had the water ready, Bob got out of his clothes, stepped gingerly into the tub, but found the water warm, and smelling of roses. He eased back into the water, and heaved a great sigh of relief. He looked around, but could see no soap, let alone any shampoo. He began to wash his face, and hair, though it definitely would have worked better with some shampoo. Hermes took one of the rounded river stones, and began to scrub Bob's back. He then relaxed, and really enjoyed the bath.

After a few more minutes of peace, with the water temperature falling, Bob got out, dried himself with a cloth and got into his underwear, scrubs, and socks. Then Hermes asked if he should like some sweet oil for his hair. Having never heard of such a thing, Bob asked to see some of the oil. Hermes showed him a small vial. Bob smelled it, and it smelled of lilacs and something else, then decided, "why not," so Hermes rubbed a small bit into his palm, then rubbed it into Bob's hair.

"Well, now I feel much more human," said Bob, "and I smell better, too. Thanks, Hermes. You know, what would be really nice right now would be a toothbrush and toothpaste."

"Tooth...brush? Tooth...paste? I do not know of these things," said Hermes. "What are they?"

"Well, where I come from, we have these things, to clean our teeth, and freshen our breath, and besides, they help prevent cavities."

"Cavities?"

"Ah, I can see that is a concept that'll need clarification."

"Master Robert, you do speak in riddles."

"I'm sorry, Hermes, It's just that I don't really fully understand yet what you do and don't know here. We'll be talking, I'm sure, and you'll get to know more about my riddles. And maybe I'll learn something from you as well."

Then Bob took up his wallet, and motioned to Hermes to come closer.

"Now, this is my wallet, and in it are papers and little bits of identification. Now this is my driver's license. Here, you can hold it. On it is my picture, as well as my birth date, my address and such."

Hermes looked at the driver's license with utter amazement. Then he looked up at Bob, then back at the license.

"Master, this is extraordinary, for the likeness is very real, it must have been made by a most wondrous artist."

Bob just laughed. It was, after all his driver's license photo, and not a nice shot of him. He thought that it made him look like he was trying to sell drugs to underage children. And to hear Hermes, it was miniature masterpiece.

"Ah, Hermes, it is just a photograph, which, in our age is done with lights and film. It is a concept that will take some explaining, I'm afraid. Let's just say that we've harnessed a bit of "magic" for our purposes, and, in this case, it's to depict with some

reality what a person actually looks like, for identification. That's the real purpose of the driver's license, just that—identification."

"There ye go, Master Robert, speaking in riddles again."

"Anyway, look here. This is money. Here are twenty-, fifty-, five-, and one-dollar bills. These are what the government prints, and it is what we use to purchase things. Now the government is supposed to keep records of just how much money is printed, and people get paid in this money for their services. It's easier than everyone carrying around bags of silver and gold."

"I, for one, would rather have a bag of gold than a piece of paper, Master Robert."

"And I would agree with you, Hermes. Gold would be so much more substantial."

"Substan…?"

"Oh, never mind."

Their deliberations were interrupted by knocking at the door. It was Aaron, and he brought the message that Craycroft would like to meet with Master Robert this morning.

"Well, I really don't have anything better to do with my time," said Bob, "so, lets go see Mr. Craycroft."

So, Bob and Hermes put on their cloaks, and headed with Aaron out the door. The morning was cold, but with no wind, and with bright sunshine, the walk was not nearly as oppressive as recently.

"So, have ye learned any of the master's magic, Hermes?"

"Nay, but I have seen his likeness, painted on a small card, with light. It is truly amazing."

When the trio arrived at Craycroft's door, Aaron took his leave, saying that he had to seek out the new commandant, Master Kerlin, for Craycroft wanted to meet with him. So Hermes and Bob were let in the Master's suite. There sat Craycroft, at table, with food and drink, reading from the little notebook.

"Ah, Master Robert, a most pleasant welcome to you. Have you dined?"

"Most definitely. When I got up just a bit ago, Hermes had seen to it that I got some breakfast, and now I've had a bath, and I feel almost human again."

"And I see that you have your own clothes on again. We shall have our tailor try to make you some clothes like what you wear. Though I am not at all certain that our cobbler could make boots like what you have on."

"That's all right," said Bob, looking down at this somewhat disreputable brown loafers. "I'm doing fine for now."

"Well, sit down, Master Robert. We have much to discuss, you and I. Now that will be all, Hermes. Master Robert and I have much to discuss. We shall call you as we need your services, thank you."

Hermes barely hid his disappointment, but bowed, then went out into the hallway to wait.

"Now, Master Robert, do sit here. As you can see, I have been reading from this notebook, prepared by lady Felicia Vincente, and it is of her life that we must speak, for it is through her life that much of our current trouble can best be understood. And her tale is a remarkable one of woe and strength."

"Let me begin by telling you of our first meeting. Now this was many a year ago, when I was but a very young man, and worked as a page here in this castle. Aye, I was a page myself, born of humble parents from one of the villages. As it was, it came upon me that the old earl, the father of our present earl, who by then was a very old man, had welcomed into his castle a new ambassador, named Gianni, and I was sent to this certain ambassador's abode with a bouquet of flowers, for the lady of the house. I was met at the door of the house by none other than the daughter herself, an astonishing raven-haired lass of such beauty as to make me weak in the knees. To this day, that memory stirs feelings in me that I dare not speak of openly, and it is probably

the major reason I never married, nor was I even interested. For if one has seen true beauty, then, it seems, none can compare."

"Well then, shortly after I was apprenticed to Master Cartho, and was absorbed in the learning of illnesses, and what he could do for those afflicted. And as you can imagine, my time and attention was taken up by this pursuit, I had no opportunity to see this young beauty. But there is one who did, in fact, have occasion to see her through her developing years, and that one was Drachma himself, who at the time was hired as tutor to the lovely Felicia. Of their relationship I cannot comment, except to say that they did produce one daughter, who became a legend in her brief time on this earth, who then herself gave birth to none other than Tom, who accompanied you here."

"Tom? The young fellow who was part of my little entourage?" Bob thought about that for a few seconds. "You know, this may sound strange, but this fellow, Tom, is the very image of one of my long-standing patients I left back home, and was, in fact, the very patient I was attempting to cardiovert when all this change happened."

"Cardiovert…what is that?"

"Well, that gets complicated, but when a person's heart rhythm gets too fast, and they begin to lose their blood pressure, and show signs that they're not getting the blood around their body very well, then we can do what is called a cardioversion, which is where we give them an electric shock through their chest, and it can restore their rhythm back to normal."

Craycroft looked at Bob quizzically, "You shall have to tell me more about that at some time."

"Ah, yes, but as I was noting," Bob continues, "this person, Tom, was one whose intelligence shone though like a beacon. He is a special one."

"Indeed, he is, and that is as it should be, as he is the grandson and namesake of his grandfather, Drachma. And he does carry the

blood of his grandmother, the lady Felicia. For now, Tom is safe, with his grandfather, but then that brings me back to our tale."

"Now through the years, lady Felicia and I did become fast friends, and many were the occasions when she and I did dine together, often with our good friend, Master Falma—of him I shall speak later. We would discuss matters of great consequence to our little island, and then she would talk with the earl, and often as not, our discussions would lead to changes that the earl would implement, through the Council of Lords. We began to feel that we were acting as advisors to the earl, and I believe that he truly felt the same. Now the one among us who had the most official duty to the earl was Master Falma, and that was because Falma, though officially acting as alchemist to the earl's house, was, if any truly were to seek an honest answer, the earl's own loremaster, which very few on this island knew about. Anyway, as time went by, there arose among the councilors, those that did suspect that the earl had his little clique of closely woven friends, and that this would become, in time, something of a sore wound to many on the council."

"In large part, it was a matter of jealousy, because the present earl became somewhat suspicious of the Council of Lords, and their misplaced wants and needs. Chief among those that have opposed the earl in recent years has been Councilor Reordan, who lives not far away, in the mansion on the hill to the west of the castle. His land holding are numerous, and it is said that he has his own private armed force, and he is said to collect taxes from those that live upon his lands, a violation of the charter from which his lands are owned, as any taxes on the lands are property of the English king, and subject to the earl's rule of distribution. And then there is Councilor Silvo, a man of unfortunate taste, who did lose many of his holdings, apparently resulting from his wife's folly, and her love of jewels, fine parties, and French wine estates. He had to borrow heavily from our friend Reordan, whose fee has been the soul of Councilor Silvo."

"So, this is the state of affairs in our ruling council, when into the turmoil is added the illness and death of some of our most esteemed potters and painters, of which you are now familiar. Then to make matters even worse, Felicia's adoptive father, Lord Carlo Vincente becomes ill, and himself is presumed dead, though I shall address that issue shortly. Just imagine, if you will, the council's fears and alarm. For their once prosperous island's future now seems threatened, and their own safety is no longer secure."

"Imagine, if you will, what Felicia must have been thinking, with her adoptive father now gone, and feeling the obligation to her only surviving relative, who is not even aware that he is any relation to her or to Drachma, and from whom she must keep the secret of her youth. And with the vultures in the council certain to strip him of what she considered to be his just reward. Then she herself becomes ill, and makes the matter more urgent than ever."

"Well, I had not been aware until lately, but lady Felicia was well aware, that this fellow, Tom, was her grandson, but she was in no position to provide anything for him in this life, as none were to know of his existence as her grandson. But our lady did seek out the aid of our earl in this matter, who was himself childless, and because of his fondness for Felicia, and also, I found out, his fondness for me as well, they devised a plan for Tom. You see, they decided that I should adopt Tom and then he would be provided for as one of the earl's own family. Now I knew nothing of this, as it was all between the lady Felicia and the earl. That is until our lady Felicia became ill, and then the earl himself, and all of the lady's plans suddenly became much more pressing. Now, implementation of her plan became paramount. Then the earl also became quite ill, as you know, and the earl then made plans of his own, and appointed me as his successor."

"Well, I tell you, I was not ready for responsibility such as this. You see, I like you, am a healer, not a leader of men. I would

prefer telling tales over flagons of ale at Barncuddy's than to stand before the Council of Lords and justify my appointments over them and their kind."

Bob sat in silence as Craycroft told his tale, thinking of how he got himself into this mess. "You know, Mr. Craycroft, I was not ready for any of this either. I was just going about my business, taking care of patients in the hospital, generally very sick patients, who were in need. I was doing the best that I could for them, though I was really tired. Then along come these messages from your Drachma, with a whole new world opening up beneath my feet, and then suddenly I get whisked off to your island, in your time, with my training and skills intact, but absolutely none of the back up or the technology of our age. And now I'm presented with the sick and injured, and have nothing to do for them besides diagnosing their ailments. Your earl is the perfect example. Here I'm presented with a sick, hypoxic individual, with obvious pneumonia, but nothing to do for him. I mean you've been giving him breathing treatments with your little mist apparatus, but I can't even give him antibiotics, because they haven't been discovered yet."

Craycroft was silent for a moment; then he said something startling. "Let me ask you, Master Robert, you speak of these antibiotics as something that can cure a person?"

"Well, it looks like I said a mouthful there, doesn't it? Let me back up a little by telling you what I know of the earl's illness. He is a man, previously healthy, who now is weakened, with trouble even catching his breath, and coughing up copious amounts of vile matter that has a peculiar color and odor. The onset of this illness was perhaps some weeks ago, and has been getting worse, or as we say, progressing. On his exam, I noticed first the fever, and then some cyanosis or dark bluish discoloration of his lips and nail beds. There was the trouble breathing and the extreme fatigue. Then upon listening to his lungs, I hear that rattling sound associated with fluid in his lungs, but I also noted that his

heart seemed normal, there was no murmur or gallop to suggest that the heart was principally failing, and there was no swelling of the abdomen or feet. So I would have to infer that he has pneumonia, which is an infection, caused by the growth and multiplication of bacteria within the alveoli, or air sacs within the lung, and that his body is trying hard to rid itself of that infection, by producing great numbers of white blood cells, as well as the lung responding by producing its own cells to try to destroy these bacteria within their own territory, but the bacteria themselves, as they multiply, produce substances which destroy the tissues in which they reside. Right now, I would say that the bacteria are winning, because he is cyanotic, which is bluish discoloration of his lips, which is caused by the lack of oxygen in the bloodstream, which, in turn is caused by the fact that his alveoli have filled up with "stuff" in such quantity that the lungs are unable to do their job."

"Now, what antibiotics can do is to kill off the bacteria in such numbers that the body is able to recover. It is the weapon that turns the tide in this war that goes on in his body right now. Now I have no way of knowing, even if we were to give him antibiotics, whether his body would recover enough to win this war, but what I can tell you is that, for the present time, it looks as though, without antibiotics, that he will lose this war, and will die."

Craycroft again sat silently, with his head in his hands.

"Let me ask you," he said at last. "If we were able to get these antibiotics, then we could, perhaps give our earl a chance?"

"That would be asking more than I believe we can do," said Bob. "You see, antibiotics are manufactured in our world by industries that produce and package them for use around the world, but do so in our time, and not in yours."

"But tell me, how do those that produce these antibiotics, do so?"

"Well, I can tell you of how the first really good antibiotic in the world got made. You see in England, of all places, there was a researcher named Alexander Fleming, who was studying bacteria and their growth requirements. Now he noticed that there was a mold that would appear on their bacterial cultures, and that wherever this mold was, the bacteria were not. In fact, it appeared that this mold was killing the bacteria. So, unlike researchers in the United States—that is where I come from—who, facing this same problem decided that the best thing to do was to build a whole new building, away from this mold, young Alexander Fleming started collecting this mold, and developed penicillin, then the whole world of medicine changed dramatically, and for the first time in human history, physicians could cure certain infectious diseases."

Suddenly, Craycroft became very animated. He got up and went to the door of his suite, and peered out into the hallway. "Hermes," he called out. "Hermes, there you are. Now listen very carefully to what I am telling you. Get you hence to the alchemist's shop. I realize that Master Falma is not there, but I want you to get Melchior, his assistant, and tell him to come right away. Tell him that Craycroft has urgent need of his services, right here and now. And you are to bring him here with you as quickly as possible. Tell him that our earl's life may depend on his getting here."

Hermes could feel the surge of energy behind Craycroft's words. "Aye, m'lord, I am off, and I shall return anon with Master Melchior. Ye have my word on that."

With that, Craycroft came back and sat down again in his seat across from Bob. His eyes had a new sparkle to them.

"Well then, Master Robert, we shall see about creating a little bit of history on our island, with your help, and Melchior's expertise.

"Now, as I was saying, I should tell you just a little about our friend, Lord Carlo Vincente."

Bob's head was spinning just a bit after the little escapade by Craycroft. He kept his composure, and said, "Go ahead, Mr. Craycroft, I'm listening."

"As I have indicated, and all on this island believe, Lord Vincente did become ill, and was thought to be dying, apparently also of this "pneumonia" which you did describe so vividly. Anyway, as the time drew near, I was summoned, by Master Falma, to come to his side in the night. Lady Felicia met me at the door to his room, and indicated that he was within, with master Falma. When I stepped into the room, however, Master Falma bade me shut tight the door, then had me go with him to the bed, but there was no one there. 'Where is Lord Vincente?' I asked. Then Falma told me a tale of mystery and of powers that both he and Drachma had called upon, and that Lord Vincente was no more, that his body also was no more with us, that it was 'sent away' into the ages, in search of great powers."

"Now wait just a minute," said Bob. "Do you mean to say that this Carlo Vincente, who came and died in our hospital, in our time and place, had been sent there by Drachma? I'll tell you that, if I weren't here myself, I might have a lot of trouble believing that."

"But, Master Robert, here you are, and that is what I have been telling you, and that you come with powers unlike any that we have seen."

Chapter Twenty

The inn was bustling with activity, even at this early hour. Barncuddy was busy with his orders for ale, and was moving about boisterously, getting the flagons and refilling those that were getting empty. He was sweating, and groaning, and keeping the younger patrons in line. He looked up from his work to notice the entrance of the odd trio of Cayman, Proust, and the younger fellow whose name he could not remember, but was the son of Diane.

"A hearty welcome to ye, my good men, and what brings ye in on this fine afternoon?"

"Well, thank ye Master Barncuddy," said the captain, "What we'll be needin' is a table for four, somewhere private, if that be possible."

"Of course, for a pair such as yourselves, but for this young lad, who comes among ye. He is none other than the son of one of my own lasses. Ho, Diane," he yelled toward the back, "I've got two gentlemen, and someone ye know out here. Come on and give these fine young fellas a table if ye will."

In a few moments, a woman appeared from somewhere in the back, whose hair was black and curly, hung about her impish face, which shone from the kitchen work she had been doing.

"Now, Master Barncuddy, ye've called me away from boilin' yer stew for this evenin', to do what? To show these men to a table…"

Then she saw who she was asked to seat.

"Eustace! Now what would ye be doin' in the company of men such as these, Have ye done something wrong?"

"No, me dear, he has done nothing wrong. He has some information that we'll be needing, some vital information." Cayman proffered. "Now, if ye'll be so kind as to find us a table, away from all this rabble."

"Very well, gentlemen, if ye'll follow me, I can show ye to a table upstairs, would that be all right, Master Barncuddy?"

"Of course, lass, of course. Why, I think ye should serve the table as well, what think ye, gentlemen?"

"Why I think we should be honored, me lads," said a grinning Cayman.

"All right, then, come this way."

The three of them followed Diane up the stairs, to a small dining room. They sat down, and ordered ale to be brought up, but Diane said to Eustace, "now, be careful, and do not drink more than yer own pint, or ye'll have to be towin' yer own way home again."

"Of course, Mum," Eustace replied, "I shan't embarrass ye, I promise."

"Now, my good woman," said Proust, "there'll be a fourth joinin' us here this afternoon, so be on the lookout for Master Kerlin, will ye?"

"Master Kerlin? Wasn't he just here last evening? Now if he's to be here too, this is going to be an interestin' meetin', eh? Now Eustace, ye be sure to mind yer manners with Master Kerlin. That's a man fer to make a lady blush. Now see, ye've got me sweatin' and stammerin' already. Well, I'll go get yer drinks, and I think ye'll be wantin' a flagon then for Master Kerlin, too. Am I right?"

"Right you are, m'lass."

Then with a toss of her head, and a practiced swish of her behind, Diane headed back down to the kitchen. Cayman and Proust stared happily at the figure vanishing down the stairs.

"Now, m'lad, that be yer own mother, eh?"

"Aye, sir, that be me mum."

"Well, then," continued Captain Proust, "what can ye tell me of what happened with old Leroy? Is the old beggar still alive?"

"Aye, Captain, at least he was when we left him at the sick bay. They had a physician there, attending to Councilor Genet. Some foreigner, apparently brought to our isle by Drachma, who actually seemed to know what he was doing, and he seemed quite calm, and not at all like the physicians I have come to know, outside of this island. Craycroft, it seems may have finally gotten someone here who knows as much as he himself does."

"My word, Cayman, ye have said a mouthful. I had no idea that ye were such a student of the healing arts."

"Well, me own mother (may she rest in peace), was a woman of some education, and did serve the old earl, not as a maid, but as his personal librarian."

"Well, Aye, now that ye mention it, I do remember Cecilia. She was called Cecilia the Wise, wasn't she?"

"Aye, that she was. Anyway, as a young lad, I was sent to the mainland for schooling, but when me mum's health became poor, I had to give it all up, and came home, and I stayed to become a guard here at the castle. Not that I ever minded, but those years of schooling just stayed with me, and every now and again, they just come out.

"Now look, here comes our ale. I thank ye Diane." Diane quickly and efficiently laid down the flagons. "Now for all assembling here, I raise this toast, that we should see to it that whatever changes we seek for the good of the isle, they be right and worthy."

Proust and Eustace quickly raised their own flagons, and clinked them noisily with Cayman's own.

"Here, here! May it be so!"

"Here, here, yourselves," said a voice coming up the stairs. "Now have you all started the party without me?"

"Kerlin! It is ye indeed. Come, we've got a goblet for ye as well."

As Kerlin joined the others at the table, Cayman noticed Diane mouthing instructions to her son. To which her son replied, "I know, Mum, ye don't have to remind me."

Then Diane blushed, and bowed, then made her way to leave, when Cayman stopped her, saying, "now, me good woman could we trouble ye for some bread and victuals also?"

"But, of course, sir. What shall ye have this afternoon? I've just been cooking some fine stew, which I think should be done, and we have some salted fish, and some fine turnips."

"Why not some of your fine stew, then, if that be all right with one and all?" Kerlin spoke, and Diane self-consciously looked down. "Well I see that none would object to your stew. How about a round, with some yeast bread, then?"

"Of course, m'lord. I shall get it for ye anon." She said, as she left, unconscious of her own use of the title, so unfamiliar to Kerlin.

Kerlin looked around at his tablemates. He noticed his good friend, Proust, and another guard that he assumed was Cayman, and the youth. "Now this would be a most unusual gathering, if I do say so myself. As you may have heard, I have had to assume some new duties, and I have been told by our earl that my new tasks shall take on more important aspects as time proceeds. So, as the newly appointed commandant of security for the earl's palace, I raise my tankard to you gentlemen and to you, m'lad as well."

They all raised their flagons, and with a crisp click, and a hearty, "here, here," they drank to the health of their endeavors.

"Now you two may be wondering why I have come to join you here. As my good friend, Proust knows, when I heard of this new threat, and your intimate knowledge of the persons involved, I thought it best that I meet with you, e'en though I would rather be sleeping."

"As well you should," put in Proust. "I told him that we could meet, and that I would report back to him, but no, he would rather meet with Cayman and Eustace himself. That'd be the kind of person he is, and that be the kind of person that I am now serving."

"Well, as my good friend Proust indicated, I am the sort who prefers to get information directly from the source, if that be possible. So that brings me to you, Eustace. Now, I know that you've told your story to both Masters Cayman and Proust, but if you'll indulge me by telling me your tale again, then I think that we can proceed towards making a plan, for as you know by now, I think we are dealing with a most dangerous and formidable foe."

All eyes turned toward Eustace, who looked down, but then stammered, "m-m'lords. 'tis a bit more than I care to do, but I shall try to tell ye all of what happened. As ye well know, I am not comfortable speaking to folks such as yerselves. I am a mere lad of the streets.

"As it happened, I was here last evening, having brought me mum some things from the market. It was getting late, but not closing time. Then, as I was leaving, I noticed this man was also leaving, and seemed to be in some kind of hurry. I decided to follow him, though I cannot tell ye why."

"Now, let me interrupt for just a moment, if I may," said Kerlin, "for I was also here, and saw this man of whom you spoke. What I need to ask is whether there be any chance this person saw you last evening? Was there even the slightest chance that he might have seen you? You shall soon learn why I ask."

"Nay, not last night, for I was certain of my cover of darkness, and if there be anything I have learned, it is how not to be seen."

"Very well, I shall believe you. And, please, go on with your story."

"Well, as I was sayin', this man seemed to be in some kind of hurry. He was all wrapped up, so I couldn't see his face, but he carried this cane with him, though he did not need it fer walkin'. Anyway, he headed fer the mansion up the hill, the one owned by Councilor Reordan. I saw him speak to the gatekeeper, and was let in. Then, as there was nothing more to see, I decided to go home."

"Did you talk to anyone at all about your night?"

"Nay, not to anyone, until today, when I talked with Master Cayman."

"Not to your mother, nor any friends?"

"Nay, not to anyone."

"Well, then, what happened next?"

"This morning, when I was walking back to the castle, I saw him again. This time he was striding toward the market, with a look upon his face that I scarce would call friendly, rather he looked as though he meant to do someone harm. It was the first time that I saw his face, and it frightened me, and I turned away. I know not whether he saw me or noticed me, but he was soon walking quickly toward the marketplace. I then followed at what I thought was a safe distance, but then, he was just ahead of me, having been stopped by a peddler, who was asking him something, but I could not say what. He then proceeded to take his cane and poke the peddler with it, but actually it looked as if he had run a sword into the old man's stomach, and the old man just crumpled to the ground, bleeding, as the stranger then pushed his way through the crowd, and went I know not where."

"Hmm, very well, young man," said Kerlin, who then noticed Diane approaching, with Barncuddy close behind. "Ah, I think our meal comes. How now, m'lass? That looks like a fine meal, indeed. Here, we'll make room for our bowls."

Diane and Barncuddy then set upon the table bowls of steaming stew, with freshly made yeast bread in a large basket. As she laid the bowl down in front of Kerlin, he touched her arm, and immediately she blushed from her ample bosom up her neck to her already ruddy cheeks.

"Now, m'lass I must ask you something."

"Wh...what is it?" she stammered. Then she looked at Eustace, and said, "now son, have ye done or said anything to embarrass me?"

"Oh, no, m'lass, he has done nothing of the sort. He has been quite a gentleman." Eustace looked down, afraid that his grin might lead his mother to think otherwise. "No, what I must ask about is a man that was here last evening. He sat back at the table near the kitchen, by the back door, and I understand he left without paying his tab."

"Oh, that one... Aye, he was a strange one, or so I'm told. Now Connie waited on that table and she told me about him. But I did see him as he went out, which is because Eustace here did bring me some vegetables, and let me tell ye that the man was not anyone I'd let me kin near, for he had danger written on his features."

"So, then Eustace did not mention that he had followed him..."

"Eustace, oh no, m'lord. Now, Eustace, what have I said about followin' after folks? Oh, no, is that what this is all about? Is Eustace..."

"No, m'lass, he is not in trouble, but what I would like to ask is whether you might spare Eustace for a time, to be with me?"

"With thee?"

"Aye, as my personal assistant."

Diane's face became redder as she digested what Kerlin had just said.

"As yer personal assistant? I...I think that would be fine. Now, would ye be needin' anything?"

"Nay, m'lass, nothing but thy blessing."

All eyes turned toward Eustace, who was grinning.

"Well, Eustace, how about it we ask you?" said Kerlin, very seriously. "What do you say to that? For I should be needing an extra set of eyes and ears, don't you think?"

"Master, Kerlin, if ye think me worthy, who am I to say no? I should be honored. Is that all right, Mum?"

"But, of course, son," said Diane, still blushing. "If that is what ye want, I can think of none better than Master Kerlin fer ye."

"Let me ask ye, Eustace, can ye ride?" asked Cayman, somewhat unexpectedly. "I know ye can manage well enough on foot, but on a horse…"

"Aye, sir I can ride, but not well. And it has been a good year since I've been on a horse."

"Well, then as ye now be Master Kerlin's new assistant, let it be my duty to teach you the finer art of horseback riding, if that be all right with master Kerlin."

"Point well made, Cayman. Aye, I think it would be good for young Eustace to learn his way around horses, and I think that you would be a fine teacher for him."

"With most hearty thanks, m'lass, we here at this table do then swear to you that we shall care for your son as one of our own."

"Here, here!" said Proust, "To one of our own."

Again, the glasses were raised in salutation.

The quartet then turned their attention to the food, as Diane left with Barncuddy to see to the others in the inn.

"Now, Eustace," said Kerlin after they had left. "What I do need to explain to you is just how and why you've found yourself in this peculiar position. You see, Master Proust and I decided that you are a most exceptional and observant, not to mention honest, young man, and we could readily use the likes of you in our aid. Now I know that you have not had the training, but that is neither good nor bad, for we can certainly train you, but your powers of observation set you apart from the other village boys.

"And then there is the matter of Master LeGace. While I do not know that he has observed you, what I do know is that he is a creature most vile, and would think nothing of destroying you if he even suspected that you were here with us."

"Then I am most grateful. I shall try to earn my keep. Now, me mum… what shall I tell her, anything more than she already knows?"

"Nay, son, it would be better if she knew little, for her sake as well as thine. Now, eat your stew, it's quite good."

"Aye, sir, I shall."

The foursome then ate in relative silence for a time, enjoying the stew and rolls, as well as their ale. Diane then came back up with a pitcher of ale. She began refilling the flagons of brown brew for the three men, but held off filling up Eustace's cup.

"Now son, I know ye think that this is some great adventure yer off on, but let me tell ye that yer still my only son, and I'll be a worryin' over ye. Here, I want ye to keep this charm to remind ye of me, fer I don't know when I'll be seein' ye again."

What she gave her son was a small, round pendant, cut from some whalebone with a carving of a ship on it.

"What is this, Mum? I've never seen this before."

"What it is, I'll tell ye, it was yer father's only thing he left me, besides leaving me pregnant with thee."

"Why, he was a sailor, then, I would believe, from this piece of scrimshaw."

"Aye, that he was, and ye know what? To this day, I've not missed him, but now, with ye goin' off, and all, I can see him in thy face, and in yer hands, and ye know, I'm going to miss ye, for I've not been without thy company, all yer days."

"Well, me good lass," interjected Cayman, "I shouldn't think that yer son should be too far gone from thee."

"Well, Master Cayman, that may be, but I do know that Master Kerlin, here, does not want my son, shall we say, exposed

to certain people, and so I don't expect that I shall be seein' much of him either. Is that not right, Master Kerlin?"

"I must admit, m'lass, that your powers of observation suit you very well. You have discerned the truth. For it is precisely for that reason that I wish to keep him with me at all times, until we have apprehended our Master LeGace. And unfortunately I do not foresee that as happening too swiftly.

"Now, if I may, I should like to study thy pendant, young man for it might prove something of value that I suspect."

"Certainly, here it be, have a look."

Eustace handed over the pendant, and Kerlin, then Proust and Cayman also studied it intently, then handed it back to Kerlin.

"Well, me lads, what think you off this little broach, does it not fit with what I told you, Proust?"

"Aye, it does at that."

"What does it tell thee?" asked Cayman. "All I see is a wondrous carving of a ship."

"Ah, Cayman, you may be a bit young, but do you remember hearing of the ship called the Tremaine?"

"Was that the whaler that sank off the island? I must have been six or seven at the time?"

"Precisely. And do you remember anything about the story?"

Cayman turned to look at Diane, and noticed that she looked pale, and avoided eye contact with the people at the table.

"Only that there were but one survivor, who managed to swim ashore, in stormy waters."

"And do you remember anything else? Do you recall his name?"

"Wait, he was a nobleman, was he not?"

"And do you recall his name?"

"Nay, that I do not."

"It was…"

"All right, he was the earl of Derrymoor," said Diane, unexpectedly. "And, so, Master Kerlin, how is it that you were able to deduce that?"

"Well, lass, I was a forest guard at the time, and I was assigned the duty of protecting the lone survivor. And, as you know, the earl of Derrymoor was he. He was nursed back to health, and did stay, at that time in the village of Champour, which I assume was your home at the time."

"Aye, it was."

"Anyway, as part of his protection, I, though younger at the time, did have the chance to visit with this earl, and though he did not have much that survived his harrowing swim to shore, he did show me this fine broach, which, as you can see, was carved of whalebone, and shows a three masted ship, which was what the Tremaine was, and though a whaler in name, was the ship owned by his family, and part of their fortune was made in whaling, as well as ownership of islands discovered by the crew."

"The family, when they learned of the disaster, did of course send for the earl, but there was a period of months before they came, and being the young man that he was, and quite good looking, he did have the occasion to sport with the young lasses of the village, and there was one who caught his fancy, though I never did meet her, did hear that she was, indeed truly charming."

Diane blushed crimson at this.

"As it happened, when it got time for him to leave, it was said that she refused to go with him, am I right? Please, have a seat, and join us, will you not?"

Diane, then, sat down at the table, took her son's tumbler, poured herself some ale, and told them all her tale of youthful indiscretion, and love for a man she knew she could never marry, and how, the night before he left, he gave her his scrimshaw broach, and a promise to send her money to help, which she never received. All she had left of that encounter, was her son, her own heartache, and that broach, which she was now bestowing on her own son, as his rightful piece of his father's memory.

"Let me ask you, then," Cayman spoke up, obviously entranced by this tale of hardship, loss and youthful love, 'has anyone heard of this earl of Derrymoor since he left our fair isle?"

"I, for one, have not," replied Diane. "but there is one here who probably has. Is that not right?"

"Verily, you have surmised correctly, m'lass." Kerlin spoke again. "For that brings our story full circle."

"Before ye continue," spoke up Proust, " might I suggest that we raise our glasses once again, in a toast to this fine young lass, who has graced us with her tale of love and loss."

"Here, here."

As the glasses were raised, Eustace pondered what he had just found out. Thinking that he was certainly in for some changes, and how he was going to look back on this moment with a certain amount of affection.

"Now to complete this tale of our newfound nobility, albeit without title or monies, let me tell you what I do know. As Diane so graciously told us, this talisman was something the earl bequeathed to her, apparently as symbolic of his lineage. What she did not say, but I have reason to believe, is that this piece of scrimshaw represents the family seal, and carries with it rights and privileges of nobility. As you recall, the earl did return to his noble home in Ireland, and I understand has married, but has not had any heirs to his estate. I know this because my own brother does work at an estate for the earl. The earl has said, in private, that, if any were to return with his seal, that they could then inherit what should rightly be theirs. But, to my knowledge, he has not said anything publicly. Nevertheless, this certainly changes how we perceive our circumstances.

"And now, let me tell you what I have found out about our infamous Master LeGace. As you know, he is an extraordinarily evil and crafty man. But what I have found out is even more alarming. Now, I know that he is in the employ of Councilor Reordan, and just what his role is for that snake I know not, but what I do know is that he has had something to do with the earl's illness, and perhaps Lady Felicia's recent illness as well."

"Oh, Diane! Come on down, I've got work fer ye." She knew that voice, it was her boss.

"Well, gentlemen, ye have certainly succeeded in turning my world upside down in a small amount of time. Now I must go. And do take care of my son, as he is all I really have left in this world."

Then she came around to where Eustace sat, gave him a kiss, and as her eyes overflowed with tears she mouthed the words, "I love thee."

Eustace whispered, "I love ye, too, Mum."

Then Diane quickly left, went down the stairs, and back to the usual chaos and clutter of the inn.

The quartet finished eating, drinking, and talking, then went down the stairs, where Kerlin paid the tab, then they stepped out into the weather that had definitely taken a turn for the worse, with a cold wind blowing off the sea, carrying with it a stinging, freezing rain. They bundled up against the elements, then headed on back toward the main keep of the castle.

They did not notice the man observing them from the seclusion of the shed by the inn. He watched as they left Barncuddy's, waited for them to turn the corner, then stepped back out into the weather, following them, but keeping just out of site. As he saw them enter the keep, he smiled, noting that it was, in fact the same youth he had seen earlier that day.

Chapter Twenty-One

Melchior was in his room when he heard the page at the door. He got up slowly, as was his custom, but somehow he knew that this was not going to be just another ordinary call. There was just too much happening too quickly, and now he was thrown into the mix, and this was even without Falma here.

He did manage to get to the door before the page started rapping again. He opened the door, and let the page come in.

"Are ye Master Melchior? The page asked.

"Aye, that be me."

"Well, then, I have a message for ye from Master Craycroft. He says that he should like an urgent meeting with ye and Master Robert of Ewe Ass, at his abode this very afternoon."

"Very well, m'lad, grant me a minute to get me cloak, and I shall accompany you. I have no idea what this is about, but I am sure it is important. Now who is this Master Robert of whom you spoke?"

"What I know is that he is a healer of great power, a foreigner from some land called Ewe Ass. He was sent here by Drachma, so…"

"Ah, Drachma was it?" Melchior remembering that he, himself was brought to the island as well by Drachma. "It does make me wonder… Well, let us be going, m'lad."

The duo stepped out into the very same weather that greeted Kerlin and his companions, as they left the inn. It was the same stinging rain, and the same brutal wind. Melchior huddled beneath his cloak, and the page did likewise, as they trudged ahead. It was truly miserable, and it was with some relief that they saw the earl's keep ahead. But then something caught Melchior's eye as they got close. It was the figure of a man, who seemed oblivious to the weather, as he stood by and watched intently, holding his walking cane, as a small group entered the keep.

"Wait, m'lad. Let us see where that man goes. There is something about him that I do not like."

The two of them huddled together, in the lee of one of the buildings across the plaza from the entrance to the keep. They kept watch until they saw the man walk away toward the main gate of the castle. Then they made their way, quickly across the plaza, and in out of the wind and freezing rain.

As they came inside, the page turned to Melchior, and asked, "Now, Master Melchior, can ye explain what we were doing, waiting outside, in this awful weather, because ye didn't like the looks of the man out there?"

"If ye must know, me young lad, that man was definitely evil. He was standing outside, oblivious to the weather, and obviously intent on watching that small group ahead of him, which was going the same way that we were. Now, what do ye think he was doing, eh?"

"I know not, now do ye have any idea?"

"Aye, that I do, but that depends on who the people in front are. Maybe we can get to the guardsmen and find out."

"Very well, let us go this way. It so happens that I know some pages who might be able to tell us something."

Kerlin arrived at Craycroft's rooms, along with his entourage. The quartet entered his rooms after they were announced.

"Why, Master Kerlin, and Captain Proust, and we have two new persons with you. Could you please tell me who they might be."

"Of course, m'lord. May I introduce Guardsman Cayman, and my new personal assistant, Eustace," he said this with a wink and a smile toward the youth. Eustace simply blushed and grinned.

"Very well, and let me say welcome. Now I have also sent for my good friend and fellow healer, a Master Robert, who is presently attending to the needs of our injured councilor and one old man named Leroy, of whom you know. I have also sent for Melchior, who is Master Falma's apprentice. So, now that we are here, let us then move to one of our meeting rooms where there should be ample room for us all." Then he turned to his page, and instructed him to watch for the arrival of Melchior and Robert, and to direct them towards the meeting room.

"Now, I shall assume that all are well fed and that your thirsts have been assuaged by your visit to Barcuddy's." All acknowledged that fact. Then they entered one of the large meeting rooms, with its large table and ample stuffed chairs, and roaring fireplace, and feeling of opulent comfort. Eustace had never seen anything like this room, and neither had Cayman, who felt acutely out of place. Sensing their disorientation, Craycroft turned to them and said, "my friends, in the name of our earl, who yet lives, and for whom I do speak, I say welcome, and please do not be intimidated by your surroundings, rather realize that this is for all of you, and that what we do and what we say here shall come directly from our hearts and our minds, and shall be for the good of our isle."

They then followed Craycroft, and sat in the comfortable chairs, all but Eustace, who stood by uncertainly.

"My son," said Craycroft gently, "you are now part of us, and a very important one at that. Here, come sit down at my right, in this seat, and let me hear of your own doings, and what you have seen and been. Do not be afraid, as I, too, started life in humility, and was a page for years, before gradually ascending to

this position. This is not what I sought, nor what I expected, but nevertheless, here I am, one of you, ascended."

Eustace sat down, humbly.

"Well, then Eustace, why don't you tell us about yourself, and what led to all these changes happening around you."

Eustace began his story, yet again, this time telling more of his own background, with Kerlin filling Craycroft in as to the earl of Derrymoor's involvement. Craycroft listened raptly, and only interrupted to acknowledge the veracity of what Kerlin was telling, and how he himself knew of both Derrymoor's doings, and of the fact that Derrymoor had left behind a child, whom he was now very pleased to finally meet.

Next Cayman filled them in on LeGace's presence, and his likely involvement with Councilor Reordan.

It was then that Aaron announced that Melchior was here, and when he was shown in took a seat shyly toward the back of the room. After being introduced to the assembled group, for his benefit, they reiterated their story yet again. But when it came to LeGace's involvement, Melchior became animated, and told them of his observation just before entering the keep, and said then that he knew the man was up to no good. And then he told them of a tale that he knew from the mainland, before Drachma came into his life, and whisked him away to this island.

"This was perhaps six or seven years ago, in the spring, that there came news of a stranger, who carried a walking cane, who began buying property in the area, and it was said that the owners, though at first reluctant, began to sell when threats were made that their indiscretions would be made public. He was said to offer them their lives, as well as the keeping of their family's secrets if they but signed on the line.

"I found out about all this when one of the members of the nobility came to see me, as I was clerking at the time in the offices of one of the law firms in the town.

"Though I was not able to take official action, as I was but a clerk, I did prepare a written statement, but I found out later that no legal writ had been filed because the family feared that any legal battle would bring about severe embarrassment and humiliation to their great name, which, if it were known could eventually lead back to the king himself. Now I cannot reveal details of the legal issues, but I can tell ye that the name of the family was tied to the estate of the earl of Derrymoor."

"My, how things get most convoluted, which is why I am glad that you are around, my good man." Craycroft then paused before laying down his plan for the group, as a way of dealing, both with the external threats, and with the internal turmoil of the council. "Now what I would propose, my friends, is that this assemblage now here in this room, plus my good friend and personal advisor, Jeanne, and Master Robert, as well Councilor Rust, shall become a new and private assembly, and, aye, that would include you, Eustace. As such we should have neither official name, nor any official powers, but we shall rule, in the unofficial sense, as an assembly of citizens. Ye shall have no authority, but shall have my undivided attention. We shall meet as often as needed, for as long as needed, and each one shall have equal voice, with none to exceed another. Now each one shall have his own duties and responsibilities, in accordance with his own special gifts, but in here all shall have equal say.

"Now, there shall remain my official retinue, including my castle guards, as well as my forest guards, who shall have official duties of protection, and there shall remain my official advisors, and official bursars and the ambassadors to the great houses of Europe, whose duties shall not be touched, as well as the numerous servants and messengers of the castle. But I do not need to tell ye that much of what happens upon this isle, happens without official sanction. As many of you know, Drachma himself has embodied this sentiment, as he has done much in the way of ruling, despite having no official title.

"And now, Master Kerlin, already officially in charge of security for this castle, I would add the responsibility for defense of this entire island, and I can think of none more worthy of this. Now Captain Proust shall remain in charge of our castle and its environs, and shall answer to none but Kerlin and me. Then guardsman Cayman, whom I am now commissioning as captain, shall be our liaison between the forest guard, and the guard within our castle, and I shall have him instructed in our use of carrier pigeons, as well as other devices of communication, so that he shall be in touch with Drachma and any external threats to our island's welfare." Turning toward Eustace once more said, "and you, my good lad shall have one of the most important roles in our assembly. I am putting you in charge of gathering information from the masses of people throughout the island, as both the eyes and ears for Kerlin, and for me. I shall rely upon your excellent sense of what is going on with all the people of the markets, the streets and the villages. And, of course master Melchior shall be in charge of all legal matters."

All this information caused quite a stir in the room. Craycroft let them all individually and collectively express their feelings, as he sat back and smiled.

Bob was in a state of agitation, and anxious to tell Craycroft about it, as he was led into the room, but he held his tongue. Before him was a room as opulent as any he had seen so far in the castle. There were tapestries on the walls, a very large stone fireplace, which was a roaring source of warmth. In the middle of the room was a large and elegant table, with chairs around for ten persons. Seated at the head of the table was Craycroft, and around him sat five persons, two of whom he recognized from earlier, in sick bay with the old man, who had been brought in with the belly wound.

"Hello, everyone," said Bob, a subtle smile appearing on his face. "I'm sorry to intrude, but I was told to come up here, that Craycroft wanted me here."

"Aye, indeed I did, and it is with honor that I introduce Master Robert to this assemblage of fine persons, who, I truly feel, shall become like family. Let me introduce these persons seated here. On my left is Master Kerlin, who is now the person charged with the security of all the island."

Bob nodded at the tall man with the piercing eyes, and the green uniform of the forest guard.

"Beside him is Master Proust, now in charge of security within the castle. And next to him is Master Cayman, whom you met, now in charge of communication between the forest guard and our own castle guard. And at the other end of the table is Master Melchior, of whom you heard me speak earlier this morning, and with whom you shall have dinner tonight. Master Melchior shall be in charge of the legal issues that come before this assembly, and will be assisting you in finding a cure, if that be possible, for the earl.

Bob nodded to the shocked Melchior, who sat with his mouth open.

"Unfortunately, Master Melchior has not heard of his new responsibility either, up until this moment," Craycroft said, with a twinkle in his eye. "But there shall be time later today for all that. And finally, here on my right is a youth, whom you also had the occasion to meet, who shall assume duties of providing me information from the markets, villages, and all the little people of this isle, which I consider extremely vital to the welfare of this island.

"And now, that brings me full circle to you, Master Robert, and to what you can bring to us, for what I have gathered here this afternoon is a group of persons with very different talents and persuasions who shall act as my own advisors. Though very unofficial, and without any defined authority or powers, they shall advise me on matters of importance to us all."

"Hmm," said Bob, "the whole thing sounds a bit Jeffersonian."

They all stared at him uncomprehending, then Bob realized the error of his assumption, as Thomas Jefferson was still centuries from being born.

"Oh, well, I'm afraid that one is for the future,' he muttered, sotto voce.

"Ah, then, Master Robert, it would seem that you are most adept at what you do, or did, where you came from, namely caring for the sick. And this much I shall promise you, that we shall provide whatever service we are able to support your efforts. And it is for this reason that I shall provide you with the assistance of Melchior, and also Falma, though he is not yet here to answer for himself, I know him well enough to say that he would be more than happy to provide whatever service he could."

"Wow, that's quite a mouthful that you just said, Mr. Craycroft. I can answer for myself, that here I am in your time and place, a prisoner, if you will, of circumstances that I had no control over, but nonetheless, here I am. Now, considering my lack of choice in this matter, I would be happy to do what I may for the good of your island, but might I also make a request?"

"Of course, Master Robert?"

"I would request that, whenever Judy does get here, at whatever time of day or night that happens to be, that I be allowed to greet her, and spend some time with her, and then, if she is willing, that she be allowed the courtesy of being my helpmate?" Bob found himself, rather unconsciously, adapting to his new language.

"That would seem more than reasonable, my friend. On that you have my word of honor."

"Then I am your man."

"Very well, then, it would seem that we are of one accord, at least as to the beginning of our pursuits. Now I should tell you that if I do need to contact you, I shall use whatever tools I have at my disposal to make contact, and that you should make every effort to attend, all of you. Even though not all have made our first meeting, I shall try to press upon Councilor Rust, and Lady

Jeanne the importance of their presence as well. Now what do you suggest that I unofficially call this assemblage, keeping in mind that I do not plan on it becoming public knowledge that such a group even exists?"

"Why do we not ask Master Robert what he would suggest?" asked Cayman.

"Aye, Master Robert, what shall we call ourselves?" chimed in Captain Proust.

"How about the Executive Committee?" suggested Bob, half in jest, realizing that he had no faith in such things in his world. "That would be as fitting as anything. Or how about the Congress?"

Eventually, all agreed that the Congress sounded more auspicious, so it was adopted as the moniker, even though none except Bob had any familiarity with the term.

"And who should take notes?" asked Bob, but he was told, in no uncertain terms, that there would be no written account of their meetings. "Then I like it even better," he said.

The meeting of the Congress then devolved into a session of jests, and good humor, when one of the pages arrived at the door, asking to speak with Craycroft.

"The sentries have spotted a party of six riders, coming this way."

"Ah, excellent! That should be the lady Judy, along with Falma, and their guard accompanying them. Now come with me, Robert, this may prove fruitful for us all. Now Melchior, why don't you come with us also. Kerlin, I am sure that you have places to go, and desperately need sleep (you see, all is not lost on me)."

The meeting was then adjourned, with as little fanfare as it began. Kerlin took Eustace, Cayman and Proust back down to the constabulary with him, and on the way, the three of them discussed their new assignments and their new life, as seen by Eustace, their youngest member. The particulars of where he would be staying, and the kind of clothing he was to wear,

and just when he was to get lessons in riding, were among the things discussed.

With Craycroft's little entourage, the discussion was more that of filling in Robert and Melchior with all that had happened before they got to Craycroft's abode, and what Craycroft had decided to do, and also involved just when and how Craycroft learned of their doings, and also the why of his decisions. Bob was most curious, because, it seemed to him, there was no precedent that he knew of for governance such as this represented, other than the Arthurian legends, of which neither of his companions were aware.

"It's really something totally new, but here, on this island, it just might work. We'll have to see. And aren't you kind of scared of the council, and what they plan to do?"

"Nay, I am not afraid of the council, for they are but common men. But I am afraid of two particular souls, namely Councilor Reordan, and this new threat, Antoine LeGace. And let me tell you what I find to fear about them. They are each only watching out for themselves, and they care not for anyone else. They obey no conscience, nor do they fear consequences. It is that which I fear most, for that is what makes them so dangerous. But it is my hope that that which makes them such formidable foes may also be that which may bring them down."

"There are those that say the same thing about Drachma, that he moves without regard to anyone else," said Melchior.

"Do you truly believe that?"

"Nay, I do not."

"And neither do I. He might act in ways not understood by others, but I do know him, and have for some years. For in truth his motivations are for the sake of those he loves, and for this island and its inhabitants. This I truly know to be the truth."

Bob then spoke up. "Now this Drachma person is one that I have met, but in something resembling dreams. Now I could describe him to you, but that would do him no justice. Now he

seemed to me to be a fierce person, but I would have to agree with Craycroft here, that he was a man of clear conscience, who was acting out of his love for his people that he deemed to be in great need. Now as to his methods, and the particular choices of persons to answer his needs, I might have some quarrel, but not his motivation."

The group then ascended the watchtower, then came out to the deck. The wind was whistling, and visibility was almost nil. Every now and then Bob could imagine seeing a small group of riders off in the distance, but realized that it would take better eyes than his to see anything.

"I'm afraid that I'm going to have to take your watchman's word on this one," said Bob. "I can't see a thing in this weather." Thinking back on his own arrival he then said, "Why don't we get a warm fire and someplace dry in which to welcome our incoming guests?"

"Aye, that would seem most prudent," said Melchior. "I also cannot see anything at all in this foul weather."

"Ah, my friends, that is already happening, as we speak. I, too, am blinded by this weather. Let us then congregate down where it is warmer, and drier." With that the small group turned inwards, and headed back down the stairs to dry, warmer rooms to await their new arrivals. Craycroft turned to his page, and said, "Please tell Jeanne to expect a few more for dinner tonight. Methinks this evening could become quite interesting."

"Aye, m'lord, I shall tell Mistress Jeanne of this."

With the wind, and the freezing rain, Judy was just about as miserable as she could be, but still, she thought about Cairn, and how he must be hurting so much from his wounds, and this merciless riding on horseback. Even a ride in some bumpy ambulance would be a clean site better than this. So when Johnny told her that he could see the castle ahead, she almost shed tears

of relief. It was true, then, that they were going to get to the castle after all. She could not see far ahead, so she trusted his word on that it was the castle that he could see. As the horses cantered along, she tried to talk to Cairn, to ask him how he was holding up, but her words were lost in the driving rain. She could see, though, that he was laboring mightily just to stay upon his mount.

My God, I hope this ends soon, she thought. *And what of Mr. Falma? Could he be coping any better than me? At his age?*

The riders then entered the village, and slowed their pace to a walk, which felt better to her tailbone, but would drag this process on even further. As they negotiated the muddy streets, she looked about, and saw no one out and about in this weather. The street then rose slightly, and turned to the right, and then back up to the left, and suddenly the castle stood in front of them, enormous, imposing, but inviting. The rest of the way, Judy just gritted her teeth, said a quiet prayer for Cairn, and held on. Then they entered the great gate of the castle, and within the gate, Judy noticed a strange man, who held a walking cane, and who smiled a most malevolent smile as they went by. A sudden shiver went down her spine as she looked at that smile. Then he turned away, and was gone.

Within the castle walls at last, the rain and wind lessened, and they turned abruptly to the left, toward the great stables. From within the stables came groomsmen running up to their horses, who then led them inside. There were men who helped Judy, Falma and Cairn off their mounts. The ground never felt so good, as Judy ran immediately to Cairn's side, and asked him how he was.

He grunted in response, and had obvious trouble standing up. "Now who'll help me get him inside?"

A couple of young men then supported Cairn and helped him into the building, with Judy right behind. As they entered there was a hallway that they walked down, then turned into a

large room with a huge fireplace, and considerable light from the numerous torches.

"Ah, they arrive! Come let us greet the cold and weary travelers." Craycroft called to the others, and they went hurriedly toward the tired, cold, stiff and sore group.

"Oh, Bob!" exclaimed a shocked and very delighted Judy. "You're here, you're really here!"

Then Bob simply grabbed Judy, and embraced her. He was speechless, and his eyes overflowed with tears of relief, and mingled with the moisture dripping from Judy's clothing. Judy's relief was physical, and she clung to Bob as if this were the first real thing she had seen or felt. Then her tears began to flood her own cheeks.

In the meantime, Melchior noticed his mentor, coming in stiffly and slowly, wet and cold, and he ran up to him, grabbed him and quickly pulled him toward the fire.

And Craycroft noticed Cairn, in his distress, and had the young men put him down by the fireplace, on the floor. Then he had his page run to get blankets.

"Oh, Bob, come over here, this is Cairn. He took a couple of arrows in my defense. There was one in the arm, which shouldn't cause too much trouble, but then there was one in his flank, which we pulled out this morning, which could be a big deal."

"Can we get him to sick bay right away? Hermes, can you run and get my things? And bring them around to sick bay." This was Bob, again in doctor mode, giving his instructions in clear, precise, and unchallengeable terms.

Craycroft just smiled, as he realized Drachma's plan seemed to be working perfectly. Now, if he could only convince the others, he might just have something for the ages. Then he went over to Falma, and put his arms around this old, frail man.

"It shall be all right, my friend. It is working so far," was what the old man said. "Now can you tell me where I may have a hot bath, some dry clothes, and something to eat and to drink?"

Chapter Twenty-Two

Tom studied the room that had been his mother's. He couldn't get over all the books. He looked at the shelves, and the various titles. Many were in foreign languages, many in English. Of the ones he could read, there was a thick volume by someone named Cartho, whose name sounded familiar to him, though he couldn't place just where he'd heard the name before. He took down the volume, and noticed that it was all handwritten in a script that was ornate, but readable. The book itself dealt with medicine, and much of it Tom was unable to even decipher, but one chapter caught his eye. It was a chapter entitled 'What We Know of the Plague of Shepperton,' and, it seemed to Tom, that he had heard something about that years ago. He went on to read. At first it dealt with individual histories of persons afflicted with this plague, and then a long discussion on the possible causes. The first case described a man of twenty two, who was a woodsman, who hunted for a living, selling pelts and meat from the woods around a rocky basin, near where there was a wetland area. One day he developed a sore throat, then a cough, fever and trouble breathing. As he got more ill, he started coughing up vile-looking mucus with blood, and developed a rash, then began urinating blood, then turned blue around the lips and hands, before dying.

As Tom was reading this, he kept thinking back to his grandmother's illness, and how she fit this description as if it had been written about her.

He then read on, and the next one was a thirty eight year old woodsman from the same part of the island, who had the same progression, including the cough, the fever, mucus production with blood, but this time a peculiar odor was noted to be present, then the rash, then he died. Then a third and a fourth case, all amazingly similar. Then, finally, Cartho was called in to see one of the persons while he yet lived, but this time Cartho was able to deduce that there was a single source to the plague, which was arising from the water, at one of the springs feeding into the wetlands. The spring, it seemed arose high in the hills, from the base of Croftus Knob.

Tom read on, about the water, and the source of this mysterious illness. He then read Cartho's scathing indictment of the great minds of medicine, and how they would look to treat the victims by bleeding, purging, and so on, without a second thought about what caused this illness, claiming that all illness was the result of body humors out of balance, and that by restoring the bodily humors to their right proportions a skilled healer could alleviate disease.

He could almost hear him muttering and cursing at those old fools, spitting out epithets, as he tried to fathom the mysteries of disease. And now, with this simple finding, that this 'illness cluster,' as he called it, had a remarkably simple source in the water of the spring, he was able to deduce that there was something in this water that, if ingested in sufficient quantity, could set a person's course down the pathway of illness. Just what that mysterious substance was, he could not be certain, but he did know, that by careful and rational observation, that someone would be able to determine an actual cause some day.

"What a remarkable discovery!" thought Tom. "I wonder if Craycroft has read this?" He knew, as certainly as if he had been

there himself, that his own mother had read this book, and he thought again about her life, cut so short in its prime, and just how lucky he was to be carrying on the tradition. "I must find a way to get this to Craycroft," he thought. "This was truly a golden find, out here in this woodland sanctuary."

Tom could not contain his excitement, so he went out looking for Angelica. He found her in the kitchen, sitting down, drinking something warm, that smelled of herbs, and the forest.

"Oh, hello, Angelica, what is that you be drinking?"

"Ah, me young Drachma, this be a concoction I make by steeping herbs and some mushrooms in boiling water, then, as the mixture cools, I pour it over some heather roots. Would ye like to try some?"

"All right, I shall."

"Well, then I'll make ye some. Just have a seat here, and tell me what brings ye out of yer mother's room with such a look on yer face that would say ye were so delighted, that moonlight could'na contain thee."

"Well, it's just this book here. It was written by someone named Cartho, who wrote of something he called 'the plague of Shepperton.' It sounds just like what my grandmother died of. And it is as if he were describing her actual illness, as if he were actually there."

"Hmm, the plague of Shepperton, now I haven't heard that term in so long, it must have been when I was but a child. Why don't ye tell me what he says in that book?"

"There's a chapter in the book about 'The Plague of Shepperton,' where he first tells about real people that have this disease that starts off with a sore throat then they develop fever, a cough that brings up mucus and blood, and then their lips turn blue, they get a rash, and then they die. But then it also talks about how he discovered that the disease was caused by drinking water from this creek that empties into some wetlands…"

"Ah, aye, I know where that creek is, it's not too far from here. It's called the Creek of the Dead."

"You know about this creek?"

"Aye, m'lad. There's much that I know. Now, if you think about it, how could I not? I have lived here, in the company of both Drachma and his men, and, of course my dear Maggie all these years. Now just because I don't read or write like one of ye does not mean that I'm ignorant…"

"Now, I didn't mean…"

"Nay, I know. But let me tell ye about it. Now the Creek of the Dead runs from high up in the mountains, from the lake which forms at the base of Croftus Knob…"

"Aye, that's just what the book says."

A slight sparkle appeared in her eye as she continued. "Does it say when the book was written? For I have some knowledge that might be of use, as well, that comes from a long time ago."

"Let me see, there might be some kind of a date. Here, on this page. He writes, 'written upon this season of Spring, in the Year of our Lord, One Thousand Four Hundred Forty Three.'"

"Now that would have made me about thirty one. Aye, the tale I have is from at least twenty years before that was written."

"Well, my dear woman, you may not be much of a reader, but your skills at arithmetical calculations is unsurpassed."

"So said your Maggie. Anyway, it would appear that this creek has quite a history. Ye see, back before there was any talk of selling pottery from Shepperton, there were various creeks and small rivers, all coming from the lake below Croftus Knob. Some were called blue creeks and rivers, others were called red, not because they were that color naturally, but it had to do with the flowers appearance on their banks, and it was said that, in certain times, when the pear trees were in blossom, that one could walk into the waters of the blue creeks, but be very wary of walking into the red creeks, for ye'd get a severe rash upon any place that the water touched. But there was one creek that ran through the

forest, to the wetland marshes, where the flowers simply would not grow upon its banks, and it was this creek, it was said, that had no fish nor any crawfish, nor even any snails within it, and there would be dead animals on the banks of this creek, even in winter. Now those that lived in the area knew better than to go wading through this creek at any time, however the unwary person could become quite ill.

"Now, this creek got the reputation, be it justly or unjustly, for killing unwary travelers. It was said that all one had to do was to pass through this creek, either on horseback or on foot, and one would be dead within a fortnight. I am not sure of the truth of these tales, but nevertheless, it seems that this creek became tamer as I grew up, for I never heard of anyone being harmed by its waters, though it retained its name, at least among them that knew of it. But now ye tell me that it was responsible for the deaths of several persons about fifty years ago. That is most strange.

"Well, then, young Drachma, what do ye suggest we do about this?"

"What I should like to do is to get this book to Craycroft, as he would know what this means, and if he has heard of the plague of Shepperton, an besides that this illness that Cartho is describing sounds just like that which killed my grandmother and is killing our earl."

"Why I think that is precisely what we should do, Tom. But since I have sworn to keep thee here until Drachma sends further word, perhaps we can send it with one of the men who would be here as couriers. So, do ye think that ye can write a letter to go with this book for Master Craycroft?

"Of course, that I could do, but I have nothing to write on, nor to write with."

"Leave that task to me, to find thee writing materials. Now, here is thy drink. Sit ye down here and drink while I look for some writing material for thee."

So Tom sat and sipped his drink, which was warm, very soothing and aromatic. It reminded him of walking through the woods, with its herbal notes. As he sat back and contemplated his circumstances, he could feel quite deeply the loss of emotional balance that sustained him through his growing years. He was now, he felt, suddenly an adult in this world of adults. He thought about how quickly this transition had taken place. In place of the carefree exuberance of youth, he now felt a burden of responsibility, but to whom? "Ah, well," he thought, "I've just been grown up about a week, so maybe it shouldn't all make sense at once."

He went back to sipping his drink, enjoying the experience. Then Angelica came back with writing paper, and a pen, with a small bottle with ink.

"All right, m'lad, now ye may write a letter to Master Craycroft, to go with the book."

Tom took the paper, quill, and ink, then sat at the table and wrote:

My Dear Master Craycroft,

As thou knowest, I am at Drachma's place, here in the Forest. I have made some unusual discoveries here in Drachma's house, and most particularly as to the presence of one whom I, of course, do not remember, but the aura of my own Mother, Maggie 'o' Killiburn is exceedingly strong. In her room there be a most astounding library, with many volumes, only some of which I am able to read.

Of particular interest to thee, I suppose, is one volume, by someone named Cartho, about whom I assume thou art more familiar than I. It is a book, mostly of a medical nature. Within the book there be a Chapter, which he entitled, What we Know of The Plague of Shepperton, which I have marked for thee.

I am certain that thou shalt find it of interest, as I did as well. Of particular note is that Angelica, who watches

Drachma's house, knows of this stream of which he speaks in his book.

With kindest regards,
Drachma, Known to thee as Tom.

He was folding his letter, when Angelica handed him a large signet ring.

"Here, m'lad, this should be thine as well. It is a signet ring that belonged to thy own mother while she lived here. I think that if ye were to use it to seal this letter, that Master Craycroft would get the hidden message as well."

"The hidden message? What…"

Angelica winked at him.

"Oh, I think I know…"

"Here, I have some sealing wax." She took the red sealing wax, and with the flame of a candle, heated the wax, until a large drop of it fell over the fold in the paper, and then Tom took the signet ring, pressed it into the molten wax, then pulled it out to reveal the face of a wolf.

"Now, we must get this to Master Craycroft in haste."

"Aye, and I was thinking, just how far away is that creek of which you spoke?"

"Now why would ye be asking that, young man?"

"Well, I was thinking, that we could send Craycroft some of the water from the creek."

"And what would he be doing with the water?"

"I don't really know, but I know that he has with him some healer with powerful magic from some distant time. I was just thinking…"

"Let me consider that, m'lad. Now, the creek is but a mile or so from here, but it is over some rough terrain. Now I know that some men are going to be about this afternoon, maybe we can sweet talk one of them into going to the creek, though I must admit, that might be a bit difficult."

"But I can go, if that should make it easier."

"Nay, m'lad, that I cannot let ye do, as I made a promise to yer grandfather to not let ye out of my sight, leastwise not yet. And besides, Harry and Ervin should be here soon. I'm certain that one of them can get yer water for ye."

Antoine LeGace studied his targets from a distance, across the courtyard. It was easy to pick out the two strangers, by their dress and by their manner. They were going into the sick bay, where he knew from earlier surveillance that they had taken the old peddler, and now they were taking in one of the guards of Drachma's regiment, obviously injured.

So, Councilor Reordan, thought LeGace, *thy plans to obtain the Lady have been thwarted by Drachma, as I suspected they would. I believe that you have a more cunning enemy than even you expected.*

He just observed for the next hour or so, than he saw them again, the lady and the stranger, coming out of the sick bay, with a small retinue of attendants, including some pages, as well as armed guards, but the forest guard remained inside. One armed guard stayed at the doorway.

He thought to himself, *well enough, I shall see what I can find out about this lady and this healer.* Then he left the premises. As he left, he pulled the shawl about him more snugly. He headed in the direction of the main gate to the castle, then made his way toward the village, hardly paying attention to the village urchins, who had observed his every move.

Jeanne and Frieda busied themselves preparing for the evening's activities. They did not know what to expect, but the evening's dinner plans had grown considerably, ever since Frieda had invited Melchior to dinner. Now, it turns out, that Craycroft was

coming, and possibly Falma, as were two healers from far away, one of whom was a lady, who would be staying with them here in this house. What started off as being a small get-together with a man to see to their legal needs, now was turning into a celebratory feast with no particular agenda. When Craycroft offered to have the meal at his place, it was Jeanne who said no, that she would be happy to serve it at her own quarters, that she was in the mood to celebrate, after her trying week. And so it was set. It had been a long time since this house had held such a feast as this.

"Oh, Frieda," said Jeanne, "I hope that the food and drink will be satisfactory, for I do not know what these people like, and dislike."

"Well, if ye ask me, what ye have cookin' in here should be a real feast for anyone's likin'. Ye have this wonderful goose, and these baked pies, and all these yeast rolls, now who would not love such a feast as this? I tell ye, if Master Melchior had known when I asked him to come to table that he'd be a walkin' into this, I'm not too sure that he'd have agreed."

"Now Frieda, I do hope ye're correct…"

Their conversation was interrupted by a page, announcing the arrival of their guest of honor, the Lady Judy, also from Ewe Ass, who awaits at the door to the hallway.

"My goodness, Frieda, can ye but see to the meal preparations, while I go and attend to our guest."

"But, of course, Jeanne, I'll see that everyone's workin' as they should. You see to the Lady."

So Jeanne went out with the page to the hallway, where Judy was waiting, and Jeanne's first impression was one of astonishment. Before her was a woman, who looked to be about thirty, but could have been any age, of such regal bearing that she took Jeanne's breath away. She was dressed in clothing from some other time and place, her face was one of undecipherable beauty. Her hair, though matted and unkempt was cut short, and her body spoke of weariness beyond measure. But it was her eyes

that really caught Jeanne's attention, for there in those deep-set brown eyes, was the soul of a woman of true virtue.

"Oh, m'lady, you are most welcome in our home. I know that you have come such a long way, and that you are most tired. But do come with me, I shall show you to your rooms, and while Frieda sees to getting our meal prepared, I shall have thee bathed and readied. Now, my name be Jeanne, and you are the Lady Judy, is that not right?"

"Oh, please, it's just Judy, Judy Morrison. And thank you, Jeanne. It has been a while since I was clean. I almost don't know what that feels like. After tramping through the snow, and getting captured, and then rescued by this Drachma fellow, and then brought here on horseback through the freezing rain and mud, a bath seems just the right thing for me now. I know that I look a fright, and smell like the back end of a wet horse."

"My, how did all that happen? You shall have to tell me about all that while we get you ready. And I do believe that we have clothing that should fit thee well, as you are the size of my mistress (may she rest in peace), and you are more than welcome to wear anything that she had."

"Well, thank you, Jeanne," said Judy, and then she followed Jeanne down the hallway, around to the right, then into a suite of rooms. Judy could not help but notice, as she came down the hallway, the beautiful tapestries and the ornate carpets on the floors, with the hallway lit up by large torches.

"Here ye be, m'lady, said Jeanne. These shall be your rooms, if ye please. Now please feel free to look around, or to sit down in one of the chairs, I shall tell Marta to get yer bath ready for ye. I shall be back anon.

Judy just sat, in the quiet of the room, and looked around. This place was one elegantly furnished abode. There was a large fireplace in the room, with comfortable chairs set around. On the table in front of her was a flask of brown ale, and a welcoming tray of breads, cheeses and dried fruits. She didn't really realize just

how hungry and thirsty she was until she started sampling from the tray. The bread was obviously fresh, the cheese was delicious, and the ale filled a need she didn't know she had. She was into her third piece of bread and was about to sample another bite of cheese, when Jeanne came back into the room.

"Oh, I'm sorry, but I didn't even know I was hungry, or thirsty. I hope this food was for me."

"Ah, of course it was for ye," said Jeanne. "Would ye care for some more?"

"Oh, no. It's just that I haven't eaten anything since yesterday, and this food was right here. Oh, and this beer, that's wonderful as well."

Jeanne just chuckled. It was good to see a lady with an appetite.

"Now, m'lady, if ye'll just come this way, I think we can pick out something fitting for ye to wear. Ye be just the right size to fit into m'lady Felicia's fine dresses. And it would give me great pleasure to find just the right dress for ye."

It was certainly an odd mixture of persons arriving at the house of Lady Vincente that evening. With Craycroft, it was, in fact, as if he were finally going somewhere he had been trying to get to for the better part of two weeks, and yet there was a sense of emptiness as well, because he knew full well who would not be there. For Falma, this was particularly sad, as he had never had the chance to see Felicia before she was so rudely taken from them, and he had been such a close friend. For Melchior, the feeling was one of great anticipation, almost as if he were a schoolchild again, getting to try out a new school, new classes. As for Bob, there was the incredible relief that Judy was safe, and his anticipation of seeing her again made things just a bit giddy. And now, with the addition of Councilor Rust, who seemed the most at ease of the group, but he also knew some of what had transpired with the council.

So, with all these mixed feelings, the group came to the door and were let in. What hit the guests upon arriving was the great smells coming out of the kitchen. To a person the aromas of roast goose, along with meat pies, breads and other baked goods spoke of winter's hold easing up. Then when Marta and Frieda brought around pints of ale, there was an even greater feeling of relaxation that came over the inhabitants.

"Now Master Craycroft, and all guests assembled in my hall," said Jeanne, as she appeared in the doorway, "may I present Lady Judy Morrison, a lady healer, new to our land, and coming from the same land as Master Robert.

There was an audible gasp as Judy walked into the room, radiant in her gown of wine red velvet, and looking every bit as regal as any had ever seen.

Bob was the first to say anything, as she smiled shyly at the guests, and went over toward Falma. "My God, Judy, I have never in my life seen you look so…so… incredible, so beautiful."

Judy smiled at Bob, then she took Falma by the arm, and brought him over to where Bob was standing.

"Bob, I want to introduce you to a man who saved my life, over and over, these past few days, and to whom I owe a debt of gratitude that I can never repay. This man is Falma, the magnificent. I don't know if he holds any titles, but that is my name for him."

"M'lady, you do me too great an honor. I am but a servant of our earl, and it was for his sake, and for Drachma's that I did what I had to for you. But let me tell you that you are a woman of power, whether you know this or not, and I believe that what I did was justified by your safe presence here."

"Oh, Mr. Falma, there you go again." Judy then hugged the old man, who blushed for the only time Craycroft could remember.

"Now, my honored guests," Jeanne broke up the tender moment, "we have for ye a meal, in celebration of the safe arrival of Lady Judy, and of Master Robert, and the safe return of our

dear Master Falma. If ye'll but follow me, I'll show ye to where ye can be sitting."

The guests followed Jeanne into the large dining room, with its massive table, its roaring fireplace, and its beautiful tapestries. On the table was a huge roast goose, numerous fragrant meat pies, yeast rolls, and assorted vegetables. At each place there was a bowl of soup, fragrant and warm. Jeanne sat down, and to her left, she had Craycroft sit down at the head of the table. The others sat down as well, and then she had Frieda also sit at the table, and then she had each one tell a little of their own story, as they each ate the soup, all with gusto. When it came time for Bob to tell of his story, all became entranced with his tale. Bob told of his old life, with its many sick patients, their illnesses, their needs, and he told them of the strange occurrences, and coincidences that led up to the apparent tacit acceptance of his position in Drachma's scheme. Then he told of his arrival on the island, and his encounter with the old man in the smelly old hut, and of his being held prisoner by the forest guards, and his journey toward the castle.

Judy had not heard of Bob's strange arrival on the island, and gave him a slight, sisterly compliment, by noting that, "Bob always seems to get stuck with the ones who least understand him, but then he finds a way to turn that relationship into friendship."

Then Judy herself began to tell her tale, which she told with simplicity, beginning with her story of the similar strange occurrences, and of her talking with Bob about them. And she told of how Bob then just disappeared, and had all the hospital and police looking for him. Then she told the tale of Josh, and how he had developed a long-standing relationship with Bob, and then after Bob disappeared, he seemed to just give up, and then died.

At this point Bob stopped her.

"I didn't hear that he died. My God, that's so sad. Can you tell me more of what happened?"

"Oh, sure, Bob. I'm sorry, I didn't realize… But, of course you had no way of knowing. Okay, I'll tell you, as I was there when it happened. I was back at work, a day after you had disappeared. I had gone to the pharmacy to get some meds restocked, when I ran into Janie, who was looking all disheveled and distraught. She told me that the hospital staff had called her to tell her that Josh was not doing well, and she should come right then, so she came. She was so glad to see me. Well, I called down to the ER and asked them if it would be all right if I took a few minutes to be with Janie. Fortunately, it was a quiet time, you know with all the snow, and they said sure, that they would page me if they needed me.

"Anyway, we went up to TSurg ICU, where we found all the usual commotion, you know with all the usual stuff going on. And I asked if we could have a few minutes with Josh alone, and Brenda, his nurse said sure, that would be okay. So when we approached his bed, I could tell that Josh was no longer there, if you know what I mean."

Bob nodded in understanding.

"As I was saying, his body was there, what was left of it, but there was no Josh. His body was just barely there, though, and soon his blood pressure fell to nothing, then his heart rate slowed way down, and he was truly gone. Just then Earl walked in, having parked the car. I took him by the hand and then I let the two of them just stay and mourn. Brenda called one of the residents, who came and pronounced him. Well, we just hugged each other, and cried. And I just stayed around, helped them with the paperwork. Then I got paged back to the ER, but before I went back, I had Janie promise to tell me when the funeral was to be."

Bob was shaken by this story, but said nothing, just sat with his head in his hands.

Judy then apologized, but said that this was a very special patient of a very special doctor. Craycroft nodded, his own loss was also on his mind. He drank away a stray tear.

After a few more moments, Judy resumed her tale, telling of Josh's funeral. Then she told of walking in the snow with Drachma, then of Josh's parents and Earl's strange dream with Drachma in it. When she got to the point of telling about driving in the snow, it was as if she were spinning fairy stories, for they had never heard of such a thing as an automobile, and the concept of actually being able to drive without the power of animals was just too staggering. They began murmuring among themselves, and comments such as fairy power, and magic stirred the air.

Then Craycroft rose up, with a look of both resignation and purpose, and took his tumbler of ale. "Now, my good friends, all, please raise your glasses to the safe arrival, upon our isle of the good Master Robert, and his lovely companion, the Lady Judy, who have come lo these many long miles, and years (though I should point out, not entirely of their own choosing), to be with us tonight."

"Here, here!" The chorus rang out, and they all drank from their cups.

As the goose was cut, and the pies were passed around, a sense of conviviality returned. Each was hungry, and eager to meet the new arrivals, who were equally eager to meet those whom they could now consider among their friends. There was laughter, there were tears, and the sharing of common thoughts and concerns. And in the end there were happily filled bellies.

Craycroft then stood back up, and addressed the company.

"Now, my very good friends, this has been a most thoroughly enjoyable meal, and for that I must thank my friends Jeanne, Frieda, and all of their servants, who have made this a most memorable evening, and a welcome relief from the drudgery of the weather and of the doings of the council. And we also remember one fine lady, who alas is not here among us this night. For it is she, among all the peoples of this island, whom I shall miss the most. And it be for her sake that I now ask for thine indulgence. For there have come up several things that Felicia would want shared with her

good friends, and while the servants clear away the dishes from this table, I would ask you all to consider."

"My dear friend," said Falma. "We are here this evening, at your request, and to celebrate the safe arrival of our new friends from a far off land. Now, I cannot speak for everyone here, but I can say that as for Melchior and me, you have both our undivided attention, and our pledge that we shall do everything in our power, limited though that may be, to assist you in your efforts, is that not right, Melchior?"

"Oh, aye, that is a certainty."

"I thank you for your support. Now, Councilor, would you be able to also offer your own aid as well?"

"But, of course," answered Rust, "by now you know of my certain confidence in you."

"Very well, then, let us get to the business at hand." He then sat down again. "Now, as some, but not all of you, know I have made Jeanne my special assistant. I was so thoroughly impressed with her honesty and integrity, that I decided I needed her to be at my side. Though I have no title for her position, many of you know her, and anything you would say to her shall be the same as saying that to me. Now this shall be true henceforth. For now, at the least, she shall reside here in the home of Carlo and Felicia Vincente.

"But that does bring me around to the next point, which has to do with all that you see about you, which is one of ownership. That would be ownership of this house and its belongings, as well as land holdings, farms, other buildings, and assets overseas. Now I know the council well enough to realize that they shall try to confiscate as much as possible for their own purposes. But we have one surprise for them, in the form of Drachma's own grandson, who is also grandson to our Lady Felicia. This is something of which the council is relatively unaware, save for good Councilor Rust, and he has not divulged this knowledge to the council, as of yet. Is that not right?"

"Nay, I have told the Council nothing in this regard."

"Well, it turns out that the lad, Tom, also called Drachma, is the one and only grandson to Felicia, whose own daughter, and Tom's mother, was a certain Maggie 'o' Killiburn, who did die, giving birth to young Tom. Now Tom was raised in the village, with no knowledge of his parentage. He then was employed by the earl as a page, and has developed a great sense of the castle and its intricacies. He has learned, only recently, of some of his background, thanks to Master Falma. He is now staying at Drachma's forest home, where, I am certain, he has learned a great deal more, thanks to the presence there of Angelica, Drachma's trusted assistant.

"Now, Master Melchior, I would assign you the task of finding any and all documents as to the paternity of young Tom, as this shall be a point of contention with the council."

"Indeed it shall," said Rust, "for they shall say that we did find some street urchin to fill the shoes of inheritance, and shall want proof."

"Now, wait a minute," put in Bob," is this the same fellow, Tom, who accompanied me on my trip to the castle? If so, that explains a lot. Now don't get me wrong, because I don't know your street urchins, but this young fellow, Tom, was something special. He was no ordinary kid, let me tell you. I sensed something very unusual in that guy. And did I mention that he is the very image of my patient, Josh, whom Judy told you about."

"Aye, that be the same lad, Tom, who did accompany you."

"Well, now, Judy, you've got to meet this kid. He's really very special, indeed. And he is the spitting image of Josh, but a much healthier version."

"Oh, it definitely sounds like I really should meet this young man."

"Now, that brings me around to my final point," said Craycroft, "which is the future of this fine, young lad."

"His future?" asked Rust. "Are we somehow to be responsible? You say he is staying at Drachma's forest home?"

"Aye, that he is, but apparently Felicia, in concert with the earl, had put into motion a plan that I scarcely can talk about. It seems that she, in her final wish, did want me to adopt young Tom as my own. I have that in writing from Felicia, along with her confession of what happened. I can share this with Melchior, as it may be the only written document as to Tom's parentage that we shall have, so it is very precious to me now."

"Wow, that is complicated," Judy could not help but add. "You've got a set of circumstances in which you have an inheritance (I assume it's quite a substantial one), that could be fought over. But now you have an heir, who is just learning of his parentage, who just happens to be the grandson of this very powerful man named Drachma, and this lovely Lady Felicia, who has decided that her grandchild should be adopted by the man appointed by the earl to rule in his place; but you also have a ruling council that wants to get its fingers on that inheritance, and doesn't like the earl's appointment. Have I got that about right?"

Craycroft couldn't help but smile at this young woman from another time and place, who so succinctly summarized their dilemma.

"My dear lady, you have said in few words, what is at the heart and soul of our circumstances. I should ask that you accompany us tonight, but I can see that you are very tired from your journey. Am I right?"

"Oh, Mr. Craycroft, you're so right. I'm just dead tired tonight, and the thought of that bed is just about more than I can stand."

"Well, then, have Jeanne bring you by my place tomorrow. For now, I shall borrow your man, Robert, as well as Master Melchior and Councilor Rust, and take them to Barncuddy's Ale House, for we have much to discuss as regards what can be done for our liege, the earl of Shepperton, who yet lives."

With that they all got up, but Judy went up to Craycroft and gave him a big, warm hug, then she did the same to Falma, who was almost asleep standing up. Finally, she went to Bob, gave him a big, long hug, then whispered in his ear, "You know I love you, and don't forget that."

Cast of Characters in the Book of Drachma

Aaron: Page of the castle

Allen of Burridge: An old carpenter

Alonza Chavez: ER nurse

Angelica: Long term companion/caretaker of Drachma

Antoine LeGace: Generally evil individual

Barbara Greshin: Cardiovascular surgeon

Barncuddy: Proprietor of Barncuddy's Ale House

Bernard: One of the Forest Guard

Blacklist: One of the Forest Guard

Blodwen: One of the Castle Guard

Brother Philip: The monk who found (and translated) The Book of Drachma

Cairn: One of the Forest Guard

Carol: ICU nurse

Carruthers: Servant to Reordan

Cayman: One of the Castle Guard

Cartho: The original Healer of Shepperton

Carlo Vincente: Felicia's adoptive father, and master of the guild

Charlie McFerris: Musician, and recluse

Charlie Stephens: Investigative TV reporter

Chris Lewinsky: Police detective

Clarice: Maid of the Castle

Councilor Rust: Member of the Council of Lords

Count Greorio: Power-hungry Italian count

Craycroft: Fifteenth century healer, locally trained by Cartho

Diane: Waitress/cook at Barncuddy's

Donovan: One of the councilors

Dowdell: One of the Castle Guard

Drachma the Elder: Enigmatic character–part intellectual, part teacher, part wizard

Earl Crabtree: Josh's adoptive father

Earl of Derrymoor: Earl with previous ties to Shepperton

Earl of Shepperton: The reigning earl, and liege lord of Shepperton

Edgar Bryant: Police detective

Ervin: One of the Forest Guard

Eustace: Son to Diane

Falma: Alchemist, Loremaster, but much more

Felicia Vincente: Grand lady of Shepperton, and grandmother to Tom

Finch: Mercenary, hired by Reordan

Fitzgibbon: One of the councilors

Frankie: Butcher

Frieda: Housekeeper to Felicia

Genet: One of the councilors

Hermes: Page of the castle

Herschel: Caretaker of the castle pigeons

Jeremy: Street urchin

Jerry Beasley: ER doctor

Janie Crabtree: Josh's adoptive mother

Jeanne: Lady-in-waiting, and confidante of Felicia

Johnny: One of the Forest Guard

Josh Crabtree: Longstanding patient of Robert's

Judy Morrison: Nurse, and friend to Robert

Kerlin: One of the Forest Guard, who becomes Craycroft's Chief of Security

Kevin: One of the Forest Guard

Leonardo: Urchin, who became Philip's apprentice

Maggie o' Killiburn: Tom's mother (and more)

Malcolm: One of the Forest Guard

Marcus: Page of the castle

Marilyn Gilsen: Robert's wife

Mark Hurwitz: Cardiovascular surgery fellow

Martin: One of the Forest Guard

McGill: One of the Castle Guard

Melchior: Apprentice of Falma

Michel: Forest Guard

Old Leroy: Old beggar, and more

Proust: Leader of the Castle Guard

Robert Gilsen: Overworked late twentieth-century Cardiologist

Reordan: Leader of the Council

Rowan: Street urchin

Sean: Forest Guard

Silvo: One of the councilors

Stoneheft: One of the Forest Guard

Tom (Drachma the younger): Page in the castle (to begin with), yet much more

Wheezer: Street urchin

Willie Minstrel: Musician

www.ingramcontent.com/pod-product-compliance
Lightning Source LLC
Chambersburg PA
CBHW071451170626
46811CB00007B/2539